BOOKS BY JUDITH KEIM

SEASHELL COTTAGE BOOKS:

A Christmas Star
Change of Heart
A Summer of Surprises
A Road Trip to Remember
The Beach Babes – (2022)

DESERT SAGE INN BOOKS:

The Desert Flowers – Rose – 1
The Desert Flowers – Lily – 2 (Fall 2021)
The Desert Flowers – Willow – 3 (2022)
The Desert Flowers – Mistletoe & Holly – 4 (2022)

Winning BIG – a little love story for all ages

For more information: **www.judithkeim.com**

PRAISE FOR JUDITH KEIM'S NOVELS

THE BEACH HOUSE HOTEL SERIES

"Love the characters in this series. This series was my first introduction to Judith Keim. She is now one of my favorites. Looking forward to reading more of her books."

BREAKFAST AT THE BEACH HOUSE HOTEL is an easy, delightful read that offers romance, family relationships, and strong women learning to be stronger. Real life situations filter through the pages. Enjoy!"

LUNCH AT THE BEACH HOUSE HOTEL – "This series is such a joy to read. You feel you are actually living with them. Can't wait to read the latest one."

DINNER AT THE BEACH HOUSE HOTEL – "A Terrific Read! As usual, Judith Keim did it again. Enjoyed immensely. Continue writing such pleasantly reading books for all of us readers."

CHRISTMAS AT THE BEACH HOUSE HOTEL – "Not Just Another Christmas Novel. This is book number four in the series and my introduction to Judith Keim's writing. I wasn't disappointed. The characters are dimensional and engaging. The plot is well crafted and advances at a pleasing pace. The Florida location is interesting and warming. It was a delight to read a romance novel with mature female protagonists. Ann and Rhoda have life experiences that enrich the story. It's a clever book about friends and extended family. Buy copies for your book group pals and enjoy this seasonal read."

THE HARTWELL WOMEN SERIES – Books 1 – 4

"This was an EXCELLENT series. When I discovered Judith Keim, I read all of her books back to back. I thoroughly enjoyed the women Keim has written about. They are believable and you want to just jump into their lives and be their friends! I can't wait for any upcoming books!"

"I fell into Judith Keim's Hartwell Women series and have read & enjoyed all of her books in every series. Each centers around a strong & interesting woman character and their family interaction. Good reads that leave you wanting more."

THE FAT FRIDAYS GROUP – Books 1 – 3

"Excellent story line for each character, and an insightful representation of situations which deal with some of the contemporary issues women are faced with today."

"I love this author's books. Her characters and their lives are realistic. The power of women's friendships is a common and beautiful theme that is threaded throughout this story."

THE SALTY KEY INN SERIES

FINDING ME – "I thoroughly enjoyed the first book in this series and cannot wait for the others! The characters are endearing with the same struggles we all encounter. The setting makes me feel like I am a guest at The Salty Key Inn...relaxed, happy & light-hearted! The men are yummy and the women strong. You can't get better than that! Happy Reading!"

FINDING MY WAY- "Loved the family dynamics as well as uncertain emotions of dating and falling in love.

Appreciated the morals and strength of parenting throughout. Just couldn't put this book down."

FINDING LOVE – "I waited for this book because the first two was such good reads. This one didn't disappoint.... Judith Keim always puts substance into her books. This book was no different, I learned about PTSD, accepting oneself, there is always going to be problems but stick it out and make it work. Just the way life is. In some ways a lot like my life. Judith is right, it needs another book and I will definitely be reading it. Hope you choose to read this series, you will get so much out of it."

FINDING FAMILY – "Completing this series is like eating the last chip. Love Judith's writing, and her female characters are always smart, strong, vulnerable to life and love experiences."

"This was a refreshing book. Bringing the heart and soul of the family to us."

CHANDLER HILL INN SERIES

GOING HOME – "I absolutely could not put this book down. Started at night and read late into the middle of the night. As a child of the '60s, the Vietnam war was front and center so this resonated with me. All the characters in the book were so well developed that the reader felt like they were friends of the family."

"I was completely immersed in this book, with the beautiful descriptive writing, and the authors' way of bringing her characters to life. I felt like I was right inside her story."

<u>COMING HOME</u> – *"Coming Home is a winner. The characters are well-developed, nuanced and likable. Enjoyed the vineyard setting, learning about wine growing and seeing the challenges Cami faces in running and growing a business. I look forward to the next book in this series!"*

"Coming Home was such a wonderful story. The author has a gift for getting the reader right to the heart of things."

<u>HOME AT LAST</u> – *"In this wonderful conclusion, to a heartfelt and emotional trilogy set in Oregon's stunning wine country, Judith Keim has tied up the Chandler Hill series with the perfect bow."*

"Overall, this is truly a wonderful addition to the Chandler Hill Inn series. Judith Keim definitely knows how to perfectly weave together a beautiful and heartfelt story."

"The storyline has some beautiful scenes along with family drama. Judith Keim has created characters with interactions that are believable and some of the subjects the story deals with are poignant."

SEASHELL COTTAGE BOOKS

<u>A CHRISTMAS STAR</u> – *"Love, laughter, sadness, great food, and hope for the future, all in one book. It doesn't get any better than this stunning read."*

"A Christmas Star is a heartwarming Christmas story featuring endearing characters. So many Christmas books are set in snowbound places...it was a nice change to read a Christmas story that takes place on a warm sandy beach!" Susan Peterson

CHANGE OF HEART – *"CHANGE OF HEART is the summer read we've all been waiting for. Judith Keim is a master at creating fascinating characters that are simply irresistible. Her stories leave you with a big smile on your face and a heart bursting with love."*
~Kellie Coates Gilbert, author of the popular Sun Valley Series

A SUMMER OF SURPRISES – *"The story is filled with a roller coaster of emotions and self-discovery. Finding love again and rebuilding family relationships."*

"Ms. Keim uses this book as an amazing platform to show that with hard emotional work, belief in yourself and love, the scars of abuse can be conquered. It in no way preaches, it's a lovely story with a happy ending."

"The character development was excellent. I felt I knew these people my whole life. The story development was very well thought out I was drawn [in] from the beginning."

DESERT SAGE INN BOOKS
THE DESERT FLOWERS – ROSE – *"The Desert Flowers - Rose, is the first book in the new series by Judith Keim. I always look forward to new books by Judith Keim, and this one is definitely a wonderful way to begin The Desert Sage Inn Series!"*

"In this first of a series, we see each woman come into her own and view new beginnings even as they must take this tearful journey as they slowly lose a dear friend. This is a very well written book with well-developed and likable main characters. It was interesting and enlightening as the first

portion of this saga unfolded. I very much enjoyed this book and I do recommend it"

"Judith Keim is one of those authors that you can always depend on to give you a great story with fantastic characters. I'm excited to know that she is writing a new series and after reading book 1 in the series, I can't wait to read the rest of the books."!

The Talking Tree

The Hartwell Women Series - Book 1

Judith Keim

Wild Quail Publishing

The Talking Tree is a work of fiction. Names, characters, places, public or private institutions, corporations, towns, and incidents are the product of the author's imagination or are used fictitiously. Any resemblance to actual events, locales, or persons, living or dead, is coincidental.

No part of this book may be reproduced or transmitted in any form or by any electronic or mechanical means, including information storage and retrieval systems, without permission in writing from the author, except by a reviewer who may quote brief passages in a review. This book may not be resold or uploaded for distribution to others. For permissions contact the author directly via electronic mail:

wildquail.pub@gmail.com

www.judithkeim.com,

Published in the United States of America by:

Wild Quail Publishing
PO Box 171332
Boise, ID 83717-1332

ISBN#: 978-0-9909329-3-2

Dedication

In Loving Memory of My Parents
whose kind spirits touched all who knew them

CHAPTER ONE

My mother's death had brought me back to upstate Barnham, New York, on this crisp April morning. Chills rolled across my shoulders in paralyzing waves as I stared at the peeling paint and darkened windows of my childhood home. Cruelty and rejection had formed its core. I clutched my hands, drew a deep breath, and told myself this place no longer mattered, but I knew better. Until I could work through past issues, I'd always be bound in some horrible way to this house and the people who'd caused such pain.

Lady, my golden retriever, stood patiently at my side. "Come, girl," I said, giving her a pat on the head. We walked toward the backyard to what I'd called the Talking Tree. It had stood outside the house on top of the hill, its branches like welcoming, loving arms. My crippled stepfather had found the hill too difficult to climb, which was why I'd chosen it as my haven away from life in the gray, shingled bungalow below.

I entered the backyard and came to an abrupt stop. My special tree was gone! I raced up the hill through overgrown grass to reach the jagged-edged stump. Breathing hard, I stared at it with dismay. What had happened? Suspicion clenched my jaw. I bet Clyde had climbed the hill after all. It would be so like him to do something crazy like this.

Lady whined and nudged her head under my hand. I sank to the ground and hugged her, feeling as if Clyde had lifted his hand and struck me once again. And even though this blow didn't carry the strength of one of his drunken rages, it hurt just the same. Tears stung my eyes.

I used to talk to that tree as I would have to the brother or sister I'd never had or the mother who'd never listened. And beneath the tree's whispering leaves that broke free from the branches each fall, I'd grown fierce with determination to one day be as free as they. I scrambled to my feet and fingered the stump's still splintered edges. Their sharpness pricked my fingers—and my heart. I should never have come here, I told myself, hating the feeling of being pulled back in time, of losing all the self-confidence I'd worked so hard to build.

I turned away and headed down the hill. Halfway, I paused to study the house. Its faded paint reminded me of my mother's gray eyes—cold and empty. I brushed aside her image and hurried over to the neighbor's house, where I would be staying. Set apart from ours by a line of pine-scented evergreens, it had an air of respectability we'd never been able to achieve. Perky white curtains softened the tiny, paned windows of her home. Light shone through the sparkling glass, like a lighthouse's guiding beam to a wayward ship. Inside, I knew, there would be peace and contentment.

At my knock, Doris Crawford quickly opened the door. "Marissa, my dear, it's so good to see you!" She beamed at me and hugged me close. "Oh, how I've missed seeing that sweet face of yours! All those thoughtful gifts, all those nice phone calls can't compare to actually holding you." Tears shone in her eyes as she looked up at me. "The years away from here have done you good. You're even more beautiful than your photos."

My tense body gave in to her natural warmth, loosening in her embrace. I used to pretend that somehow things had gotten mixed up when I came into the world, and Doris was the mother I was *supposed* to have. But even in the unhappiest of circumstances, fate can sometimes be kind. In this case, she'd given us one another.

"I've missed *you*!" I stepped back and studied her. It had been ten years since I'd seen her. Well into her sixties and barely five feet tall, Doris still held herself with confidence. Keen intelligence shone from her blue eyes. A ready smile lit her round face, subtracting years from her age. To me, she'd always been beautiful.

I gave her another squeeze and followed her inside.

Doris indicated a seat at the solid, round, pine table that was the heart of her warm kitchen.

I inhaled the smell of coffee and settled in a chair. It seemed surreal to be back here, sitting in the same chair where I'd spent so many hours seeking kindness. "I saw my Talking Tree. What happened to it?"

Doris handed Lady a treat and took a seat opposite me. She sighed and gazed into my eyes.

"Not long after you left, I heard shouting over at your place. I looked out and saw Clyde struggling to climb the hill, carrying a power saw." She shook her head. "Your mother followed and stood with him on top of the hill, arguing, trying to stop him, but you know how determined he could be..."

"She tried to stop him?" I drew my lips together. That didn't sound like the mother I knew.

"Clyde shoved her out of his way and went at the tree," Doris continued. "For a moment, I thought it might fall on the old fool."

"It would have served him right."

"I know. He was furious when you left. And he knew how much you loved that tree. I guess that's why he wouldn't give up until it was down."

My hands knotted. Clyde was such a twisted man.

Doris got up and poured each of us a cup of hot coffee, giving me time to rein in my emotions. She handed me a mug and rejoined me at the table.

I took a grateful sip of the hot liquid, letting it slide down my throat in a soothing swallow. "Better tell me what you know about the accident."

Doris took hold of one of my hands. "What with Clyde's medical condition, your mother was driving as usual. She apparently went off the road and hit a tree. The cops said she was drunk. She never made it alive to the hospital."

"And Clyde?" My nostrils flared with dislike. "How is *he*?"

"Clyde suffered internal injuries. They had to use the Jaws of Life to get him out of the car." Doris clucked her tongue. "I'm told he's causing a ruckus in the hospital."

"I don't want anything to do with him," I said with a firmness I felt to my toes. "I came home for my mother's funeral." It was supposed to be a way to help put my relationship with her in better perspective so I could move on with my life. I knew I'd eventually have to deal with Clyde, but being back in Barnham was harder than I'd thought.

"I understand, believe me, but there are things you don't know. Your mother came to see me not long ago and asked me to keep some papers for her. After her death, I did as she instructed and looked through them, then turned them over to Brad to check for any legal issues." She gave my hand a squeeze. "Marissa, your mother left the house and everything in it to *you*, not *him*."

My jaw dropped. "Why didn't she leave it to him?"

"It seems they never married."

"Whaaat?" My voice quivered. "She stayed with him, out of a sense of ... of ... what? Love? I've always thought ..."

My mind spun. I gripped the edge of the table. My mother Margaret had kept her maiden name of Cole, as some women do, but why had she endured living with a man who constantly insulted her and abused her child? One she wasn't bound to by marriage? None of it made sense. It never had.

Doris patted my back. "It's hard to understand. She was a very private person. Her clients loved her ... "

"Clients? You mean the people she cleaned house for?" I knew it sounded harsh, but I couldn't help myself. Our house had been filthy, filled with cigarette smoke, the pungent smell of stale beer and the acrid aura of anger.

Doris's eyebrows shot up. "She was a hardworking woman. You have to give her that, Marissa."

My cheeks flamed at the disapproval in Doris's voice. "Sorry, but I never understood why she worked so hard at other houses and did nothing but sit around and drink at ours. You know that's all they did, drink and fight. God!"

Doris sighed. "It was awful, I know. That's why I helped you leave."

I swallowed hard. It was more than the drinking. Doris didn't know all the details. No one else did. An image of Clyde staggering into my bedroom, drunk, flashed before my eyes. Even now, terror made my heart gallop in nervous beats. If I hadn't been so careful, so strong, who knew what might have happened?

Doris gave me a worried look. "Are you all right?"

I unclenched my hands and shook off the memories. "I guess I'll have to talk to him after all. We have a few things to settle."

"You probably should see him in the hospital, get things cleared up before he's due to come home. There are other living options for him."

My body turned cold at the thought of dealing with Clyde. But my initial purpose of the trip here was about facing the past and letting it go, even if it included a confrontation with him. I rose, wishing I could magically sprout wings and fly back to my safe home in Atlanta. "I'd better get it over with."

"Do you want me to go with you?" Concern showed in

Doris's eyes. She rose and stood beside me.

I shook my head. "Thanks anyway. This is something I need to do. Alone."

Lady lumbered to her feet and looked at me expectantly. I turned to Doris. "Okay if she stays?"

"Sure. I miss Champ. That old hound dog and I spent many long hours together." She gave me an encouraging hug. "Good luck, dear."

I nodded, well aware it would take a lot more than luck to get through this visit and let go of the past.

My gut fisted as I pulled up to the hospital. I felt as if I were about to come face to face with a tornado. Clyde had always been a whirling mass of destruction, lashing out with stinging words and hands that struck viciously.

Inside, the hospital was much as I'd remembered—three stories of small, yellow-painted rooms filled with the pungent odor of antiseptic, the beeping of machines, the sad looks on people's faces, the quiet hush of death.

I took the elevator to the surgical ward, my hands as cold as the New York winters I'd once known.

Standing outside the open doorway to his room, I paused to straighten my clothes and to make sure my thick sweater hung loosely. My heart pounded in warning beats. I swallowed hard, took a deep breath and peered inside the room.

Tubes and monitors surrounded a man who looked much too small to be Clyde. He turned his head and looked right at me. The wicked gleam in his eye sent me whirling back in time. He used to look at me like that before he tried to grab me or say something disgusting to me. I gripped the door frame. I'd gotten the correct room, all right.

"So, it took your mother's foolishness to get you here."

I folded my arms in front of me and willed my voice to be steady. "This isn't a friendly visit, Clyde. We need to discuss something."

"You think so?" His mocking laughter erupted into racking coughs. The color of his face changed to an unhealthy red. "Sit down, girl."

Ignoring the wave of his hand urging me forward, I stood just inside the doorway, not about to fall for his show of friendliness. "They tell me you're going to recover."

"What do they know?" he snarled. "While they think I'm sleeping, I hear 'em whispering about me in the hallway."

Paranoia. That's all it was. I blurted out the question that had rubbed my mind raw. "Why didn't you marry my mother?"

Clyde's lip curled. "She wouldn't have me. 'Said I wasn't good enough for her."

I blinked in surprise. "Why did she hide that fact from me? You stayed together all those years. Why?" I shifted from one foot to the other nervously. Had he forced her to stay with him? Played some sort of abusive mental game with her?

"Why? That's easy. She wanted to remain hidden. Thought she'd be safe that way. An Army buddy of mine told me where she lived. Why else would she have taken me in? I kept her secret so she'd be safe. That's why."

I shook my head in disbelief. My mother hadn't seemed afraid of anyone but him.

"You didn't know her," he challenged, wagging a finger at me. "She worked for cash under the table. No way people could trace her that way."

"What are you talking about?" *Was he crazy?*

"It had somethin' to do with her family. She didn't want 'em to know anything about her."

Disgusted, I pressed my lips together. He was such a

manipulator. "You're lying. She had no family. She told me so several times."

He waved me closer.

I stayed right where I was. No way would I get anywhere near him. I already had the weird sensation I'd shrunk in size.

"I remember everything, Clyde. Everything. And now I know you even chopped down my tree. How sick is that?" I heard the hurt in my voice and didn't care if he heard it too. Ruining the tree was another way for him to strike out at me. I'd never understood why he hated me so.

He was quiet. Tears shone in his eyes. If I hadn't known him better, I might have been tempted to think time had changed him.

"I couldn't stand seein' your mother sittin' up there by that goddamn tree, cryin'." Clyde's voice was raspy with emotion.

"Crying? Why? That doesn't sound like my mother at all."

The hateful gleam came back to Clyde's eyes. "Because, you stupid bitch, you left! It was all *your* fault."

Clyde's words drilled into my chest. "What do you mean, *my* fault? My mother told me to get the hell out and never come back. That's exactly what I did."

"She was drunk when she said it," Clyde said. "You know she didn't mean it."

"Like you didn't mean anything when you were drunk?" I fought for control, furious that once again he'd twisted things around so it was my fault my mother had been unhappy. Sadness had always wrapped around her like a tattered shawl that couldn't warm her. Lord knew I'd tried.

"Aren't you even sorry for all the things you did?"

Clyde's weathered, veined face crumpled. He swept a hand through his long gray hair, bundled in a ponytail as outdated as he. "You want an apology? Okay, dammit, I'm sorry. There. Satisfied?"

I couldn't respond. His words were there, but the emotion was not. It was just another lie, another way to try and influence me. "What are you going to do when you get out of here?"

"Go back home. Why?"

"That's what we need to talk about. It's *my* home now. Mother left it and all the contents to me."

"Whaaat?" Clyde's eyes rounded into dark circles of surprise. His hands drew into broad fists. Fighting the needles and monitors that held him back, he tried to sit up. His face grew purple with rage.

"That bitch! After all I done for her!" The familiar fury etched on his face made my body grow cold. I cringed and backed away, as I'd done so many times before.

An IV needle popped out of his arm. He yelped in pain.

I hurried from the room. "Nurse! Nurse!" But even as I called for help, I didn't care if he lived or died.

Outside, I calmed myself. I'd faced Clyde and stood up to him. But so many things were unsettled. I'd thought this trip would be about endings, but after Clyde's curious ramblings about my mother, I couldn't stop thinking that it might be a beginning. Somewhere I might have a family after all.

CHAPTER TWO

I awoke in Doris's guestroom and stretched. It felt like old times, rising in the cozy warm four-poster bed, hearing the sounds of Doris making coffee and inhaling its enticing aroma. Gratitude filled me. Doris had taken me in when things were too tough, too violent to stay in my own house. Even now, she was my protector.

I leaned over the edge of the bed and patted Lady's head. She lay on the floor, faithfully guarding me. At the touch of my hand, her tail thumped the rug in happy, drumming beats. I smiled and leaped out of bed, eager to be outside in the crisp spring sunshine.

Slipping on a pair of jeans and a sweatshirt, I studied the framed photograph of me Doris kept on the bureau. As much as I didn't want to admit it, I had the same physical features of my mother—smoky gray eyes, auburn hair, and a heart-shaped face. But I'd vowed to never, ever be like her. I wanted a very different life, one filled with love and tenderness from a man I could trust and children who would always know I loved them and would take care of them. First, I had to leave my old self behind and become the woman ready for all that.

Lady nudged me, and I turned and hurried downstairs after her.

As I entered the kitchen Doris smiled at me and handed me a cup of coffee. "Good morning."

"Thanks." I accepted the mug gratefully and gave her a quick peck on the cheek before heading out the back door with the dog.

Outside, steam rose from the hot liquid and greeted me with a moist, satisfying kiss. I stood in the quiet of the cool early morning and decided, like it or not, I needed to set up a meeting with Doris's nephew, Brad Crawford. He was a lawyer who could help me straighten out the mess on my hands. The faster I could get things resolved in Barnham, the earlier I could return to my safe, predictable life in Atlanta. There, I could work on my issues. Here, I could not.

As a young girl, I'd adored Brad, the basketball star of the high school and one of the few kids who'd been kind to me. Now, he was back in Barnham, in a law practice with his father.

Nerves jangling, I went inside and called his office. An assistant agreed to put me in a slot at ten o'clock.

Later, in the privacy of my room, I eased pearl earrings through my lobes and swept back the lock of auburn hair that fell across my brow. I brushed stray dog hair off my black slacks and tugged on my soft pink sweater, telling myself it didn't matter what Brad thought of me. But that was a lie. I wanted him to see me as a woman, and how I'd changed from an insecure girl into a more confident adult.

On schedule, I pulled up in front of the yellow-brick building that housed the law offices of Crawford and Crawford. New small quaint storefronts, so different from those in Atlanta, lined the street nearby.

Inside the law office, a gray-haired woman greeted me from behind a reception desk and indicated a seat. I waited, wondering what the years had done to Brad. My own had been busy, trying to resolve my past through therapy and forging a future by working and continuing to take night courses in telecommunications.

"Mr. Crawford will see you now." The pleasant-faced receptionist studied me with unabashed curiosity. "It's the first door on the left."

I swallowed hard and stood, then headed down the hallway to his office.

Brad rose from behind his desk and strode toward me. A smile brightened his face. "Come in!"

He was even more handsome than he'd been as a teen. His hair, the color of caramel, was swept back from his face, showcasing his strong features. His brown eyes lit up, and his welcoming gaze settled on me. He held out a hand. As his fingers wrapped around mine, a jolt of energy shot up my arm.

I stifled a gasp of surprise but I noticed his eyes widen and realized he'd felt the same connection. Rattled, I didn't know what to say.

He cleared his throat. "It's good to see you, Marissa. It's been a long time. Have a seat."

I gratefully sank into a leather chair and crossed my legs, still shaken by my reaction to him.

He lowered himself into a plush leather chair behind his massive oak desk and steepled his fingers, settling his gaze on me. "You look great."

"Thank you," I managed to say, drawing upon my years of pretending I was just fine when I wasn't at all.

"Aunt Doris told me you're aware that your mother's house and its contents are yours. There's also a small savings account of a couple thousand dollars. It's a pretty simple matter."

I let out a sigh of relief. "Good. I'd like to get back to Atlanta as soon as possible." What an understatement! I couldn't wait to bolt and get back to my comfort zone where no one knew about me with my mother and Clyde.

Brad smiled. "Aunt Doris was hoping you might consider staying. She told me you work for MacTel in Atlanta. A new telecommunications company has opened up in Syracuse. It wouldn't be a bad commute."

My stomach clenched at the thought of living in Barnham. It would be like erasing all the things I'd done to build my new life. I shook my head. "That's nice, but I'm very happy in Atlanta."

He studied me. "Marissa, I know how tough your life was."

My lips grew stiff. "Leaving was the only answer."

"I know." Brad cleared his throat. "Let's talk about your present situation."

The tension left my body as we made a list of things to be done. I'd sell the house as soon as I could. It would be another way to get rid of the past. God knew I could use the money. My school debts alone were overwhelming.

At the end of the discussion, Brad rose. "I'm here to help you in any way I can."

He held out his hand as I stood.

I took it, rocked again by the surge of energy between us.

Brad gave me a searching look, and I fumbled for something to say to smooth over the awkward moment. "I ... I never wanted to come back here."

"I can imagine how you feel. It's funny how things sometimes turn out."

I turned to go and stopped. "Brad? There wasn't any mention of other family members in the papers that Doris gave you? Clyde mentioned she had a family after all. Was there something we missed?"

Brad shook his head. "No. Sorry."

Disappointment stung my eyes. As a young girl, I'd always dreamed that somewhere my real family, a kind, loving family, the family I was meant to live in, was waiting for me. Clyde must have been lying again.

###

As soon as I pulled into Doris's driveway, she came to the front door, an anxious look on her face. "Did the hospital call you?"

I frowned. "No. Why would they?"

"It's Clyde. He's taken a turn for the worse. They don't expect him to live."

I caught my breath. A myriad of emotions spun through me—alarm, satisfaction, and a flash of guilt for being happy that I might not have to deal with him, after all.

Doris led me into the kitchen. "We'd better call them." She dialed the number and handed me the phone.

My hands shook as I waited for the receptionist to connect me to the proper floor. Heaven knows, many times I'd wanted Clyde dead.

"This is Marissa Cole," I began when the doctor's voice came on the line. "I'm returning your phone call regarding Clyde Breeden."

"I'm sorry," came the response. "He passed away a few minutes ago. His heart just stopped beating. We tried to revive him, but we couldn't."

Shaking all over, I hung up the phone and sank down on a kitchen chair. The man who'd terrified me was gone. I'd never have to worry about him again except, perhaps, in my nightmares. The terror of him, real and remembered, fell away from me, leaving me feeling lightheaded with relief. I held my head in my hands and burst into loud, noisy tears.

Doris wrapped her arms around me, and I turned my face into her comforting, safe, soft body.

"Let it go. It's over, Marissa. It's time to move forward and live your own life the way you want, without all this baggage."

"I love you, Doris," I murmured. Though we'd kept in touch, feeling her arms around me was so much better than hearing her encouraging words. Nothing I'd ever done for her over the years equaled my abiding thankfulness for all she'd given me.

"I love you too," she said softly.

I pulled away and swiped at my eyes with the back of my hand, breathing deeply.

"You can do it, Marissa," Doris said firmly. Her sympathy, I well knew, went only so far.

I tried to smile and wiped my tears away. Doris was right. I had to get through the last of my duties here before I could return to Atlanta. Then, maybe, I could deal with the past and finally forget I ever knew a place called Barnham.

Arriving at Bailey's Funeral Home for my mother's service, I was surprised to see a few cars in the parking lot. I shot Doris a questioning look.

She shrugged. "Your mother's customers, I suspect."

Chester Bailey, owner, and chief mortician greeted us at the door. His dour look, dark clothing, and somber manner suited his role. "Welcome. We're ready for you," he said in a soft, soothing voice. "You understand your mother's ashes won't be ready for a few weeks?"

I gave an inward shudder and nodded.

I'd chosen the flowers on the small, non-denominational altar. The huge spring bouquet symbolized promise to me. Perhaps my mother was in a much better place. This one had, apparently, been hell for her.

I noted the dozen or so people seated in chairs in front of the altar—all of them strangers. A few waved at Doris.

We took our seats, and the minister rose.

The service was very traditional. The clergyman obviously didn't know Margaret Cole. The kind, loving woman he described bore no resemblance to the absent, cold mother I knew. My eyes remained stubbornly dry. Not out of spite, but simply because I hadn't known her. Not as a woman, and certainly not as a mother—she was never there for me when I needed her most. I simply outgrew the desire to have her in my life. It was almost as if a stranger had vanished.

At the end of the short service, a well-dressed elderly woman approached me. "I'm Jane Houghton. You must be Marissa. Your mother often spoke of you. I'm so sorry for your loss."

I blinked in surprise.

"Margaret was a great help to me over the years. I came to count on her." Jane studied me and then continued. "She was a sad woman who remained a bit of a mystery to me. She had the marks of good genetics—fine features, her carriage, her natural style. I always wondered about that." She smiled. "You have it, too. Fine bones, as my mother used to say."

"Thank you," I mumbled, caught unaware by what Jane had revealed about my mother.

Jane turned away to greet someone else, and Brad approached me. "The flowers look nice. Doris said you special-ordered them."

"Thanks. They remind me of spring in Atlanta."

"You said you were selling the property." Brad gave me a crooked grin. "I don't have any plans this weekend. If you need any help hauling stuff, just give me a call."

"No plans with the family?" I asked, curious about his life.

"My parents are away on vacation." He grinned again, reminding me of the impish boy I'd always admired. "And much to my mother's distress, I'm single once more."

Surprised, I was oddly pleased by the news. "Thanks for the offer. I'll see how it goes."

"I don't know what to say about Clyde ..." he said, hesitating.

I sighed wearily. "It's a closed chapter—over and done with. He had no relatives. I'll see that he gets a decent veteran's burial and that'll be the end of it."

He stared at me thoughtfully. "That's good of you, considering everything."

He walked away to greet another guest, and Doris approached. "Ready to go?"

I turned away from watching Brad and looked at Doris. "Brad's never remarried?"

Doris shook her head. "Eight months of being married to Amber Johnson really soured him on that. In that short time, she charged up his credit cards, took all the wedding gifts for herself and tried to leave him high and dry." She clucked her tongue. "He says he'll never marry again."

From across the room, he caught my eye and grinned.

After a quick bite to eat at Doris's place, I stood outside the house in which I'd grown up, trembling like the frightened teenager I'd been. Lady remained at my heels. Taking a deep breath, I forced myself to place the key in the front door lock. My hands shook so badly, I could hardly find the opening.

At the clicking sound of release, I pushed the door open and jumped back out of the way, as if the tainted memories of the house could escape into the fresh air and strike me down with their dark force.

I stepped inside, hurried over to the windows and opened the shades to allow the sunshine to filter in. Light was what I needed to fight the darkness in here, I told myself. Blinking at the sudden brightness in the living room, I turned away from the windows. Stale cigarette smoke hung in the air, a gray pall that spoke of so many things.

My gaze settled on the worn, fake leather couch.

Resentment burned inside me at the memory of Clyde's behavior. No doubt he'd continued to spend most of his time there, lounging, watching television, drinking. I could almost see him sitting there, his white undershirt barely able to contain the bulge of his stomach, graying whiskers covering a face whose skin had gone spidery with drink, his beady eyes following my every move.

I glanced at the blue overstuffed chair by the bookcase in the corner of the room—my mother's favorite spot. It, too, looked worn and shabby. I brushed my hand across my eyes, trying to erase her image from my mind. There wasn't a thing I wanted in the house, though pride would force me to clean things up a bit before putting the place on the market.

It was all such a waste, I thought, thinking of the family I hoped to have someday. I wanted it all—love, laughter, and lovely things around me. Foolish as it sometimes seemed, coming from my background, the dream of a real family of my own had never died within me. But now was not the time, nor this, the place.

Sunshine glared through the windows and cast an unforgiving eye on the filth inside. I glanced around, repulsed by all I saw. It would be a huge job to clean up the place, but I swore I would do it well. No one in town would know that Marissa Cole had lived in such squalid conditions right under their tilted noses.

I marched to the bottom of the stairs and looked up to the floor above. "Come, girl." My voice quivered as I called to Lady. Heart beating wildly, I took one step up the stairs, then another. Each one sent me farther back to an unhappy time. At the top of the stairway, I headed for my room, not sure what to expect. Pausing at the doorway, I let out a gasp. The room was spotless. The old spindle bed under the sloping roof was just as I'd left it. My ancient rose-colored quilt still covered it.

The white teddy bear Billy Whipple had won at the state fair in the eighth grade lay on my pillow and peered back at me with a quizzical expression. He'd given it to me as a token of his undying, boyish love. Tears stung my eyes as I lifted the stuffed bear and hugged it tightly. It had listened to my dreams of one day living an entirely different life. Yet, when it had come time to leave home, I'd left it behind, wanting nothing from my past to spoil my chances for a better future.

I opened the white painted chest in the room, one drawer at a time. Some of my worn sweaters from high school were still there as if the whole room had been waiting for my return. Was that why my mother had kept it ready?

I sank onto the bed, confused. She'd been such a painful puzzle to me. Jane's words came back to me. The woman she'd described to me was someone I didn't know. Now, I doubted I'd ever come to understand my mother.

As agreed, Brad arrived at Doris's place at six to take us to dinner. He and Doris exchanged quick hugs, and then he cheerfully helped her with her coat. Observing the easy affection between them, I felt a prick of envy.

Seated at a nice table by the window inside Antonio's restaurant, Doris's gaze flitted between Brad and me, a happy smile on her face. Doris sometimes liked to take matters in her own hand, and I suspected what she was thinking—her two favorite young people would make a nice couple. She'd have to forget her fantasy. It would never work. Clyde had damaged me more than even he would've guessed. Relationships were not easy for me—a romantic one, more difficult yet.

Doris jabbed me with her elbow, playfully. "You should have seen the article in the local paper about Brad and the other businessmen in town. He's famous in these parts."

Brad shifted in his seat uncomfortably. "Now, Aunt Doris, don't start." He turned to me. "We've begun a campaign to lure suburbanites in nearby Syracuse to move to Barnham. The small downtown area is being renovated by new retailers who are attracting more and more customers."

Listening to him talk about what the campaign entailed, I wondered if Brad was as nice as he seemed. As we sat at dinner, several women waved at him, one outrageously flirtatious. A couple of men tipped their heads as they walked by. Another man stopped to shake his hand. Brad accepted the attention graciously without letting it go to his head. By the end of the meal, I was beginning to realize he really was a great guy—like he'd always been. What, I wondered, had gone so wrong with his marriage?

As Brad drove us home, Doris broke the silence in the car. "Antonio's is the best restaurant in town. Didn't you think the food was wonderful, Marissa?" She turned around in the front seat and beamed at me, prompting me to say something.

"Yes, very nice." The chicken piccata I'd ordered was excellent. I was pleasantly full.

"Brad is so good to me." Doris patted him on the shoulder. "He's the nicest young man I know."

He caught my eye in the mirror and winked. I held back a laugh. Doris was nothing, if not persistent, in trying to get the two of us together. It wouldn't happen. I was anxious to leave town, and he never wanted to marry again.

After helping each of us out of the car, Brad led us to the front door, where he gave Doris a quick peck on the cheek. Before I could step away, he gave me a kiss to match. Caught by surprise, I rocked back on my heels and lifted my hand to my cheek, still feeling the heat and the tenderness of his lips.

Brad grinned at me and bid us both a cheery goodnight before turning and bounding down the front porch steps.

CHAPTER THREE

Old memories fought with common sense as I once more faced the battered front door of the house I now owned. I swallowed hard, reluctant to enter. I couldn't afford to have someone else do the dirty work for me nor did I want to. This task was like ridding me of the past. I told myself the house was empty. No one was inside, no one would yell at me, no one would grab my hair in fury, and no one would try to grope me or leer at me with drunken lust.

"Lady, heel," The dog nudged my left leg and stayed by my side as I opened the door.

Trying not to inhale the odor of rotting food, I went to work in the kitchen. In no time, I filled two large garbage bags with food-encrusted dishes, and dirty pots and pans. I discarded opened jars of food, along with tattered boxes from the cupboard shelves. Lifting the soiled cushions off the seats of the maple captain's chairs, I tossed them in a garbage bag and washed my hands. I sank down into a chair, as confused as ever by my mother. Lady rested her head in my lap. I stroked it, loving the comforting feel of her soft fur.

"What a mess!" I said into the empty room.

Lady perked her ears as if she knew I meant more than the condition of the kitchen. My mother's whole life had been a mess—one I would never understand.

The sound of a truck disturbed the silence. I rose and went to the front door. Drexler's Disposal Service was delivering the dumpster I ordered. I waved the driver to the back of the house.

Out back, a burly man with a gray fringe of hair around his bald pate jumped out of the truck he'd pulled up to the kitchen door. He checked to make sure the heavy container had settled properly.

He offered his hand to me. "Bud Drexler. You said you're selling? Can I take a look see? The wife and I are lookin' to downsize, now that the kids are gone. I'm real handy." He indicated the house with a nod of his head. His dark eyes seemed to take in every forlorn detail. "Figure this place could use a handyman."

I held up a hand. "Once I get things in order I'll be glad to have you come inside. Give me your card and I'll call you when things are ready." I didn't care what the man might offer for it, I'd jump at the chance to unload the place.

"Fair enough. Like I said, name's Bud Drexler." He searched inside his tan work shirt pocket, pulled out a business card and handed it to me.

I glanced at it while he climbed back inside his truck. He bobbed his head, and I waved, gripping the card so hard it bent. I might be able to sell the house sooner than I'd thought. Relief coursed through me. This soulless house was my last link to the past.

Just after noon, Doris knocked on the front door. I wiped my soapy hands on my jeans and went to answer it.

"Thought you might want to take a break for lunch," she said, offering a tentative smile. Her gaze swept the room behind me, and her eyes widened.

"Come on in. Give me a minute to get my thermos, and I'll walk over with you."

"My!" Doris said. "I had no idea the place was such a mess. I've never been inside." She made a clucking noise. "Don't you want to hire some professional cleaners?"

I shook my head. "Not a chance. This is more therapeutic

than a double session with my shrink. Opening up the windows, letting the fresh air in, and cleaning up the mess inside, makes it seem as if I'm doing just that to my past."

She patted my hand. "Good for you."

Lunch was tuna salad and a frank talk with Doris about Brad.

"You know he's always had a soft spot for you." Doris gave me a hopeful look.

I looked at her tenderly. "Doris, I know what you're trying to do and it won't work. I've got a life I love in Atlanta and Brad is a big wheel here. Besides, I'm not very good at loving relationships."

She gave me a steady look. "At some point, Marissa, you have to learn to trust people."

I squirmed in my seat. It wasn't the first time I'd heard those words. I wished I could let myself go, especially with someone exactly like Brad.

Munching on a cookie, I left Doris and returned to the house to do a thorough cleaning of the refrigerator and stove. Mid-afternoon, I took a break, and sat on the back stoop, staring at the spot on the hill where the Talking Tree had stood. It was such a waste to have chopped it down, I mused, but so typical of Clyde's mentality.

Sighing at what I couldn't change, I checked my watch and dragged myself back indoors. The living room would have to wait until Brad could help me move the furniture. Most of it would go into the dumpster; some could stay for whoever wanted it.

I picked up a box of plastic garbage bags and climbed the stairs into my mother's bedroom. Starting with the closet, I leafed through the items on hangars. Surprisingly, many of my mother's clothes were of good quality, nice enough for me to know that my mother's income wouldn't pay for them.

She'd probably picked them up at Goodwill.

I carefully folded several items and tucked them in bags for charity.

In the very back of the closet, a white blazer hung on a padded hanger. I lifted it out and held it up for a closer look. A multi-colored coat of arms was woven into the pocket. The name *St. Andrews* was stitched in navy blue above the emblem. From its softness, I guessed the blazer was made of cashmere. I'd never seen it before.

I took the jacket off the hanger and tried it on. It fit perfectly. The faint yellow tinge to the cloth made me realize it must have hung there for some time. Closing my eyes, I tried to recall any mention of St. Andrews. The emblem looked like it belonged to a school of some kind—a private one, no less. Why was it hanging in my mother's closet?

Sliding the blazer off my shoulders, I started to add it to the discards in the bag for charity then held back, unwilling to let the mysterious jacket go. Had someone given it to her? Like some of the other clothes?

I set the blazer aside and sorted through the bottom drawer of her bureau, sweeping up a bunch of sweaters to toss into a bag. At the clink of something falling on the pine floor, I looked down. A gold ring winked in the sunlight as it rolled along the wooden surface.

I picked it up and studied the delicately carved flowers that covered the wide band. It was so beautiful I couldn't imagine my mother wearing it. The initials M.C. and B.B. were engraved inside. MC surely stood for Margaret Cole.

"Who was B.B.?" I whispered.

I sank onto the bed, lost in thought. Many times I'd asked my mother about my father. All she would tell me was that he'd died in a military action. That's how Clyde Breeden came into our lives. He'd promised Tim Hartwell, an Army buddy of his, he'd pay a visit to Margaret Cole and her daughter if anything happened to him.

So, as far as I knew, Tim Hartwell was my father. My mother would never verify that. In fact, she became irrationally upset if I pressed her for information about him. A drunken episode usually followed. I'd checked my birth certificate, of course, but it made no mention of any father. After a while, I gave up. I didn't try to find his family; instead, I concentrated on escaping mine. Now I wondered if I'd made a mistake in not pursuing the subject of my father more strenuously.

I slipped the ring on the fourth finger of my right hand. It looked good there, and I liked the idea that my mother must have loved someone enough to keep the ring hidden all these years. I'd always hoped that my mother and father had loved one another, but now I doubted it. The initials T.H. were not in the ring.

Still wearing the ring, I loaded my car with bulging plastic bags of her clothes to take to Goodwill. Tomorrow, as much as I hated the idea, I'd clear Clyde's room of everything, though the mere thought of touching his things sent a shudder across my aching shoulders.

"Looks like you could use a fresh cup of coffee," Doris said when I trudged into her kitchen and collapsed in a chair, exhausted.

"Sounds wonderful."

"Catch your breath," she said, getting to her feet. "After you do, I've got something to give you."

At her closed expression, suspicion gripped me. "Something to do with my mother?"

"A sealed envelope addressed to you. She gave me this,

along with some papers, approximately three weeks ago. I put them away, certain I wouldn't have to go through them for some time, if ever. After all, your mother was quite a bit younger than I am."

Doris handed me a light blue envelope, along with the cup of coffee.

My mother's spidery handwriting spun my name across the front in blue ink. Dread welled inside me. What was my mother going to say in this letter that she couldn't say to me in person?

Upstairs in my room, I sat on the bed and stared at my mother's thin, wispy, almost flowery handwriting. It suited her, I supposed. She was thin and willowy, her hair a flaming red until early aging dimmed its glory. For most of my memory, there was no fire left in her. She was bent and broken, like a young tree caught in a violent storm.

Odd, I'd never thought of her as young, yet I realized as I sat there thinking of her, she was only in her late teens when she had me and not much past fifty when she died.

Gritting my teeth, I remembered my therapist's instruction to gather in my whirling emotions and deal with them one by one. Pain, anger, and sadness battled and were brought into line.

I ripped open the envelope. My mother's words stared up at me, challenging me to maintain my control. I studied every word, my vision blurring.

"Marissa, if you're reading this letter, I'm dead. I'm sorry we couldn't be friends, but it was too much to ask of me. It wasn't your fault; the heart of me was destroyed long before you were born. I ask something important of you. I want my ashes to be scattered at sea at Briar Cliff in New Hope, Maine.

There, you may have a better understanding of my life. Margaret Cole."

Furious, I bunched up the letter and threw it across the room. She'd signed her full name, for God's sake, as if I didn't know who in hell she was.

"Dammit to hell," I fumed. "She still hasn't told me anything about her!"

Trying to conjure up a sympathetic picture of my mother, I let my anger out in short, puffing breaths. The image that came to mind was of a straggly-haired, red-headed woman whose face didn't seem to know whether to puff from the alcohol she drank so heavily or to shrivel from the nicotine that drew her skin into lines of distress.

What I remembered most were my mother's eyes, an unusual shade of slate gray that complemented what once had been thick red hair. As beautiful as they were, the defeat in them had made me want to turn away. She was an unhappy woman. I always knew that.

I grabbed a pillow and punched it, too mad to hold back. I'd read in magazines that New Hope, Maine, was a small seaside village in the south of the state, known for its seasonal estates, made famous when the first President Bush summered in Kennebunkport.

I sat on the edge of the bed, breathing hard, staring at the crumpled paper on the floor. There were too many unanswered questions. The answers might help me understand my mother and allow me to forgive her for all that had gone on. I had to know more.

Hurrying downstairs, I called for Doris.

Startled, she looked up from the book she was reading. "What is it?"

I took a seat on the edge of the living room couch. "My

mother wants her ashes scattered in New Hope, Maine. What do you know about it?"

Doris cleared her throat. "Your mother came to see me not long ago. She handed me a bunch of papers and asked if I would help her. We had coffee and talked about what she wanted me to do if something ever happened to her."

"Did you do that often after I left? I mean, have coffee together?"

Doris shook her head. "She seldom stopped by. I was really surprised when it happened."

"What did she say?"

"She never mentioned your name but we both knew who was on her mind when she gave me the papers. She said she'd been thinking of her death recently and wanted me to handle things for her."

My breath came out in a shocked whoosh. "She'd been worrying about death?"

"Call it a premonition or what you will. Some people have an impending sense of their death. Apparently, your mother did."

"Did she tell you anything about her childhood? Or New Hope, Maine?"

Doris shook her head. "Not one word. I found it difficult to know what went on inside her head. I've never understood the relationship between her and Clyde." She clucked her tongue. "It wasn't healthy or happy."

"I wish there was someone I could talk to about her."

"Jane Houghton, who spoke to you at the funeral service, may know something. She was your mother's biggest client."

I tucked that piece of information away, torn between wanting to know more and leaving the painful past behind. I held out my right hand and indicated the gold ring I'd found.

"Look what I discovered among my mother's sweaters."

Doris leaned closer. "It's lovely. Absolutely lovely."

I twirled it on my finger. "It has my mother's initials inside and those of someone named B.B. I don't know who B.B is, but it can't be my father. I'm pretty sure his initials were T.H."

Doris patted my hand. "I'm sorry I don't have answers for you. Your mother was a very private person. She didn't allow anyone to get close to her."

"That says it all, doesn't it?" I commented sadly.

"Are you going to do as she requested?"

I shrugged. "The funeral home is supposed to contact me when her ashes are available. I'm not going to make any decision until then." I rose, too frustrated to sit still. "Guess I'll take Lady for a walk. I've got to get some fresh air."

Doris gave me an understanding nod.

Outside, I was drawn to the Talking Tree. I climbed the hill and paced at the top, circling the stump of the tree, my thoughts in turmoil. My mother thought a trip to New Hope would explain her behavior through the years? That wouldn't do it for me. If she'd wanted to tell me something, why in hell hadn't she tried to reach me? Anger burned inside me. My mother had kept her distance from me to the very end. Eleanor Boswell, my therapist, used to tell me that the day would come when my mother and I could meet and talk about the hurtful past without too much damage. She'd been reluctant to push for a meeting until I was stronger.

Now, it was too late.

Jane Houghton's home sat in the nicest section of Barnham, an area abutting the small grassy square in the center of town. In the middle of the square, a monument rose to the blue sky like a raised sword, honoring the local men who had fought and lost their lives in World War II. The homes that lined the square were all relics of that time, standing stately and tall, like proud, aging matrons.

Her house was a large Victorian painted a pretty tan and trimmed in white with burgundy and green accents. I stood on the broad sweep of a porch, waiting for her to respond to the doorbell. Questions circled my mind. I wondered what relationship my mother had had with this woman who seemed to know more about her than I did.

She greeted me with a broad smile. "Come in. It's so lovely that we'll have a chance to talk."

Following her through a wide hallway, I felt intimidated by her refined appearance. She wore a gray flannel skirt, a pale blue sweater and a string of pearls, which from their luminescence must have cost as much as I earned in a month. I brushed at my denim jeans, wishing I'd worn something different.

"Thanks for taking the time to see me. As you can tell, I'm working at the house again today."

Jane smiled. "I'm sure there's a lot to be done. It's always that way. I don't know what my sons will do when it comes time for me to move out of this old ark of a place. Forty-eight years is plenty of time to collect all kinds of things. And I've certainly done that."

I chuckled along with her.

"I was a new bride when David, that was my husband, moved me into this house," Jane explained. "I'm thinking about moving to Florida to get out of the weather here. It's become a more definite goal with your mother gone. She's the one who kept this house looking so nice. She came to me when my husband was dying, over fifteen years ago. Not too long after you left." Her blue eyes pierced mine.

Feeling vulnerable and exposed, I crossed my arms in front of my chest.

Jane waved a hand of dismissal. "I don't know all the details, nor do I want to. Your mother was very reserved. I didn't poke into her business and she didn't poke into mine. I do know, though, that she was a very unhappy woman."

We sat in the living room, which would have been properly called the parlor in earlier times. The high-ceilinged room was filled with large antiques and heavy dark furniture that suited the style of the home.

Jane stirred in her seat. "I tried to talk to her about her drinking, you know."

My eyebrows shot up. "What did she say?"

She shook her head. "Typical active alcoholic. She denied everything, said she just had some drinks to quiet her nerves. When I mentioned it again, I thought she was going to up and leave me. I decided as long as she did good work for me, and she did, that I should mind my own business. We got along just fine after that."

Studying Jane, an idea came to me. "You gave her all the clothes, didn't you?"

"She loved nice things. One day I caught her at my closet door, caressing a cashmere sweater of mine. She turned to me with a dreamy smile on her face and told me that she'd worn such clothes once."

I leaned forward. "Did she say anything else, like where she'd worn those clothes?"

Jane shook her head. "No, but I decided then and there, that when it was time to lay certain clothes aside, Margaret would get them. She loved receiving new items for her wardrobe."

"I ... I don't know much about my mother," I stammered. "We didn't get along. She never told me anything about her childhood, her family or anything else. In fact, she said she had no family. Now she's left me a written request to scatter her ashes at sea in New Hope, Maine. I have no idea why. Does that name or the name St. Andrews mean anything to you? Has my mother ever mentioned them to you?"

Jane shook her head. "As I said, Margaret didn't share much information with me. I do think that as unlikely as it seems, she came from a good background. She loved nice things and knew the difference between quality and show. Also, as I mentioned to you at her service, she was once a beautiful woman. You look just like her, you know."

A shiver crossed my shoulders. I couldn't get my mind around the idea that my mother was thought to be beautiful. I certainly didn't feel that way about myself.

Jane confessed she had nothing else to tell me about my mother. I checked my watch and rose. Brad was due to arrive at my mother's house any minute to help me with the furniture.

"Thank you," I told her, extending my hand.

"Your mother would be very proud of you," said Jane.

Tears stung my eyes. Even if they might be just a social nicety, Jane's words meant a lot to me.

I left Jane's house knowing a little more about my mother—enough to make me think that the well-preserved cashmere blazer in her closet must have been hers. Still, I had to know more.

CHAPTER FOUR

Brad's SUV was sitting in the driveway when I arrived at the house. I parked behind it and went to look for him. I heard Lady bark and hurried into the backyard just as Brad threw a stick for her. She bounded after it, her paws pounding the grass in excitement.

"Sorry, I'm a few minutes late."

Brad turned and grinned at me. "It's okay. Lady and I were having a little fun. " A breeze caught a lock of his hair and formed a curl over his forehead. His cheeks were flushed from the cool air. In his jeans, he looked ... well, fabulous.

Broad-shouldered beneath his sweater, he strode toward me. His long legs moved with strength and purpose.

I warned myself to ignore the stirrings of attraction. I'd tried to have normal relationships with other men but had ended up embarrassing myself when past memories caused me to panic at anything too sexual.

"Ready to go inside? We've got lots of work to do."

Brad grinned and flexed his muscles in a mock show of strength. "I didn't go to the gym this morning. 'Figured this workout would take the place of that."

I returned his smile. "I really appreciate your help."

Brad followed me into the living room and let out a low whistle. "I didn't know things were this bad." He fingered a hole in the drywall where I suspected Clyde had thrown something. He stared at the stuffing oozing from the rips in the worn couch.

"You should have seen the place when I started cleaning it

out. I'm donating the books to the library and other things to charity, but the rest of the stuff will be thrown out. I don't want any of it."

"I can see why. Where do we start?"

I pointed to the couch where Clyde had sat, leering at me, quizzing me on what I'd done at school, making suggestive remarks about anything he could. Looking at it now, a shudder traveled through my body.

Brad lifted one side of the couch, and I grabbed hold of the other end. We half carried, half dragged it through the kitchen and out the back door. "There," grunted Brad, hefting it into the dumpster. It landed with a noisy thump.

We dumped all the living room chairs, including the blue chair that had been my mother's favorite. We moved the bookcase and the floor lamp beside the chair to the garage where a pile of things was accumulating to be given away. We rolled up the threadbare area rug, and Brad dragged it out the door.

"Whew! That's better." I gazed at the empty room, feeling a tiny part of my past fall away.

"Anything else?" A smudge of dirt darkened the tip of Brad's nose.

Caught up in the moment, I lifted a finger to wipe it off.

He smiled and took hold of my hand.

My heart raced at the way he was looking at me. I knew he wanted to kiss me. I wanted it too. He was so handsome, so nice.

Brad took hold of my hand and drew me to him. I told myself to relax. But memories of Clyde grabbing hold of my hand and pulling me close kept intruding, twisting the sweetness of this moment into something ugly. I jerked away.

"What's wrong?" Brad asked, surprised.

"Nothing." I felt sick and ashamed.

Brad studied me.

I looked away, wishing things were different.

After a few awkward seconds, Brad said, "Well, I guess we'd better get busy with the stuff upstairs." He turned away.

"Brad?" I couldn't let his tender gesture go. Struggling to overcome my tortured memories, I reached for him, remembering all the times my therapist had encouraged me to do something exactly like this. Standing on my toes, I lifted my face up to his. His lips met mine, soft and sure, tasting of toothpaste, clean and fresh.

When we broke apart, Brad gave me a look of gentleness that warmed my insides. "God, Marissa! I've wanted to do this ever since high school." He wrapped his arms tighter around me, making me aware of his arousal.

The safe place in my mind evaporated. Overcome with memories too real to deny, here in this house with its horrible history, I shoved him away with all my strength.

"Jesus! What's wrong?" Brad looked as shocked as I felt.

"God, Brad! I'm sorry, so sorry," I managed to get out. "It's not you! It's me!"

Shaken, I ran from the room, out through the kitchen and up the hill to where the Talking Tree had once stood so proud, so comforting.

"Marissa?" Brad came up behind me. "I'm sorry. I didn't mean to come on so strong. I guess I got carried away."

I turned to him. Hot tears burned my cheeks as they slid down. I lowered myself to the ground. "I'm just too emotional with all that's going on with my mother's death and all."

There was no way I was about to tell him that Clyde used to grab me any chance he got, sometimes forcing me to touch him. Or that my mother had done more than ignore my distress. I ran my hand over my cheek. She'd once hit me, sending me to the floor, calling me a whore. No, I'd die before

I told him or anyone else any of that.

Brad took a seat beside me and gave me a look of concern. "I don't think it's a good idea for you to remain here at the house alone. Why don't I stay and help you clear out the rest of the things?"

Grateful beyond words, I nodded. I'd thought by cleaning out the house myself, the work would symbolically rid me of my bad memories and enable me to put Clyde and my mother behind me. But it was too difficult to pretend the past was over. It wouldn't be over until I knew who she was, who my father was, who I was.

Brad and I worked steadily, quietly, avoiding talk of what had happened between us. By the end of the day, the dumpster was overflowing, and the one-car garage held a number of full boxes, along with a few pieces of furniture, to go to Goodwill. Besides the jacket and the ring, the only thing I saved for myself was the white teddy bear that had sat on my bed throughout my teen years. It seemed only right that the little bear be given freedom, too.

Later, Brad and I sat on the back stairs in silence, catching our breaths, relaxing our tired bodies. I glanced over at him. Though he'd been mostly quiet throughout the afternoon, the tightness of his lips had spoken volumes. He knew my earlier reaction was caused by more than the issues with my mother.

He reached out and lightly stroked my cheek with his fingers.

My heart filled at his kindness. He was a good man. I wished I was able to return affection as easily as he gave it.

I wanted to get out of Barnham as fast as I could. I called

Bud Drexler and told him I was ready to talk to him about selling the house. Brad had told me that the housing market in the area was on an upswing because of the new businesses coming to town. I didn't care what I got for the place as long as it allowed me to leave and close this chapter of my life forever. I'd look elsewhere for the answers I now wanted.

I met with the Drexlers and gave them a tour of the house. Whereas I saw the house for what it had been, Bud was able to envision what it might become. And the house was in a nice area—a quiet, peaceful neighborhood close to the heart of the town. Bud made an offer and I immediately accepted it, well aware he was getting it for a bargain price.

Brad drew up the purchase and sale agreement for us both to sign. I let out a relieved sigh when Brad assured me a closing could take place without my presence.

I locked up the house, happy I'd never have to come back to Barnham.

Doris greeted me at the door to her house. "The Drexlers are buying it?" Her eyes filled.

"They'll be good neighbors."

She followed me upstairs. "You sure you can't stay a while longer?"

I put my arm around her. "Thanks, but I have to get back to Atlanta. I talked to my boss and he needs me."

A short while later I loaded my suitcase into my old blue Honda. Eager to be on the road, I waved good-bye to Doris, helped Lady into the backseat and got behind the wheel.

Doris stood at the edge of the driveway, clutching her hands. "Keep in touch, hear?" Tears glistened in her eyes.

Determined to be brave, I forced a reassuring smile. "Thanks for everything, Doris. I'll call you. Like always." For all the bad in my life, there'd been some good things, too. Doris was one of the best.

In town, I parked in front of Brad's office and cracked a window open for Lady, letting the cool air in. Then, mindful of her, I hurried inside to Brad's office to sign the papers for the sale of the house. He rose from behind his desk. "Aunt Doris called to say you were leaving town for good."

"Yes. With the house off my hands, there's no reason for me to stay any longer."

Brad walked over and gingerly wrapped his arms around me.

I stiffened and then relaxed for a moment before pulling away. Even though he might be a tempting reason to try it, I couldn't stay in Barnham any longer.

He stared at me for a moment with his brown eyes and, as if waiting for permission, lifted my chin before gently placing his lips on mine.

Trusting him, I closed my eyes. It felt so good to savor the taste of him, to feel his gentle touch.

He released me and caressed my cheek. "Stay well, Marissa."

I smiled and turned to go. I'd just reached the door when he called, "Marissa?"

I stopped and turned. "Yes?"

He paused and then shrugged, apparently thinking better of what he'd wanted to say. "Be safe."

"Thanks," I said softly and let myself out of his office.

Traveling down Interstate 81, through the hills and valleys of Pennsylvania, into Virginia, and then following the Appalachians into Georgia, my thoughts stayed on Brad. He was the kind of man who would make some woman very happy. I hoped someday I'd have the courage to try for the brass ring of love and family with someone exactly like him—

just not someone from Barnham.

My lips curved when I pulled into the driveway of the small house I rented outside Atlanta. Letting out a satisfied sigh, I stepped outside the car and stretched.

Lady barked as if to warn the neighborhood canines that she, once more, was in charge of her own territory. Glad to be home, she pranced in delighted circles.

I stood a moment and studied this well-loved home with its gentle soul. The clapboard house was tiny but cheery, painted a bright yellow with crisp white trim. Red tulips in front of neatly trimmed bushes bobbed and bowed a greeting in the breeze. I breathed in the warm spring air, reveling in the change in temperature. I'd left winter behind. It was symbolic, I thought, to be back in Atlanta's spring weather, where new life was emerging in colorful glory. Here, I could begin a whole new segment of my life.

I lugged my things inside with renewed energy. Lifting the white blazer out of the suitcase, I slipped it on and stood in front of the mirror, studying myself. If, as Jane Houghton and others had said, I looked exactly like my mother, why had she let herself go? I squinted to blur the image. My reflection was striking in the rich-looking school blazer.

A flash of anger brought me up straight. There were so many unknowns to deal with. I didn't even know if it would be worth the trouble of trying to find out who my mother was when she hadn't cared enough to try and find me. Unable to deal with the old painful issues, I ripped the jacket off, disgusted with the whole affair. Better to let it go, I told myself. Our tale was an old, sad story with no new chapter. And I had to move forward.

I settled back into my old life, slipping into the familiar

pattern of going to work each day and to school two nights a week. Before I'd left town, I was seeing Eleanor Boswell, my therapist every Wednesday. I decided to see her again. The visit to Barnham had raised issues I'd thought were settled.

She smiled as I slid onto the big leather chair in front of her desk and twisted my hands in my lap.

"How was it, going back home?" Eleanor asked.

I let out a sigh. "It was hard being there, remembering so many things. But I confronted Clyde in the hospital and it felt good. He was such a bad guy. He even chopped down my tree."

Eleanor's eyebrows lifted. "The Talking Tree?"

"Yes. Doris, my neighbor, told me he did it right after I left. Pretty sick if you ask me."

"Why do you think he did that?" Eleanor asked softly. She leaned back in her chair, waiting for my answer.

"Because I'd bested him after all."

She gave me a satisfied look. "Who else did you see when you were there? Anyone else besides Doris who's important to you?"

"Brad Crawford." My voice sounded foolishly breathy but I couldn't help it.

Her eyes gazed into mine. "Want to tell me about him?"

I took a deep breath and all my thoughts about him tumbled out of my mouth—how I'd secretly adored him since high school, how handsome and kind he'd become, and how he'd tenderly kissed me good-bye. My cheeks flamed with embarrassment, but I held nothing back.

She leaned forward. "Sounds like you're making progress, Marissa."

I smiled. He was the best man I'd ever met.

Eleanor broke into my dreamy thoughts. "This experience with Brad can be helpful to you, Marissa. Good friendships are built with trust over time."

"What if I want it to be more than friendship?"

Eleanor's lips curved. "Ah, I hoped you'd admit that. I saw it in your eyes, heard it in your voice when you mentioned his name. That's something we can work on. But opening your heart to someone else means you're going to have to take a chance—be vulnerable, share control. Are you ready for that?"

I wondered if I could do it.

Several weeks passed. Eleanor and I did exercises on trust, control, and forgiveness. She encouraged me to reach out to others, allowing people to become close to me.

Sari, one of my girlfriends at MacTel, began to meet me after work one evening a week, sharing a light meal and lots of talk. She'd always been outgoing, so I was surprised when she told me she'd lost her parents at an early age and had been raised in a harsh foster home. Her story made it easier to bond. She listened carefully to some of my past. "Jeez, Marissa, I'm sorry. That Clyde was a total pervert. Thank God I never had to cope with that."

Encouraged by her reaction, I told her about my last meeting with Clyde, feeling my spirits rise as I recalled how I'd stood up to him before hurrying for help.

"Y'all went through a bad time. Survivors, that's what we are, girl!" Sari raised her glass.

I grinned and tapped her glass of wine with my Coke. That clink of glass on glass sounded a note that cemented our friendship.

After spending years of trying to hide every detail of my life, I found it exhilarating to finally talk about it. I realized that others weren't going to blame me for Clyde's behavior, say I'd encouraged him, call me a whore like my mother had so cruelly done.

I wasn't the only one who'd had difficulties growing up. Sari had too, and it had made her stronger like I wanted to become.

One night, while I was sitting in my kitchen finishing a hasty meal, the phone rang. Thinking it was Sari, I picked it up. "Hey there! Feeling better? I missed you at work today!"

"Marissa?"

My pulse began to pound. "Brad?"

"Yeah, it's me. I've been thinking about you and wondering how you're doing. You know, checking up on a client."

I smiled. Lawyers didn't check up on clients at eight o'clock at night. "A client? Really?"

Brad laughed. "Aunt Doris and I were talking about you. She misses you, you know."

"She's a wonderful woman—so kind, so good to me."

"Yeah, she's pretty special."

"And how are you?"

"Good. Good. The Rotary Club is keeping me busy after office hours. We're putting together a softball team. Our first game is against the Kiwanis Club. Guess who's pitching for us?"

"You?"

"No, Bernie Duncan. Remember him? He's lost most of his hair and he's forty pounds heavier, but he has one helluva fast ball."

I laughed. The Bernie Duncan I'd known was a skinny kid with bushy black hair.

Any awkwardness between us eased. By the time we hung up, I wondered if this might be the beginning of a real friendship like Eleanor had suggested. I hoped so. I liked Brad. A lot.

Brad called at least once a week, usually more. His calls quickly became precious to me. We talked about everything—

the weather, our jobs, the latest happenings around Atlanta—everything but the reason he kept calling and the reason I waited so eagerly for those calls. Building a friendship was enough for me for the moment. I'd never had anything of the kind with any other man.

Then, Chester Bailey called from the funeral home to say that my mother's ashes had been delayed but were finally "ready".

My mouth grew dry. I found it difficult to think of her bottled up, just crumbs of the person I'd sometimes hated. "I won't be able to pick them up until the end of the summer, if then," I explained, putting it off.

"No problem. We can hold them here for you."

Brad flashed in my mind but I quickly decided I wasn't ready to return to Barnham. "I'll let you know when I can come for them."

I hung up the phone, rattled by my mother's request to go to Maine. Carrying her ashes there seemed such a macabre business when I still had so many mixed feelings about her. She'd just dumped the task on me. Why?

During my next session with Eleanor, I asked, "Why didn't my mother protect me from Clyde?" It still hurt to think of it.

Eleanor was quiet and spoke thoughtfully. "I believe, in many ways you've previously indicated, that your mother was unwilling to deal with your life so she wouldn't have to face the reality of hers."

"She never wanted me around." I wondered if I'd ever be able to get past the pain of knowing that. She'd allowed me to be tormented, and had refused to listen to me when I needed her most. What kind of mother would do that?

Driving home from Eleanor's office, I gripped the steering wheel, recalling the time I'd come home from Jr. High School, excited about trying out for the cheerleading squad. Clyde was sitting in the kitchen, sipping a glass of amber liquid—probably whiskey. When he found out why I was late getting home, he'd chortled. "Know what girls like that want?"

I'd cringed, knowing something crude was about to come out of his mouth.

He'd tapped his chest with a fat finger. "Men like me. That's what they want."

Sickened, I'd moved to get out of the room, to get as far away from him as I could. In a flash, his hands grabbed me by the wrist and he jerked me back, landing me in his lap.

I'd struggled to get free, panicking, as he grabbed my breasts and stuck his hand between my legs. I'd jabbed his stomach with my elbow as hard as I could, and was finally able to wrest my body away from him. Crying, I'd run out of the house and up the hill to The Talking Tree, where I'd be safe.

Recalling this, my knuckles turned white on the steering wheel. The sickening feeling of his hands all over my private parts slithered its way through me like a hideous snake. Oh, yes, Clyde Breeden had been a mean, disgusting man who'd found it easy to cow an innocent, young girl without a mother to protect her.

At home, I went to my closet and pulled out the white blazer. I couldn't let the story of my mother go. I'd do as she'd asked. Maybe then I could learn to forgive her.

I'd just settled down at my desk when Sari approached me with a smile. "Hey, Marissa, Rico has a friend at work, Mike Willis. I've met him and he's a real nice guy. We've got four tickets to the Braves game on Saturday. Want to double date with us?" Her dark eyes sparkled in her brown face. "He's a Brad Pitt look alike. I swear."

"Sounds like fun," I forced myself to say, though my

stomach squeezed at the thought of going out with a stranger. Suddenly, I saw the silliness of my worries. I wasn't the scared little girl I'd once been. I was a grown woman in control over my life. I wouldn't allow him or any other man to hurt me.

Brad called later that evening. "How're you doing?"

"Great. I'm making new friends. In fact, I'm going on a date this weekend."

"Really?" I heard something in Brad's voice, maybe dismay, and I smiled. When the time came to *really* test this new concept of being in control of dating men, I wanted it to be with him.

"Sari is fixing me up with a friend of Rico's. We're going to a baseball game."

"Sounds like fun," Brad commented in a lackluster tone that thrilled me.

After small talk about the trip his parents were on, he said, "Well, I better go. I'll phone you in a few days."

I hung up, already looking forward to his next call.

Saturday night was sunny and clear, a perfect late spring evening. Rico and Sari pulled up in his red Ford truck at exactly five, as planned. I watched from the window as a tall blond man got out of the back and walked toward the front door of my house.

My stomach felt as if hummingbirds were hovering inside, their little wings a blur. I opened the door. Kind blue eyes assessed me. A smile crossed his face. "Wow! Sari was right. You look just like Julianne Moore."

I laughed. "She told me you looked exactly like Brad Pitt."

He stirred uneasily, and we laughed together. He was nice

looking, but he and Brad Pitt didn't even resemble cousins, and I knew Julianne and I didn't have much in common either. As we climbed into the backseat, Rico and Sari smiled from the front seat of the truck.

Sari winked at me as I buckled up. "Nice night for a ball game, huh?"

I grinned. "The Braves better pull through this time."

Rico and Mike threw baseball stats around, filling the truck with their chatter, leaving me to my thoughts. I glanced at Mike out of the corner of my eye. He seemed like a nice guy, easy-going, comfortable with himself. I leaned back against the seat and listened to the banter between the men, content to chat with Sari from time to time. Rico joined the throng of vehicles lined up for the stadium, found a place to park and we headed into the ballpark with the rest of the crowd.

Sari pulled me aside. "Isn't Mike nice? Good looking too?"

I smiled. "Yeah, he seems real nice."

"I can tell he likes you already." Sari gave me a smug look, and I couldn't help laughing. She prided herself on being a matchmaker. She'd taken credit for more than one romance in our office.

Rico took hold of Sari's hand. "The crowd is heavy and I don't want to lose you."

Mike clasped my hand and we all walked inside together. We bought cold beers, hot dogs, and chips and headed to our seats.

Seated between Sari and Mike, I cheered as loud as they, caught up in the tenseness of a tie game. The game ended with a Braves win. The people all around us made a hasty retreat to the exits.

"Great game," said Rico. "No sense getting caught up in the crowds. It takes forever to get all the cars out of the parking lots."

Sari flashed me a grin. "Why don't you two sit here and talk. Rico promised to show me one of the suites his uncle's company uses."

Mike and I exchanged knowing smiles as Sari and Rico left.

"They aren't too subtle, are they? So, tell me a little bit about you. You work with Sari. What else do I need to know about?"

I told him about the computer programming courses I was taking at night. "I'm hoping to become a project manager."

"Yeah, I've got my eye on a promotion at the marketing company where Rico and I work." He studied me. "I like you a lot, Marissa." His gaze settled on my lips and he leaned toward me.

His lips met mine, still salty from the chips we'd been munching on. When we pulled apart, we smiled at one another. The kiss was sweet but I couldn't help comparing it to the two kisses Brad had given me. Those had rocked me to the core. All the way home, an image of Brad lingered in my mind and I knew I had to see him again.

The spring weather turned summer like. I pulled out the winter-weary pansies along the side of the house and worked the sun-warmed soil, preparing a place for the pink and white begonias I'd bought.

Kneeling on the ground, nestling the young plants in the nourished dirt, I thought of Brad, as I did so often. The careful, safe life I'd constructed over the past several years wasn't what I wanted after all. After being with him, I wanted so much more, including love with a good man.

Instead of waiting for his phone call, I punched in his number. "Brad? I'm coming to Barnham to pick up my mother's ashes."

"You're going to take her ashes to Maine, after all?"

"Yes. I think it'll be an opportunity for me to settle up with the past. I need to know more about her. Until I do, I'm not sure I can truly forgive her for some of the things that went on. She wanted me to do this. She must have had a good reason, don't you think?"

"I hope so. But unexpected reunions with family or friends like this might blow up in your face. It happened to a client of mine."

We talked for a while longer and agreed to see one another. But as I hung up the phone, I couldn't stop wondering if he was right and it would be a mistake to go to Maine.

CHAPTER FIVE

Once I'd made up my mind to return to Barnham, I could hardly wait to go there. The timing was perfect. The Drexlers wanted to settle on the house sooner than I'd originally thought, and I'd be there for the June closing they'd requested.

The drive, which had seemed so short on my earlier trip, now seemed to take forever as I made my way north. Just in time for the eleven o'clock closing, I pulled in front of the yellow-brick building that housed the law offices of Crawford and Crawford. I opened the car door for Lady and heard someone call my name. Brad descended the marble steps of the building with a broad smile. Lady lunged toward him, wagging her tail, pulling me off-balance. Laughing, I let go of her leash and watched as she leaped up on Brad and greeted him with licks of her pink tongue.

Brad patted her and then walked over to me. Casually putting an arm around my shoulder, he hugged me close. "I'm glad you decided to come back."

"Me, too," I murmured. His smile made me feel warm and wonderful.

When we went inside, a tall, well-dressed man was standing by the receptionist's desk. Though his hair had gone gray and there were signs of aging that Brad had yet to acquire, I knew immediately he was Brad's father—the resemblance was uncanny. He gave me an appraising look.

"So this is Marissa, come back to town," Brad's father boomed.

I froze as everyone in the office turned to stare. Swallowing hard at the attention, I held out my hand. "Nice to meet you."

He grasped it firmly and searched my face. "Jim Crawford. I've heard a lot about you. Glad to meet you at last."

Brad shifted his feet, as uncomfortable as a twelve-year-old at a middle-school dance.

I hid a smile.

"Gotta go down to the courthouse," Jim said, giving Lady a pat on the head. "See you later, son. You, too, Marissa."

Shaking his head, Brad led me into his private office. "Not always easy being in business with my father. My parents worry too much. He heard me talking about your visit and now they have invited us to the club for dinner. They want to get to know you."

My body turned cold. I was just finding my way in the dating game. This was much more than I was comfortable with.

"So, how about it? Will you come to the club with me tonight?" His chestnut eyes settled on me.

I felt my body draw into itself and then scolded myself. It would be the perfect opportunity to put to use all the self-esteem exercises I'd worked on over the last few years. In my mind, I could hear my trusty therapist Eleanor say, "Marissa, you can do it."

"Sure, I look forward to it," I replied evenly, though the thought of a parental inspection in this particular town made a part of me want to turn tail and run.

"Great!" Brad's face lit with pleasure and I was glad I'd agreed to it. He checked his watch. "I've got the settlement for the house set up in the conference room. The Drexlers are in another room. They just finished signing."

He showed me into a small room. A pitcher of ice water and several glasses sat alongside a glass bowl of mints in the middle of a long conference table. I settled Lady under the table, grabbed a mint and walked over to the tall window overlooking the front of the building. Cars were parked in front of the storefronts a few doors down. I thought once again of all that Brad was doing to make the town a good place to live. If things were different I might be tempted to stay.

I turned as the Drexlers stopped at the doorway.

Bud Drexler's wife, Pam, a heavy-set, pleasant woman, grasped my hands kindly. "We're so happy to have your house. It has a lot of potential. Now that the kids are grown, we'll have a nice, cozy place of our own. Shame about that tree out back, but I love to garden and I'm going to fix up the backyard real good."

She thought I was only looking for good people to own the house. She had no idea how much I wanted to get rid of it and permanently close that chapter of my life.

The mechanics of selling the house proved to be easy. All the paperwork had been prepared ahead of time, so it became simply a matter of having the figures explained to us and having each of us sign the papers. At the end of the brief meeting, I was handed a check for just over thirty thousand dollars. My hands trembled as I stared at it. Never, in my entire life, had I had so much money.

Bubbling with good cheer, the Drexlers departed.

"So, what are you going to do with all that money?" Brad's eyes twinkled.

"The first thing I'm going to do is deposit it in the bank next door. Then, I'm going to pay some overdue bills and figure out what to do with the rest of it." I grinned at him, thrilled with the idea of having such choices.

"Sounds good. How about my buying you lunch to celebrate?"

I shook my head. "Thanks, but I promised Doris I'd stop

by. She's waiting for me."

Holding onto the check as if it were a million dollars, I led Lady over to the bank.

The woman behind the teller's cage beamed at me. "Marissa Cole. Margaret's daughter, I heard. Real nice lady. She used to do some housework for my mother."

I smiled, wondering at the number of people who seemed to have known and liked my mother. During my years away, had my mother changed so much? My heart sank. If so, why hadn't she bothered to contact me?

Those troubling thoughts lingered in my mind as I drove to Doris's house.

"Marissa!" Doris's welcome cry from her front porch warmed my heart. I pulled into the driveway, got out of the car and hugged her. Lady pranced around our feet, barking excitedly.

We strolled into the house arm in arm, chatting easily. It felt good knowing I could come to town, free from the house next door, free to enjoy being with one of the sweetest women I'd ever known.

Doris fixed a chef salad and poured glasses of iced tea for lunch. We sat at the kitchen table, eating companionably.

Still thinking about the comments the teller at the bank had made about her, I asked Doris, "Did my mother change a great deal after I left home?"

Doris studied me a moment. "She started attending AA meetings not long after you left. I think it was right after Clyde chopped down your Talking Tree."

My jaw dropped. "I had no idea."

"Another reason she and Clyde grew apart. I have to tell you in all honesty that she'd do well for a while, and then she'd fall off the wagon. But I do know she tried."

I sat back in my chair, feeling as if I'd been punched in the stomach. I would have done anything I could to have helped my mother through those times. "If only I'd known." Regret brought tears to my eyes.

Doris patted my hand. "Now, now, there's no point in stewing about it. It's over and done with. I believe your mother was a much happier person after she began trying to beat her addiction to alcohol and drugs."

"When she was sober, why didn't she reach out to me? Isn't that part of the program?"

"Yes, but she told me she couldn't bear the pain of looking back too long or too often."

I leaned forward. "Did she ever mention her family? Clyde said she had a family, after all. Do you think it has anything to do with New Hope, Maine?"

"Oh, hon, I honestly don't know what to think. She never mentioned any family to me. And if Jane Houghton couldn't tell you anything about it, I don't suppose anyone else could."

"Who was my mother's sponsor at AA? Do you know? Maybe I could ask her."

Doris's eyebrows shot up. "I thought you'd guess. Me."

"You? Why didn't you tell me?" I sat back. "Oh, I remember now. Anonymity is part of the program."

"We became more than neighbors, though I wouldn't call us friends. Your mother would never open up about the past. I tried to get her to let her guard down, but she was a very wounded woman, not about to give anything of herself away. And though she never challenged me on it, she resented the fact that you and I were close."

I let out a frustrated sigh. This was more like the mother I knew. It was so like her to take exception to anything that made me happy.

"When do you plan to return to Atlanta?" Doris asked. "Can you stay longer this time?"

"I haven't decided when I'll go back home. It might not be right away. Maybe I'll take care of my mother's ashes." As soon as the words were out of my mouth, I realized I'd already made up my mind to go directly from Barnham to New Hope. "I have vacation time coming and my boss is away for two weeks. It'll be perfect timing if I go now."

"What about Lady?" Doris asked. "Do you want me to keep her while you're gone?"

At the mention of her name, Lady's tail thumped against the brick-colored linoleum. I leaned over and patted her on the head. "That'd be wonderful. She's comfortable here and it'll give me the freedom I need to snoop around a bit."

Doris grasped my hand, her brows knitted with worry. "Don't get your hopes too high, Marissa. If your mother had truly come from a nice family, her life would have been a whole lot different. You do see that, don't you?"

I gave her a noncommittal shrug. I hadn't a clue about them. I didn't even know if they really existed. But I could dream, couldn't I?

I gave myself a last look in the mirror before heading down to meet Brad. The black sheath I'd recently bought looked great with the faint tan I'd achieved working in my garden at home. A string of fake pearls and matching earrings added just the right touch. The gold ring on my right hand kept attracting my attention. I hadn't taken off my mother's ring in weeks. Just wearing it made me remember the better times between us—the moments we'd shared a rare laugh or a pleasant look. And, somehow, I felt stronger wearing it.

Brad's eyes lit up when I entered the living room. His gaze took in all of me. He grinned. Doris stood beside him, giving us both a doting smile.

"You look great," Brad said. "I like whatever you did to your hair."

I smiled and lifted a hand to the cascade of red curls, caught up in a clip. Summer humidity tended to make my curls stronger, bolder.

"A very handsome couple, I'd say." Doris put her arms around us as she walked us to the front door. "Go, enjoy yourselves!"

Doris shut the door firmly behind us as if she could make her dream of the two of us together come true by forcing us to be alone.

Brad and I exchanged amused glances.

"Well? Shall we go?" he asked.

I smiled, though I dreaded making an appearance at the upscale club. In this small town, I'd felt little more than a shadow as a child.

Brad handled the car easily as we wended our way up the curving road to the club's front entrance. A sign, carefully lettered in gold, announced The Barnham Country Club was a private golf club, open to members and their guests only. The clubhouse itself was a low-slung white-painted brick building that overlooked rolling hills of green.

A valet opened the car door for me. I drew a deep breath and exited. Brad held my hand as we entered. He gave my fingers a squeeze of encouragement, and I let out the breath I'd been holding.

Pausing at the entrance to the dining room, I recognized Jim Crawford right away. He was unmistakable as he spoke jovially to the waitress in a voice loud enough for me to hear from a distance. The trim woman sitting opposite him was pretty, with the same honey-colored hair as Brad.

Jim scrambled to his feet as we approached his table. "Hi there, son. Hello, Marissa."

Ellen Crawford smiled and offered her hand as she was introduced to me. I took it, returning her smile, surprised by how tiny she was. I hadn't remembered her being so small. But then, as a child, most adults had seemed large and powerful.

Brad held out a chair for me and I took a seat, conscious of the stares the other diners cast our way. No doubt word would get out that I was back in town. Like many small towns, this one had an information network many countries would fight for.

"Doris tells me your mother's house has sold," Ellen said.

"We had the closing today," Brad said.

"That's why I'm here, and to take care of a few other things."

"What do you know about New Hope, Maine?" Brad asked. "Marissa has some business there."

Ellen turned to me, a look of surprise on her face. "Have you ever been there?"

I shook my head.

"Isn't that the place where we stayed in the B and B that cost me a fortune?" Jim asked Ellen.

"Yes." Ellen laughed softly. "New Hope is a very exclusive little place. Oh, it has its fishing people and retail owners, of course, but mostly it consists of huge homes lining that part of the coastline. It's comparable in style to Kennebunkport, where the Bushes have their summer home."

Was Briar Cliff one of those homes? I wondered. I hadn't found anything about it on the internet and the image that had just been painted for me did not match the mother I knew. Maybe she had visited the area at some time in her life. That would explain it.

The waitress approached the table carrying a tray of empty tulip-shaped glasses and a dark green bottle, which peeked out from a moisture-coated silver ice bucket.

Jim beamed at me. "I thought a little bubbly was due—to celebrate the sale of the house."

"Oh, Jim, how nice," Ellen murmured. "Champagne makes any occasion special and this is special indeed for Marissa."

After the wine had been poured into each glass and the bottle returned to the ice bucket, Jim lifted his glass.

"To happiness!"

At Brad's wink, I raised my glass and felt my cheeks grow hot even as the cool liquid played effervescent games in my mouth.

"Are you planning to move back to Barnham?" Jim asked me.

Brad shifted uneasily in his chair, and I had the distinct impression that Ellen wanted to kick her husband in the shins.

"I don't think so. I really like Atlanta." In truth, I couldn't imagine coming back to Barnham, not even when my circumstances had changed so much.

"Good for you. A friend of mine from college moved there many years ago. She loves it," said Ellen, smiling pleasantly. I detected a cool undertone in her voice, and there was no mistaking the way she patted Brad's hand consolingly.

Brad frowned at his mother and turned to me with a smile.

The conversation throughout the meal remained light and pleasant, but by the time we rose from the table, I was glad the meal was over. His parents had treated me kindly, but I'd felt as if I didn't quite measure up.

"Will we see you again?" Ellen asked as she clasped my hand good-bye.

"I'm not certain," I answered truthfully. "Doris is keeping my dog, Lady, while I go to New Hope. Then, I'll have to return home."

Ellen reached for her son, giving him a warm hug and a kiss

on the cheek.

We left them and went outside, waiting for the valet to deliver the car, each of us lost in thought.

His brown-eyed gaze settled on me. "It's early. What do you want to do now? Any place you want to go?"

My heart pounded. "How about showing me your house? Doris says it's nice."

Brad studied me a minute. The hidden meaning behind the suggestion filled the atmosphere with sexual tension. His eyebrows lifted. "Really?"

"Sure. Why, not?" With someone like Brad, someone I could really trust, I might be able to finally let go of my past inhibitions.

We were quiet as Brad drove to a street in the middle of the nicest section of town, an area behind Jane Houghton's house on the town square. Though my hands had turned ice cold, I was filled with resolve. I told myself not to worry, I was in control.

We pulled into the driveway of a Cape Cod that had been enlarged at one end. Creamy white with dark green shutters, it resembled a scene from on a postcard from New England. A white picket fence enclosed a portion of the yard, behind which I got a glimpse of a small garden. In front of the fence, yellow marigolds lined up, little rays of sunshine captured in a moment of time.

"It's lovely," I murmured as Brad stopped the car.

He gave me a rueful grin. "It's the one good thing I got from the marriage. Amber took almost everything else." He shook his head. "Nasty business, divorce."

I patted his arm sympathetically. "Let's go take a look."

We entered the house through the back door. A small but well-laid-out kitchen greeted us. I noted the pots and pans hanging from a large metal hook over the stove set in an island

and realized they weren't just for show; they exhibited signs of much use.

"You like to cook?" I asked, pleased by the thought.

Brad grinned and patted his stomach. "It started out as a necessity and ended up a hobby. Frozen dinners get very tiresome after a while."

There were other signs of his hobby as well. A small crockery pot on the counter by the stove held a bunch of seasoned wooden spoons and other kitchen utensils. A wooden spice rack hung along one side of the island, within easy reach and was loaded with an impressive array of herbs and spices. Two black bar stools were pulled up to a dark granite counter separating the kitchen from the dining room. Though it lacked a woman's softer touches, the kitchen was welcoming.

"C'mon, I'll show you around." Brad took my elbow and I followed him into the dining room, which held a bare mahogany table surrounded by six matching chairs. Nothing else. The living room, off the front hall, was compact and cozy. A brick fireplace painted white was offset by bookshelves that held a number of books scattered about randomly. One overstuffed chair sat in the corner of the room.

The den lay off the living room. A huge TV, assorted stereo equipment, and gadgets of every kind filled the room, barely giving space for the leather couch that lined one wall.

"This is where I spend most of my time, with all my stuff." Brad gave me a boyish grin.

"It's a nice house, Brad. I like it."

"Yeah? You haven't seen all of it. The bedrooms are upstairs." His gaze bore into me. There was no mistaking the desire in his eyes or the implied invitation.

A shiver of anticipation crawled through me. This is what I wanted, what I'd worked toward, letting my own desires overtake any ugliness from the past. "You want to show me?"

"Okay?" he asked softly.

"Yes,"

He took my hand and led me to the front hallway. I paused at the bottom of the stairs and said a silent prayer that things would go well. Being back in Barnham had brought up some of the old memories of Clyde. Damn him!

"You all right? Your hand is cold," Brad murmured, rubbing it with his thumb as we climbed the stairs, one scary step at a time.

I forced a smile and reminded myself to breathe deeply. This time, I would do it. This time, I would let Brad get close to me, be intimate with me. This time, he would set me free from the bad memories.

Upstairs, Brad went through the motions of showing me two small empty bedrooms, divided by the bathroom they shared. But we both knew what was on his mind. And mine.

We walked into a large master suite, which held a king-size bed, two easy chairs, and two large bureaus. A skylight in the cathedral ceiling appeared open. I walked closer to it and stared up through the opening in the peaked roof. Stars in the sky winked at me as if to say everything would be all right. Cicadas chirped a summer tune that drifted through the air.

I smiled at Brad. "Love the skylight! I almost feel as if I'm outside."

"You like it?" Brad came up behind me. "I designed the room myself."

"It's great." I moved over to the bow window on the outside wall. Perched on the cushioned window seat, I gazed out at the woods behind Brad's house. Dimly lit by the lights in the kitchen, the dark outlines of trees formed a backdrop for the velvet lawn that stretched to meet them.

Brad came over to me and pulled me to my feet. Grinning,

he wrapped his arms around me. "Forget the house." His lips came down on mine, tentatively soft at first and then with growing firmness as I responded.

Pulse racing, I leaned into him, inhaling his spicy scent for comfort. Brad's arousal left no doubt that he was ready for more. I automatically pulled back, then, told myself to relax and enjoy the moment. But the pounding of my heart echoed in my ears, blocking out my wishful words.

"You okay?" Brad's eyebrows formed a vee of concern.

I made myself smile, then turned my back to him. It was now or never. "Unzip me."

In seconds, my dress lay in a pile at my feet. Standing in my black lacy bra and matching panties, I squeezed my eyes shut, so unsure, praying to get the whole thing over with.

"Marissa?" Brad reached for me.

I fought to loosen the tension that gripped me. "It's okay," I murmured, wishing it were so.

He unhooked my bra and pushed it out of the way, freeing my breasts. His fingers circled a nipple and squeezed gently. I bit my lips to keep from crying out. Memories of mean fingers, pinching too hard, fought against the pleasure of Brad's gentle hands. Brad unbuckled his pants and pulled off the golf shirt he'd worn under his blazer. I watched him, my stomach churning at the bulge in the front of him.

My body cold with terror, I turned away. Tears betrayed me, oozing out from beneath my eyelids. Stop, I silently pleaded, but I couldn't stem their flow.

"Jeesus!" Brad murmured, and dropped his arms. "You're crying! What's wrong?"

My eyes flew open. I gulped noisily. "I can't do this. I just can't."

Brad stood next to the bed, hands on hips, his face registering a range of emotions, hurt among them.

Sobs shook my body. "I'm sorry ... I want to be with you, but I guess I'm not ready yet."

"Okay. We won't go any further." Brad grabbed his clothes and went into the bathroom.

As soon as he left the room, I quickly hooked my bra and slipped on my dress. The whiny sound of the zipper mocked me. Grabbing my shoes, I bolted down the stairway and out the front door.

Outside, in the cool night air, I started walking as fast as I could. Shame filled me. Doris had told me how hurt Brad had been by Amber, how vulnerable that had made him. And yet I'd tried to use him to pursue a selfish need of mine.

The sound of a car's engine brought me out of my melancholy thoughts. I turned. Brad's SUV pulled over to my side of the road. He lowered the window.

"Get in! I'll drop you off at Doris's house."

I kept walking, mortified to face him.

The car rolled along the edge of the road, keeping pace with my stride. "Look, Marissa, you shouldn't have run out like that," Brad called through the open window. "I know how awkward this is but let's talk it over. And, I don't want you walking alone along this road at night."

I stopped and half-turned to him. I couldn't look at him. "I'm almost there. I can see Doris's house."

He swore softly, and I was grateful for the darkness that cloaked my face, hiding my humiliation.

His black SUV hovered beside me, humming like a giant bumble bee on the attack.

As hard as I tried, I couldn't ignore him. I wanted to tell him everything but I knew if I got started I wouldn't be able to stop.

Brad pulled the truck up and over the curb and parked it in front of me, blocking my way.

He jumped out and took me by the shoulders. I couldn't turn away.

"Look, Marissa, I understand how difficult this is for you. We don't have to go from a kiss to making love, all at once. There are a lot of steps in between." He gazed into my eyes. "I'd like to take those steps with you. Okay?"

I swallowed my tears. "Of all the men I'd known in my life, you're the one I trust the most." It had scared me to death that I'd wanted him so much. "This is all so new to me, wanting you like I do. And yet I still couldn't go through with it."

Brad lifted my chin and gently brushed his lips against mine, making my body go soft. Our kiss ended and I rested my head against his chest. He was such a good man. I wondered if I would ever be able to show him what I truly felt.

Brad walked me to Doris's front porch and, lifting a hand to my cheek, cupped it. "I'm going to chase the ghosts away, Marissa. No matter how long it takes, I'll do it. I swear."

Tears of gratitude stung my eyes. My emotions rode high at his acceptance and plummeted low at my inadequacies. I watching him return to his vehicle. Taking another deep breath, I straightened my dress, opened the door and went inside.

"How'd it go?" Doris emerged from the kitchen with a big smile. She came to a sudden halt. "My stars! What happened to you?"

Lady bounded over to me, wagging her tail. I brushed back a lock of disheveled hair and knelt to embrace her before facing Doris.

"I walked home. It's a long story. I've decided not to wait another day to go to New Hope. I'm leaving early tomorrow."

Doris arched an eyebrow. She knew my haste had everything to do with the events of the evening. But I couldn't tell her or anyone else what a mixed up mess I was.

CHAPTER SIX

The next morning, the patter of rain on the roof woke me. Cracking an eye open, I glanced out the window. Raindrops fell softly against the windowpane, dripping in silvery streaks. I rolled over in bed and stretched, telling myself to cheer up, that it would be a good time to travel, that traffic would be lighter on such a gloomy day.

I jumped out of bed, padded over to the chair in the corner of the room, and slipped on a terry robe. Downstairs, I met up with Doris.

"You're serious about leaving today?" she asked, setting down her coffee cup.

"Might as well get it over with."

Doris fisted her hands on her hips. "I hope whatever happened last night isn't what's sending you away. If you're running from something or someone, you know as well as I do that life isn't that simple. Problems don't just disappear."

I scuffed a bare foot against the linoleum floor, wanting to say so much, knowing I couldn't. I glanced up. Doris was studying me carefully.

I tried to sound casual, though the truth of her words stung. "I was going to go to New Hope, anyway. I've pushed up the timing a bit. That's all."

"Well, when you're ready to talk about it, I'm here. I just hope you're doing the right thing." Doris's knowing look forced me to lower my gaze. I didn't think even the Talking Tree would've helped untangle the feelings that filled me.

After a quick breakfast, I loaded my suitcase in the car.

Lady shot me a begging look to join me, but I ignored her and turned to give Doris a hug good-bye.

"Take care now," Doris said softly. "Let me know when you arrive so I know you made it safely."

A short time later, I was sailing along on New York's Dewey Thruway, heading east. I had no idea what to expect when I got to New Hope. Briar Cliff wasn't on the Internet. There'd been a time in my life when I'd desperately wanted to know if Tim Hartwell was my real father. But knowing he was a buddy of Clyde Breeden's had dampened any enthusiasm for investigating it further. When my mother refused to talk about him, I told myself it didn't matter, that neither he nor anyone else could get me out of the mess I faced at home. That was something I had to do on my own.

Frustration once again gripped me. She could have sought me out after she'd fought her alcoholism and drug addiction. We could have tried to make amends. I knew making amends was part of the program. But that wasn't my mother's style. Never a giving person, she'd held bits and pieces of information about herself close to her chest, like treasured jewels death had turned to glass.

By late afternoon I'd traveled as far as Portsmouth, New Hampshire. I was too tired to continue. I pulled off the highway into the seaside town, searching for the motel I'd seen advertised along the road. New Hope was within a one-hour drive but I wasn't ready to make a final push to get there; I wanted to be refreshed when I hit the town.

The Seaside Motel was a three-story brick building that looked decent. I pulled up to the front, under the small portico, got out and stretched beneath its protective roof.

When I entered the building, an older gentleman looked up

from the front desk with a querying glance.

"I'd like a room for tonight,"

The man's weathered face didn't change a bit as he got up. He took my credit card with his rough hands.

"I'd like a non-smoking room. How much is it?"

"All the same. Seventy-two dollars."

I smiled. "Okay. I'll take it."

Remaining silent, he rang up the charge and handed me a room key. "Top of the stairs. Third door on the right."

So this is New England, I thought, amused by the man's abrupt manner, so like the jokes I'd heard. I went out to the car and pulled it into the parking lot for the night. Glad to see a break of blue in the sky, I rolled my suitcase inside.

The next morning, I got an early start and drove up Route 1 along the Maine coast. I passed Wells and Kennebunk and finally saw the sign for New Hope. I drove into the tiny village perched on the water's edge and was immediately charmed by the weathered wooden buildings containing a number of small, colorful, upscale shops. I parked the car in the public lot in the center of town and got out.

The distinctive crisp, salty tang of the air rolled around me as I walked down the street. The cries of seagulls swirling above me caught my attention, and I looked up into a deep blue sky. Excited, my rapid heartbeat kept pace with my steps as I walked down to the docks next to the commercial area. This small town, oozing New England charm, was picture postcard perfect. Patty's Place advertised a hot fisherman's breakfast. The tinkling of a bell announced my arrival as I swung into the restaurant and perched on a stool at the breakfast bar.

"Yep. What'll you have?" asked a sharp-featured woman with graying hair.

"Cup of regular coffee," I answered promptly, smiling to

myself. The waitress reminded me of the bad witch in the Wizard of Oz.

A steaming cup of coffee was placed in front of me, along with the tab. I took a grateful sip. I'd been so anxious to leave the hotel, I'd foregone breakfast.

"Want a splash more?" Patty asked, a few moments later.

I shook my head. "No thanks. Can you tell me if there's a place called Briar Cliff around here?"

Patty's eyes narrowed. She looked me over carefully. "The Hartwell estate? What do you want with them folks?"

The restaurant grew quiet as stares of curiosity were thrown my way. I squirmed at the unwanted attention.

Estate? My jaw dropped. "I ... I honestly don't know." A shiver coiled snakelike down my spine. *Hartwell estate?* I'd once thought Tim Hartwell might be my father. My God, was it true?

Patty clucked her tongue. "Yup, the place they call Briar Cliff is up the road a bit. Keep close to the coastline. It's there with all the others. Can't miss it."

Patty leaned on her elbows in front of me. "Old lady Hartwell hasn't been seen in some time. Some say it's bad health. Don't know the truth of it. She weren't a friendly one. Always thought she was better than most, ya know. The other one's odd, too. Two old ladies by themselves up to no good, if you ask me."

She straightened and brushed her apron off, still studying me. "Don't know what you want with 'em. Don't care."

Silently digesting this information, my stomach whirled. Why had my mother sent me here? Was Tim Hartwell my father, after all? I finished my coffee, rose and paid the bill. I left a good-sized tip. Patty had earned every bit of it. Talk of the Hartwell estate and strange old ladies had me on edge. I couldn't imagine what it meant. I had my mother's gold ring and a white blazer but little else to help me solve all the riddles.

Outside once more, I breathed deeply. Patty's words spun in my mind.

The tangy scent of the salt water surrounded me as I walked back to my car. A playful cool wind lifted a lock of hair off my forehead. First things first, I decided. I'd agreed to take care of my mother's ashes, and that's what I intended to do.

I slid behind the wheel of the car and followed Patty's directions north of town. Large estates peeked out at me from behind stone walls or wrought iron fences. The homes sat comfortably alongside this winding stretch of road that followed the jagged shoreline. Large rocks lay interspersed between creamy sandy beaches that stretched toward the water. The mournful cries of seagulls dipping and rising in a whir of white wings in the blue sky added to my anxiety.

I looked carefully at the entrances to the houses and finally noticed a simple white wooden sign with bold, black letters. "Briar Cliff". I slammed on the brakes. The sign was mounted on a stone pillar beside a driveway blocked off by a wrought-iron gate.

My heart pounded. I pulled off to the side of the road, climbed out of the car, and stared at a large, three-story, brown-shingled home. A sunroom extended from one side. At the other end of the house, I could see the curl of a wide porch which swept across the front of the house overlooking the ocean. The house was enormous. My little rental in Georgia would fit inside the sun porch alone.

My mind spun as I got back into the car. I had to figure out how to scatter my mother's ashes at Briar Cliff without facing the inhabitants inside. Then I could tackle the puzzle of Tim Hartwell.

I drove slowly until I spied a wide spot at the edge of a road.

A battered red truck was parked there, leaving me enough room to pull in my small Honda.

After I parked, I stood beside the car, studying my surroundings. Good-size rocks and sparse, leggy green grasses were intermingled with beige sand. A worn path wove from the parking spot to the edge of the water approximately one hundred yards away. It appeared to be a public right of way. On either side of the path, fenced off from this open area, were massive houses similar to Briar Cliff.

I opened the trunk of my car and placed the urn with my mother's ashes into a large canvas bag, hoping it wouldn't be conspicuous. I didn't know if what I was about to do was legal.

Kicking off my rubber thongs, I placed them in the bag, along with a bottle of water and a tube of suntan lotion.

The warm sand felt soft beneath my feet as I picked my way through the grasses. A feeling of wonder came over me. I stopped. Had my father walked here once? How did my mother know this place? How was it connected to me?

At the water's edge, I stuck my toe in and shivered at its coldness. The water's temperature was a far cry from the gulf coast in Florida I'd once visited for a long weekend.

I headed down the wide beach toward Briar Cliff. A gull swooped overhead and squawked. The water was at low tide, allowing families to gather together along the exposed expanse of sand. I smiled, watching the children run to the water's edge and back again in seemingly endless circles. I held the canvas bag close to me. At this time of day, I wouldn't have the privacy to do what I needed. Still, my curiosity drove me on. I couldn't turn back now without viewing Briar Cliff.

The weathered houses I passed rested like toughened old matrons, fat and full, bravely facing the vagaries of New England weather. People sat on many of the broad porches facing the water, chatting away, oblivious to my tenseness.

Awe took my breath away as I recognized Briar Cliff. A sweeping porch lined the front of the house, curving around to one side. The sunroom on the other end displayed wide, tall windows that tantalized me with their open views. I stood and gazed at the estate that perhaps my father had lived in.

Out of nowhere, anger stabbed me. I'd had to struggle for every small thing, working at the local burger joint after school and on weekends, watching the other girls my age flirt and gossip while I waited on them and endured their catty abuse. *Why?* The word pounded inside me like a throbbing heartbeat. If my father had this kind of financial means, why hadn't he offered to help us? Why hadn't my mother asked for enough help to get us by? To get away from Clyde?

I caught a movement on the porch of Briar Cliff and hurried away. I didn't want to face anyone there until I learned more about them.

I walked back down the beach, wondering how best to learn their story. At the car, I stowed the canvas bag with my mother's ashes into the trunk and took off. My next stop would be the local library.

A small red brick building housed the New Hope Library. It was located one street away from the white, wooden Town Hall. Compared to the other buildings in the center of town, the two-story library appeared to be relatively new. It welcomed people into it through black, wide, double, wooden doors.

I pulled into the parking lot, surprised to see it nearly full. Volvos, BMWs, and SUVs of every variety were parked side by side. I checked my watch. Eleven o'clock.

At that moment, the doors to the library opened and a barrage of mothers with small children emerged. I grinned. It must be story time.

I got out of the car and went through the double doors,

determined to find out about these Hartwells. Maybe then I'd know more about who I was.

The bespectacled woman behind the circulation desk smiled at me. "May I help you?"

I gripped my hands together hopefully. "I'm interested in a family who lives here—the Hartwells. Can you direct me to a place where I might find out about them?"

Her eyebrows shot up above the rim of her glasses. "The Hartwells? I probably know as much about them as anyone. My mother used to work for Arinthia Hartwell many years ago before she and her husband had children."

My mouth went dry. Here, at last, was a chance to learn about my father. "What do you know about Tim Hartwell?"

The librarian glanced around as if to make sure nobody else was near. In a low voice, she said, "Such a shame. Handsome man, had everything in the palm of his hand, the family business and all." She clucked her tongue. "Defied his mother, went off to join the Army and was killed. His name is on the town memorial at Town Hall."

"Did...did he have any family of his own?"

"Tim? Not that anyone knows ... I doubt it. He was, well, different ... not one for the girls, if you understand." Her cheeks grew red.

"Did he have any brothers or sisters?"

"A sister, but there was a tragedy there, too. It's really a sad family in many ways. And they're very private people." She studied me a moment. "Why do you ask?"

"I'm doing a study of my genealogy," I fibbed. I couldn't hide the disappointment in my voice. I hadn't realized how much I'd hoped to discover a family that could become mine.

She gave me a sympathetic look. "I hate loose ends. If you like, I can look up some old newspaper articles. Tim Hartwell's obituary should be in there."

"Thanks." If nothing else, I might be able to see a picture of the man who'd requested Clyde Breeden to enter my life.

While I waited for the librarian to return, I looked up the name Cole in the local phone book. Nothing.

The librarian brought a cardboard box over to the table where I sat.

"Look through this film and you'll see a number of articles about men from New Hope. I believe you'll find an obituary for Timothy Hartwell in there. If I remember correctly, he died over twenty years ago. It should be one of the films near the top."

"Thank you." I followed her into a small cubicle where a microfiche machine sat and put a film into the machine, adjusting it until I got a clear image.

The name Hartwell popped up after several others. I blinked and zeroed in on it, staring at the picture of a young, thin man in uniform. It was difficult to see the details of his facial features, but his stance gave the impression of self-containment, with a shy smile. I leaned closer. His nose was straight and narrow. I touched my own, so different. Disappointment stung. Clueless, I read the obituary. Son of Arinthia and Herbert Hartwell. No mention of brothers, sisters, grandparents. Frustration ate at me. What in the hell did Margaret Cole have to do with them? Nothing. Not a damn thing.

Discouraged, I returned the box of film to the librarian.

"Anything else I can help you with?" she asked pleasantly.

I shook my head. "No, thanks. I'll be on my way."

I left the library, and dejected, kicked at a small stone in the parking lot. My mother had sent me on a wild goose chase. I should have known better. I pressed my lips together. If I were smart, I'd scatter her ashes, drive back to Barnham to pick up Lady and return to my solitary existence in Atlanta.

Life there was at least predictable.

I checked my watch. Naptime in this family seashore location would be a good time to wander the beach again. I'd find a place among the piles of large rocks strewn along the shoreline and let the waves wash my mother's ashes out to sea—and out of my life.

Toby's Take Out was not far from the library. I stopped for lunch and sat at a picnic table in the small outdoor pavilion and, deep in thought, ate my lobster roll. If, as the librarian told me, Tim Hartwell had no family of his own, perhaps my mother had never told him about me. I shook my head, remembering the librarian's description of him. Another thought interrupted. Clyde had said my mother never wanted to be found. Why? Was it something to do with the Hartwells? I lowered my head, so confused I couldn't think.

After lunch, I wandered the streets, window-shopping at the quaint little shops filled with elegant offerings while my mind whirred. No, I wouldn't leave. Not yet. There were too many unanswered questions. I decided to check into one of the motels in town. I needed more time to get a better sense of what might have gone on here with my mother. Those unanswered questions prickled my skin and my mind.

The Harborside Inn sat beside the small harbor. I was shown to a room that had a tiny balcony overlooking the water. Sailboats and other watercraft filled the harbor. After the bellman left, I stood outside on the balcony, becoming caught up in the charm of the scene before me.

The cool breeze wafted about me. The sharp grating sound of motor boats offset the quiet movement of sailboats skimming the water outside the harbor. Tourists wandered the streets, strolling arm in arm or laden down with packages. Walking beside their parents, children seemed to dance on their feet, endlessly busy, while babies slept in strollers. Cries of excitement and even the sound of tired whiny voices made me envy such family scenes.

I checked my watch and went inside. I put on the bathing suit I'd thrown into my suitcase at the last minute and donned a pair of shorts and a T-shirt. My hair had grown bushy and wild in the humidity, so I tucked rebellious strands inside my *Braves* baseball cap and spread suntan lotion on my face and body. Defiant freckles had already appeared, scattered across my nose and cheeks.

I left the hotel and drove along the winding road that led out of town once more, eager to complete my task so I'd have time to enjoy a pleasant evening before returning to Barnham.

As I arrived at my earlier parking spot, the red truck pulled out and I quickly pulled into the empty space beside a yellow Jeep.

I got out of the car, took a deep breath and lifted the canvas bag out of the trunk of the car. Hefting the bag over my shoulder, I walked with purpose down to the edge of the water, noting with relief the beach was all but empty.

In front of Briar Cliff, I waded to the cluster of protruding rocks a small distance out in the water and climbed onto the largest one. The waves rushed in and filled a pool formed by the rocks and pulled away again, taking the water with it. It was the perfect place for distributing the ashes in privacy.

I crawled down onto a lower rock near the mouth of the opening, where the water was most active, and crouched. Carefully, I lifted the urn out of its canvas bag and stared at it. An eerie feeling gripped me. A person's body had been reduced to ashes—my mother's body. The phrase "from dust to dust" came to mind, and I thought of the mystery of life.

I reminded myself that the ashes were just that, and not a person's soul, and slowly opened the urn. Lowering the mouth of it to the surface of the water, I let the ashes dribble out as the waves pulled back, carrying them out to sea.

Thinking of the many wasted moments and years between my mother and me, my eyes filled. Sorrow filled me for all we'd lost. I brushed at my eyes and giving up, allowed tears to roll down my cheeks. It was good, I supposed, to finally cry for my mother and all that was and all that might have been.

I watched as the last of the ashes washed to sea. Then I dug a deep hole in the calmest part of the pool and buried the empty urn. It was over. I'd done what my mother had asked.

I picked up my empty canvas bag and sighed with relief. I jumped off the rocks and waded to shore, studying the movement of water at my feet.

"Hey! What do you think you're doing?"

Startled, I glanced up at the young man standing on the shore, hands on hips, looking rather put out with me.

I held the canvas bag close to my chest, even though all evidence of my activity was gone. I thought about walking away without saying a word but kept wading through the water toward him. After all, I'd done nothing wrong.

As I drew nearer, I observed the stranger more closely. Dark hair drooped in a lock above a wide brow. Startling blue eyes studied me as I took in his masculine physique, dressed in blue plaid Bermuda shorts and nothing else.

I stepped onto the dry sand, and he approached me. His height made me feel small or maybe it was the swagger in his walk as if he owned the whole beach. A shadow of dark stubble covered his cheeks, giving him a manly look that balanced his fine, almost pretty features.

"What were you doing? My aunt wants to know," he said.

I bristled at his imperious tone. "Something personal, not that it's any of your business. Who are you?"

He held out a broad hand. "Sorry. Hunter Hartwell."

"Of *the* Hartwells?"

He smirked, "Whatever the hell that means."

"Is Arinthia Hartwell related to you?"

"She's my aunt, why?"

"I heard about the family in town and was wondering about them. That's all." I could feel my cheeks flush at the lie of omission. Hoping my sunburn covered it, I pulled my cap down.

"Between you and me, she's an old biddy."

I blinked in surprise. Emotions warred inside me. If I could wangle a way to meet her, I might be able to find out more about my father. Maybe even my mother. I couldn't ignore the possibility.

"Any chance I could say hello to her? Or see the house? I've admired it and I'm, ah, doing a study of old homes along the Maine coast." I hated the fib, but I knew I'd regret it if I didn't take advantage of this opportunity.

"You really want to see her?" Hunter's eyes held a bit of mischief, but otherwise, he seemed harmless.

I nodded, hoping I wouldn't regret it.

"She's in a wheelchair."

I hesitated.

"Don't worry," he said, "there's a companion with her. My aunt doesn't have much to do at the moment but stare out at the beach. That's why she caught sight of you."

"I'd like to meet her."

We headed up a pebbled walk to the house. "Do you live here?" I asked.

"I used to summer here as a kid, but my family has always lived in Portland. We tried to get her to move out of this house. It's way too big for her. But Aunt Arinthia is a very stubborn woman. Despite everything that's happened to her body, she's as strong-willed as ever."

I absorbed this interesting piece of information as we

climbed the front steps of Briar Cliff.

A white-haired woman was seated in a wheelchair on the porch. Standing next to her an attractive, gray-haired woman stood guard.

Bright blue eyes raked over me as Hunter led me to Arinthia Hartwell. She lifted her right hand ever so slightly from the armrest of the wheelchair. I realized from her lack of movement and the way the left side of her face drooped that she must have suffered a stroke. I raised her hand and gently shook it.

"Hello, Mrs. Hartwell."

She mumbled something, and I looked at Hunter in confusion.

"Better ask Simone what she said," he remarked, indicating the companion with a nod of his head. "She's the only one who can understand her."

"Try again," the companion said quietly to the old woman.

I listened to the unintelligible sounds and was amazed when Simone calmly said, "She wants to know who you are and why you're here."

I chose my words carefully. "My name is Marissa Cole. I'm visiting for a couple of days, sightseeing, and I'm interested in all the beautiful old homes along the coastline of Maine."

Arinthia's blue eyes bore into mine. A shiver traveled down my back. I swear she knew there was a whole lot more to my story than that. I didn't dare say another word. There was no reason to let the ghosts out of my closet if Tim Hartwell wasn't my father.

Arinthia made more garbled sounds and motioned to Simone to come closer. I stood awkwardly, my gaze flitting from one part of the porch to another, trying to see as much of the house as I could.

Simone spoke. "Arinthia wants to know if you're from these

parts. She thinks she might have seen you in town."

I smiled and shook my head. "I live in Atlanta and have for several years."

"Well, anyway, she'd like us to have some refreshments. Won't you come inside?"

I hid my surprise and slowly nodded.

Hunter gave me a sympathetic look and motioned me toward the front door. "If Auntie wants you to do something, I'd suggest you do it," he said *sotto voce*. "No one goes against her wishes."

He led me inside to the sunroom. The afternoon sun slanted into the room, softening the edges of the several tall, multi-paned windows. The light from the windows accented the green tropical plants that leaned toward the outside as if they wished they could join the rhododendrons outside in the garden.

Heavy white wicker couches and chairs were scattered around the room, covered with bright floral cushions of green, yellow and pink, all of which reminded me of pictures of English gardens. The tinkling sound of water caught my attention. I turned and discovered a small water fountain in the corner of the room.

"Have a seat." Hunter indicated the couch with a sweep of his hand. "Simone will be here shortly with my aunt." He checked his watch. "It's time for her medicine."

I chose one of the single chairs and sat on the edge of the seat.

"So, what do you do in Atlanta?" Hunter asked. He leaned back against the couch and stretched his long legs out in front of him, totally relaxed.

"I'm an administrative assistant for a telecommunications company. But I'm going to school to get my college degree in computer programming."

He studied me, and I wished I was wearing something more glamorous than denim shorts and a T-shirt.

"Do you stay here with your aunt from time to time?" I asked politely.

He let out a snort. "Not a chance. We'd be at one another's throats all the time. I visit on a regular basis, though. It's important. As the only remaining male in the family besides my father, I'm going to inherit her share of the paper mills my great-grandfather founded. I figure I owe her a visit or two, whenever the mood hits me."

Simone rolled Arinthia into the room and Hunter immediately sat up straight, like a schoolboy caught out of his seat. Arinthia glanced at me, and if she could smile, I'm sure she would have.

A round, pleasant-faced woman wearing a white apron carried in a silver tray laden with glasses of iced tea and a plate of cookies. *Did people really live this way?* The whole scene made me think I'd magically gone back in time at least a hundred years.

Simone smiled at my awe and eyed my baseball cap with silent meaning. I removed the hat I'd plopped on my head, allowing my long red curls to fall around my shoulders with abandon.

Arinthia made a garbled sound and grabbed her throat.

Alarmed, I saw that her eyes had widened and her mouth hung open, causing spittle to dribble down her chin. I glanced away.

Simone stood and gave me a look of apology. "I'm sorry. I think this is too much for her. Why don't you young people sit and enjoy the tea and cookies? It would be a shame to waste them."

Arinthia and Simone made a hasty exit.

Hunter lifted his shoulders and let them drop,

unconcerned. "She has these episodes from time to time. What the hell, let's go ahead like Simone said, but I'm about to have a beer instead. What about you? Do you want one?"

I shook my head. "Actually, I was looking forward to the tea. Thanks, anyway."

He left me alone in the room. I sipped my tea silently.

Hunter reappeared with a bottle of Heineken in his hand. "Can't stand tea," he said, shaking his head. "Don't know why I have to put up with this play-acting, but it'll be worth it in the end."

I decided he wasn't so handsome after all. Not with an attitude like that. I gulped down the last of my drink and stood. "I'd better be going."

He shrugged. "Whatever. I'll walk you to the door."

We'd reached the front hallway when Simone came hurrying down the hallway.

"Wait, Marissa! I have a message for you."

Simone approached and placed a hand on my arm, preventing me from leaving. "Arinthia asks if you would come see her tomorrow morning. Around ten o'clock, say. Will you do it for her? She apologizes for her abrupt departure."

I caught my lip between my teeth. Would one more day in Maine hurt? "All right. Tell her I'll be here at ten."

Hunter frowned at me and turned to Simone. "What's going on?"

Her face became devoid of expression, a process I found fascinating. "I think it's one of her quirky ideas, but who are we to keep her from her wishes?"

CHAPTER SEVEN

As I walked along the beach, I was jolted back to the present by the shouts of children splashing in and out of the water while their parents closely watched them. Observing women in skimpy bikinis, I was reminded that Arinthia was still living in an old-fashioned world where matriarchs could rule by the fistful of money they promised to leave behind. I knew I'd never be part of such a scenario.

I made my way to my car, anxious to get back to my motel room. In my room, I rubbed lotion over my face and limbs to soothe the sunburn that was beginning to sting and decided to stroll among the shops once more. My mother had sent me here. Perhaps she'd walked these very same streets. The idea seemed so foreign to me.

Outside, I gazed at the old houses and shops lining the narrow streets and tried to imagine what the town might have looked like when my mother was young.

A small, red clapboard building housed the County Historical Society. Maybe I could shed more light on her background.

Inside, I strolled through the small rooms, studying photographs and reading about the sea captains who originally built some of the larger homes in the area with widow walks. Briar Cliff was shown in a photograph and mentioned as being one of the summer homes built and maintained by families who owned paper and pulp mills in the state. I thought of Hunter. He, too, would soon be among those in that category.

After I left the Historical Society building, I walked over to the town hall. The white clapboard building, three stories tall, sat in the middle of town next to a small grassy square. A cupola sat atop the roof, making it appear more like a church. Not your typical government building.

I climbed the concrete stairs that led to the entrance and opened the black wooden door. Inside, the vestibule was sparsely furnished and empty. A large marble plaque, mounted on the wall facing the front door, caught my eye. I drew close and saw that it contained a list of townspeople who'd died serving their country. My eyes followed the alphabetical listing until they found *Timothy C. Hartwell* listed. I traced the name gingerly, my mind racing with excitement. Had Clyde Breeden really been friends with Tim? My lip curled at the thought. Knowing now what kind of background Tim had come from, I doubted it. There must be more to the story. Otherwise, why would my mother have welcomed him into our home?

On my way back to the motel, some of the old resentment toward my mother resurfaced. She'd left me with more questions than answers. Irritation ate at me. Why hadn't she ever opened up to anyone about her past? I didn't understand her now any better than I ever had. I let out a frustrated sigh. I probably never would.

I returned to the lobby of The Harborside Inn and headed to the elevators, intent on a refreshing shower.

"Marissa!"

Startled, I whipped around.

Hunter rose from a chair in the lounge area. "I thought you might be staying here." He flashed a broad smile as he approached me. "I came by to see if you'd like to go to dinner with me. It's the least a native like me can do for a stranger to these parts."

I stopped. What harm could one dinner do? It was my choice. This would be the same thing as going to the baseball game with Mike. And maybe I could uncover more information about the family that intrigued me so.

"Thanks, that sounds nice."

Hunter gave me another bright smile. "Great. I'll pick you up at six. We can have drinks out on the deck at Harry's, here in town, before going to dinner."

"Okay. See you then."

I waved good-bye. He seemed harmless and would, I hoped, be a source of much-needed information.

Upstairs in the shower, the cool water felt good on my overheated skin. I thought of Hunter Hartwell. He seemed to have it all—good looks, a settled future, a stable family. But I didn't like his overly eager desire to inherit what he considered to be his, nor his contempt for his aunt. I decided to enjoy the evening, comfortable I'd never see him again.

I put on a shell-pink dress I'd bought on sale at Macy's, and added the pearl necklace and earrings. The simple, sleeveless sheath looked even better with the slight color I'd picked up from the beach. I lifted my red curls and bunched them together with a clip at the back of my head, letting them have their way in the humidity. I stepped back, studied myself in the mirror and decided it would do.

At six, I took the elevator down to the lobby and arrived in time to watch Hunter extract himself from a small red Beemer convertible parked in front of the motel. He was wearing tan slacks and a wine-colored golf shirt that showed off his well-tended body. I could almost hear Sari let out a soft murmur of approval. Hunter Hartwell wasn't of interest to me personally, but he was, I had to admit, a real hottie.

Hunter gave me a slow whistle as I stepped outside. His blue eyes sparkling, he approached and lifted my hand to his lips. "You look great."

He held onto my hand and walked me over to the car, glancing my way with a wide grin that made my mouth go dry. I hoped he didn't have the wrong idea about the date. Nervous about the evening ahead, I slid into the passenger's seat and waited for him to get behind the wheel.

We drove a few blocks along the waterfront and pulled into the parking lot of a large, gray-shingled, two-story building with a huge outdoor deck that overlooked a backwater.

I twisted to open the car door.

"Stay right there," Hunter said. He got out, ran around to my side of the car and stood by while I crawled out as gracefully as I could in the slim skirt.

Hunter clasped my hand and held tight. "No way am I going to let you walk through the bar without staking a claim on you. The guys will go nuts. And wait 'til Sam sees you—it's going to blow her mind. Now, maybe she'll get off my back."

I frowned. "Who's Sam?"

He tugged me toward the building. "One of my sisters."

I came to a stop. Things were moving way too fast. "She's here now?"

"I called her and told her to meet us so she could see you for herself."

What kind of game was he playing? I wondered, wishing now I hadn't been so quick to accept his invitation.

He tugged on my hand. "C'mon. We've got a great evening ahead of us. I promise."

One evening, I told myself. That's all. Hopefully, I'd learn more about the family I had once thought might be mine.

The inside lounge was rustic but charming with its sailing décor. Nautical flags, pictures of racing sailboats and other marine items hung from the walls and ceiling. Hunter flung an arm around my shoulder as we crossed the dimly-lit room toward the outside deck. I shifted out from under his arm as casually as I could.

Outside a large wooden deck overlooked dark swirling water below. I stood blinking in the sunlight until I was finally able to see a number of people seated at tile-top tables.

"Over here, Hunter."

From a nearby table, a young woman about my age waved to us with a thin arm. I studied her as we approached. Her dark hair, worn straight and loose, gave me the first clue that this was Hunter's sister. Closer inspection proved me right. Her features matched Hunter's, though her eyes were a pretty gray instead of bright-blue.

Hunter held my chair while I got settled. Then he moved around the table to give his sister a light kiss on the cheek.

She gave him a glassy-eyed look. "So you've got a looker, not a hooker, this time, bro. Don't tell me it's serious. She looks too nice."

Hunter's eyes narrowed. "Dammit, Sam. How long have you been here drinking?"

She smirked. "Since you called me. I decided I'd better get a little mellow before meeting your latest woman because as your older sister, I'm supposed to keep an eye on you."

Hunter groaned, and I fought the urge to get up and simply walk away. But something inside me held me back. I was not Hunter's "woman" as Sam so weirdly put it. Neither was I going to simply accept her rudeness. It reminded me too much of my home life growing up.

Hunter placed a hand over mine. "Sorry, Marissa. I didn't know Samantha would be in one of her nasty moods. We can leave right now if you want."

Sam glared at Hunter. "Don't call me Samantha. You know

I can't stand that name." She threw me a challenging look and gave Hunter an exaggerated innocent look. "Afraid she can't take the Hartwell heat?"

"You're drunk, Sam," I answered quietly. "You don't scare me. In fact, I feel sorry for you."

Sam pushed back from the table so fast her chair made a loud scraping noise. She jumped to her feet. "You think you're good enough to be a Hartwell? Well, let me tell you something. You're not!"

She stomped away. Others on the deck stared from her to me in shocked silence. I sat in my seat, frozen with mortification.

Hunter shook his head. "Sorry about that. I should have known better. Do you want to leave?"

I held Hunter back from rising. "Wait! Maybe it's better if we stay here a while and let things die down a bit. Then we can go."

"Good idea," he quickly agreed. "People around here are used to Sam, anyway. The ones that aren't, don't live here."

The waiter appeared, and I ordered lemonade. Somehow alcohol didn't seem appropriate at the moment. Hunter ordered a double scotch on the rocks. A single malt of some kind, he explained to me.

"Tell me about your sister, Why doesn't she like the name 'Samantha'?"

"She and my other older sister, Allison, or Al, as she's sometimes called, were supposed to be boys. My mother, in an effort to placate my father, allowed the girls to be called by boys' names. The thing is, they've always known they were a big disappointment to my father."

"That's hard," I said with genuine sympathy.

"Samantha thinks she should get part of the business. She interned there during summer breaks from college and even went on to get her MBA and law degree from Harvard. But the family rules are very strict. It's the men in the family who are supposed to get the business."

"What about your aunt? I thought the business was hers."

"Only through inheritance from my uncle. She can hold onto it, but after she dies without children or grandchildren of her own, it reverts back to the males on my side of the family. My father thought he'd inherit the business when his older brother, Herbert, Arinthia's husband, died."

"But he didn't?"

Hunter shook his head. "No, his brother's side of the family wanted to keep it to themselves. It's been a family disagreement for years. Now, with Arinthia having no heirs, we have a chance to take a turn at running it. My father wants me to do that for him, and Arinthia has finally agreed."

"You don't sound very enthusiastic about it."

He shrugged. "I want the money and all the benefits, of course, but things have changed in the paper and pulp business in Maine. The Feds are always snooping, what with OSHA and all the dioxin stuff of the past ..."

I recalled there'd been several investigations into the toxic chemicals that were produced by what were described in the news reports as "craft" paper mills. It wasn't a pretty picture in Maine or in the Southeast. One of my bosses at work had family members who sold pine trees from huge tracts of land they owned.

"But if Sam wants to run it, can't you have her help you?" I asked.

"Nah. She's a woman and the men won't like it."

My sympathies shifted to Sam. It didn't seem right in this day and age for a woman to be punished because she was a woman. The whole Hartwell family seemed to be living in the past.

The crowd doubled on the deck and the noise rose to a level that made further conversation impossible. People stood at the railing and filled every available space at the tables. Hunter picked up the bill from the table and got to his feet. I rose and began to weave my way through the strangers.

Hunter grabbed my arm. "Hey, there's Al. Let's say hello."

I turned and frowned, wondering which woman in the crowd he was talking about. Then I saw her. A tall, stunning girl with sun-streaked blond hair that swung at her shoulders as she talked and laughed. Three men appeared to hang onto her every word. I envied her ease with them. As we drew closer, I heard her say, "I hate my job. It's so boring."

She saw Hunter and gave him a teasing grin. "Speaking of boring, here's my brother now."

I noticed the tension in Hunter's jaw and realized with amusement that he was irritated by her remark. Brilliant blue eyes raked over me as she put an arm around her brother, placating him with an affectionate hug. She released him and held out a hand to me.

"I'm Allison Hartwell. Who are you?"

I tried not to wince as she grasped my hand a little too firmly. "Marissa Cole."

"You new in town? I haven't seen you before."

"Aren't you going to introduce me?" asked one of the three men standing next to Allison.

She shrugged. "Marissa, this is Will, Bob, and Duncan. But, hey, they're all here with me." She let out a chuckle and I couldn't help smiling at the pure impishness of her grin. Somehow it was charming, and I could see why people would be drawn to her. She sparkled with life. The contrast between her and her sister was remarkable.

"Well, we'd better go," said Hunter. "We've got reservations at *Chez Si Bon*."

Allison's eyebrows shot up. She studied me openly.

I pretended not to notice as Will said, "You gonna be in town long?"

I shook my head. "I'm just visiting. Actually, I'm leaving tomorrow."

Hunter took my hand and led me through the crowd. Outside the building, I paused to catch my breath. Before I could object, Hunter put his arms around me and pulled me close.

"You were the most beautiful girl on the deck. I think Al was a little jealous."

"Hunter? Is that you?"

He immediately dropped his arms and turned to face a leggy blond walking toward us with purposeful strides.

"Bettina! What are you doing here? I thought you were in Boston."

"Obviously." Her frosty gaze swept over me, chasing a shiver down my back.

Hunter cleared his throat. "Bettina, this is Marissa Cole. She's visiting Aunt Arinthia. Marissa, Bettina Browning."

I let Hunter's lie go. "Nice to meet you."

Bettina's eyes narrowed. "How do you know Arinthia Hartwell?"

I fumbled for an answer.

"It's a long story," Hunter interjected, making a point of checking his watch. "I'll tell you about it later. Right now, we have to leave or we'll be late for dinner. I promised my aunt I'd show Marissa a good time."

Bettina stood by as we climbed into Hunter's car. The look she gave me as I turned to wave good-bye was murderous. I shuddered and wondered what hornet's nest I'd stumbled into. The stinging remarks and undercurrent of tension between Hunter and his sisters, and now with Bettina, were a warning to me that the people surrounding Arinthia were like buzzing bees circling a honey-filled hive. I turned to Hunter, questions on my mind.

"Guess you want to know who she is." He gave me an abashed grin. "Bettina Browning and I have an understanding of sorts. Or at least our families do. We're due to become engaged this fall, as soon as my aunt turns the business over to me. The Browning family owns a paper company and, if all goes well, we could merge the two paper businesses under the direction of Willard Browning, Bettina's father."

"And you're happy with those plans?" Who made arrangements like that anymore? I wondered.

Hunter shrugged. "Bettina's all right. She and I have been more or less together for years."

It was the way Hunter said it—without passion or deep-rooted respect. I thought of Brad Crawford and the way he'd kissed me—with both the passion and respect I needed. That's what I wanted when and if the right time came.

Hunter pulled into a parking lot next to a two-story white wooden building. Bright blue awnings protected large picture windows overlooking the lawn which spread a layer of bright green grass between the parking lot and the house.

"*Chez Si Bon* is a lot better than the funky name implies." Hunter helped me out of the car. "They brought a chef up from Boston, a guy who used to work with Lydia Shire. He's really good."

Inside, white linen tablecloths covered round tables. Vivid blue napkins brightened the tables, blue-stemmed water goblets accented the lincns, and little blue vases filled with what looked like miniature white Calla lilies completed the color scheme.

The maitre d' greeted Hunter by name and ushered us to a table in the corner.

"You and your lady enjoy," he murmured, casting a sideways glance of admiration my way.

Hunter smiled at me as he picked up the wine list. "I owe you one for covering up for me when I told Bettina you were visiting Arinthia. She can be very jealous."

With good cause, I thought, and listened as the waiter began to tell us of the evening specials. My mouth watered at the suggestion of chilled, cooked lobster with a light lemon-cream sauce and I ordered it, along with a small pear and blue cheese salad.

The evening passed pleasantly. Hunter and I carried on harmless, friendly conversation, with little new information revealed about the family. Finally, I couldn't stand it anymore.

"Do you know of anyone named Margaret Cole?" I asked. My body tensed with hope.

He thought a moment and shook his head. "Why? Is she a friend of yours?"

I hid my disappointment. "Not really. Just someone I knew."

The waiter arrived at our table and I let the matter drop.

Dessert was a gooey chocolate torte that Hunter and I shared. I couldn't help noticing, though, for every bite I took, he took two.

After dinner, we stepped outside into the cool, briny air. Stars twinkled in the dark sky above us and I felt like winking back. Hunter kept the top down on the convertible as he drove me back to the motel. The moon smiled down on us as we followed the coast back to New Hope. I realized I'd miss the small picturesque town huddled along the Maine shoreline.

"I like New Hope. It's so pretty. In some respects, it will be hard to return to Atlanta. No ocean and all."

His lips curved into his now-familiar lopsided grin. "Why don't you stay?"

I shook my head. "I have to go back. I've got plans." But I couldn't help wondering if the safe future I'd planned so carefully was the future I really wanted.

At the motel, Hunter swerved into a parking spot, got out and opened my door. When I stood up outside the car, Hunter grinned confidently. "How about a goodnight kiss?"

I smiled and stepped back. "Thank you, Hunter, for a wonderful evening."

His eyes widened and I realized not many girls turned him down. He gave my hand a squeeze. "Okay, then. You're going to see Arinthia tomorrow morning?"

"Yes, I'll make a quick stop on my way out of town."

"I may join you. If not, have a nice trip home."

Upstairs, in my motel room, I undressed and slipped on my favorite oversized T-shirt. Turning off the lights, I stepped out onto my balcony and looked up at the stars in the cool air, wondering how my mother might have fit into life here. My trip had been fruitless. Still, I was happy I'd made the journey. And now that I'd seen the place that must have been so special to my mother, I realized I owed it to me—and to her—to find the truth behind the lies.

After packing the car, I drove to the entrance of Briar Cliff. The gate was open. I drove past the stone pillars to the back of the house, climbed out of the car and walked toward the side porch. Rounding the back corner of the house, I came to a quick stop. Arinthia was sitting in her wheelchair, facing Simone, practicing vocal exercises. They stopped when they noticed me.

Simone smiled. "We're working on getting Arinthia back to her old self. Knowing Arinthia as well as I do, it will be just a matter of weeks before she's better than ever."

"Wonderful," I said, having read about the remarkable recovery of some stroke victims. I approached Arinthia. "Are you doing physical therapy every day?"

She nodded and I clearly heard her say, "Ya." I thought of Hunter and wondered what his reaction to Arinthia's "recovery" would be. His family so clearly wanted her out of the picture.

Simone smiled. "Arinthia is anxious for you to see the house and to spend some time with her."

My gaze swerved to Arinthia. She held out an unsteady hand to me.

"Fine." Wondering at all this attention, I took her hand in mine.

Arinthia's eyes filled with tears, and I was glad I'd agreed to come visit her. She seemed such a lonely, unloved woman.

Simone opened the door, and I helped wheel Arinthia inside.

"This way." Simone indicated the large living room on my right.

It looked exactly like I thought it would—right out of a magazine. A huge stone fireplace dominated one wall, flanked by white bookcases that held *objets d'art* and a collection of books. A large cream and green Oriental rug covered most of the golden pine floor. Overstuffed couches and chairs in subtle patterns compatible with the rug were scattered in conversational groupings amidst small antique tables. The room gave the impression of an elderly grande dame—worldly and wise and accustomed to the best.

"This way," said Simone, and I followed her into the adjoining dining room, as elegant as the living room.

A large, oval mahogany table was surrounded by many high-backed, carved chairs. A side table held a silver coffee service and a built-in corner cupboard displayed a variety of silver and crystal pieces. It, like the living room, seemed a scene out of the past, when quiet elegance reigned.

After the quaintness of the other downstairs rooms, the kitchen was strikingly modern. When I remarked on it, Arinthia mumbled something and Simone interjected, "We upgraded it when the sunroom was added on. I came to work for Arinthia many years ago when she and her husband decided to move from Madison to New Hope before the children were born. This house has been in the family for generations."

"This is where her son grew up?" I thought of Tim.

"And her daughter."

"Her daughter?" I turned to Arinthia. My gaze fell on her watery eyes.

She looked away from me.

"Thea was a beautiful girl. She was gone too young," Simone said softly, and held up her hand, cutting off any of my questions. "It's a painful topic for Arinthia."

I followed them to the stairway, understanding now why I felt such tenderness for Arinthia. Her life had been filled with pain and disappointment.

"You want me to go upstairs?"

Simone gave me a discreet nod and assisted Arinthia into the motorized chair lift.

At the top of the stairs, I helped Simone maneuver Arinthia back into the wheelchair so we could continue our tour.

Arinthia's room was unmistakable. It dominated a corner of the house and had a full view of the ocean, the gardens to the side and, in back, the distant view of the winding road along the shore.

I counted six bedrooms before we arrived at the last one. I felt Arinthia's eyes on me as I walked into the room, immediately drawn to the pink and white décor. Without asking, I knew this had been Thea's room. I strolled over to the window and pulled aside an ecru damask curtain. Leafy green branches of a huge tree all but blocked the view of the ocean, and I was reminded of my talking tree. I turned around and found Arinthia staring at me.

"Theee-a," she said and lowered her head so I couldn't see her face. I observed her shaking shoulders and knelt before her.

"I'm sorry,"

Simone tapped me on the shoulder. "Time to go," she whispered, waving me to my feet.

Impulsively, I leaned over and gave Arinthia a kiss on the cheek. "Good-bye, Mrs. Hartwell. It was nice to meet you."

She remained silent as I left the room.

"Thank you for coming," Simone said at the front door. "She insisted I ask you to visit, but I didn't realize it would upset her so. I'm sorry it turned out this way. Can I offer you some refreshments?"

"No, thanks, I'm on my way back to New York, and should get started."

Simone's eyebrows shot up. "New York? I thought you were from Atlanta."

I smiled. "My dog is staying with a friend in New York. From there, I'll go home."

"Safe travels then."

After descending the back steps, I walked out onto the lawn to get a closer look at the tree at the northeast corner of the house. I stood a moment, looking up into its lush, green umbrella and sensed a movement at Thea's bedroom window. Somehow I knew Arinthia was there. I gave her a small wave and continued on to the car.

###

The drive back to New York seemed to take no time at all. My mind kept busy, reliving every moment in New Hope. The family I'd hoped to find did not exist; I was right back where I started—with a gold ring and a white coat as the only clues to my mother's past.

I'd taken care of her ashes and was free of her obligation. What happened from this point forward would be of my own choosing. And though I was terribly disappointed with the results of my visit to New Hope, I vowed not to give up the search for the truth behind my mother.

CHAPTER EIGHT

I pulled into Doris's driveway and heard Lady's high-pitched welcoming yelp. The front door opened and Lady came bounding out of the house in a frenzied rush to greet me. Happy to see her, I put my arms around her neck, and let her lick my face all over.

"You made good time!" Doris gave me a hug. "I've got a meatloaf in the oven and was getting ready to call Brad to see if he wanted to join us."

The memory of Brad's pained expression burned in my brain. I was so ashamed of the way I'd tried to use him.

Doris studied me. "Maybe I won't call Brad."

"Do you mind? I'd rather not see him."

"No problem," Doris said, but I could tell from her tone of voice that she didn't approve my running away from an awkward situation.

"Come along." Doris grabbed hold of my suitcase. "Lady and I are dying for your company."

I smiled, grateful as always for Doris's acceptance of me—flaws and all. Giving my shoulders a shake to loosen sore muscles, I reached into the backseat of the car and lifted out some gifts I'd picked up for Doris that morning in the hotel gift shop. Following her inside, I kept my eyes averted from the house next door, reminding myself it no longer had anything to do with me.

At dinner, I filled Doris in on all I'd done and seen in New Hope. "It's a pretty town. I can't imagine what it or Briar Cliff has to do with my mother. Nothing about it makes sense."

Doris clucked sympathetically. "Well, you've done as your mother asked. That should make you feel good."

I sipped my after-dinner coffee. "I've completed my mother's request, but there's a whole lot more I need to do for myself. I can't let go of the idea that somewhere there are people who knew Margaret Cole as a young woman, people who could help me solve the mystery of who she really was."

She patted my hand. "There must have been a reason your mother never told you about them, Marissa."

"What about my father? I want to know about him, too. How do I know who I really am? Where I came from?"

She gave me a worried look. "I understand about finding your roots, but sometimes it doesn't turn out well."

I took another sip of coffee, inwardly vowing to continue my investigation.

The next morning I rose early, eager to get back to Atlanta. It had been a full, busy week but I was ready to return to the quiet life I'd built there. After breakfast, I stowed my luggage in the trunk of the car and helped Lady into the backseat.

Doris gave me a hug. "When will I see you again?"

I shook my head sadly. "I don't know."

"I suppose there's no reason for you to ever return, with your mother gone and the house sold." She pulled a Kleenex out of her pocket and dabbed at her eyes.

I put my arms around her. She was more my mother than my own had ever been. "I'll keep in touch with you. I promise."

"And Brad?"

I shook my head and remained silent. I'd ruined everything. Besides, long-distance relationships seldom worked.

I pulled out of the driveway, feeling like the young girl who'd taken flight several years ago. Only this time, I knew where I was going.

#

The little house I lived in outside of Atlanta never looked better to me. I let out a sigh of relief when I pulled to a stop beside it. Home.

After I got things settled inside, I took Lady for a walk. Strolling down the sidewalk, I thought about my visit to Maine. After years of avoiding anything to do with my family, I was now obsessed with finding out about both my parents.

I quickly settled into my old routine at MacTel. My boss had returned from vacation with renewed energy, which meant in addition to my usual workload, I was kept busy with a number of extra projects. I didn't mind. It kept me focused on things other than my mother's family.

Over the Labor Day weekend, I decided to take it easy, do nothing more strenuous than deciding which movie I wanted to rent. I fixed a chef salad for dinner and sat down to enjoy it. The trilling of the phone interrupted me. I picked it up, expecting to hear Sari or one of my other girlfriends.

Brad's deep hello startled me into silence.

"You there, Marissa?"

I nodded stupidly, then spoke. "I'm just surprised to hear from you."

"I finally realized I'd have to call you 'cause you were never going to call me."

The familiar feeling of embarrassment washed over me. "Brad, I'm so sorry about what happened. I just can't be myself in that town. I know it was a rotten thing to do, try to use you like that."

"Yeah, well, I've had time to think about it and I guess I'm sort of flattered you thought of trusting me like that. Let's put it behind us."

A wave of relief washed through me. I'd told myself to

forget him, but he'd stubbornly remained in my thoughts, filling me with a yearning only he could fulfill.

"You okay with that?" His voice sounded unsure.

I swallowed hard. "Yes, it's a good idea. I've missed our talks."

"The thing is," Brad continued hesitantly, "I want to see you again. I was thinking I'd fly down there one weekend. Maybe next week? What do you say?"

I remembered the way we'd been able to talk, the gentleness of his touch, the warmth I felt when I was with him. "I'd like that very much." My voice cracked. I was lying. I'd *love* it!

"Good. That's settled then."

I heard the happiness in his voice and smiled. Maybe this time, away from Barnham, I could show him how much I cared.

Over the next few days, I tried to concentrate on my job, but my excitement over seeing Brad kept me dropping pens, staring into the distance, reliving moments with him.

"What you got going on, girl?" Sari asked one morning as I settled behind my desk. An impish smile spread across her face. "Gotta be a man. Right?"

I felt giddy as a school girl, telling her about Brad's visit.

She gave me a nod of approval. "'Bout time you got interested in someone." She moved her chair closer to my desk and lowered her voice. "I think Rico is getting ready to pop the question." She and Rico had been going together for over two years. He was a real looker who was a genuinely nice guy. We all drooled over him whenever he showed up at the office.

"You know what to answer, right?"

Sari laughed. "Yeah, I know what to say all right. I've been practicing ooh-ing over the ring and saying yes."

We laughed together.

In preparation for Brad's visit, I went through the house, straightening forgotten cluttered corners and adding a few homey touches here and there. The day before he was due to arrive, I splurged on a mani and pedi and had my hair trimmed.

The airport was a forty-five-minute drive from my home if, and it was a big 'if,' there was little traffic. Luck was with me. The Friday evening traffic moved along without the normal number of wrecks. Each mile that brought me closer to the airport added another level of excitement to my already nerve-wracked body.

We'd agreed I'd meet him in the baggage claim area of the airport. I parked the car and went inside, anxiously checking my watch. His plane had landed late. I hurried over to the waiting area at the top of the escalator and searched the travelers rising up to the main level from the trains below.

My heart leaped with joy when I saw the top of Brad's head. The rest of his body came into view and his broad grin at the sight of me made my pulse jump happily. Smiling, we stared at one another.

He stepped off the escalator, and I moved toward him. He dropped his leather suitcase at his feet and swept me up in his arms. Laughing, I inhaled the smell of his spicy aftershave lotion and leaned against his chest, thrilled by the sound of the pounding heartbeat beneath his golf shirt.

He raised my chin and kissed me. His lips were soft and firm, gentle, yet filled with an urgency that sent frissons of excitement through me. We drew apart and stood in the middle of the crowd, smiling at one another, alone in our joy.

"Hi," I said shakily, still rocked by his kiss and the sexy way he was looking at me.

"It's good to see you." He cupped my cheek in his hand and gave me a smile that sent my pulse soaring.

"You, too." I took his hand.

He picked up his suitcase and followed me out the door.

We got settled in my car and headed north. I couldn't help stealing glances at him as he told me about the flight. He looked so handsome with that sandy hair of his and those shining brown eyes.

"You wouldn't believe what Bud Drexler and his wife Pam have done to your old house," he told me. "It's starting to look really good. He's adding on a big family room and Pam told me they're going to paint the house a bright cream color."

I smiled. "I'm so pleased for them. The house I knew was ugly in so many ways. What else is going on?"

"I took Aunt Doris out to dinner last night. She told me 'You bring that girl back here.'"

We laughed. She loved both of us.

As we approached the city, I turned to Brad. "It's late. Want to try and grab dinner downtown?"

"Sure. Know of any place special?"

"Sari was telling me of a new place at Lenox Square in Buckhead. It's supposed to be a really cool spot. I've never been there."

"Let's give it a try."

Salud was the so-called new, hot, "watering hole" for the hip in Atlanta. We walked into the dimly lit bar and looked around. I spied an empty high-top table and quickly moved through jostling elbows to get to it. We sat, and soon a waitress, clad in a low-cut white blouse over a pair of black shorts came over to our table to take our orders. She winked at Brad. "What'll you have, hon?"

He glanced over at me. "What do you want, Marissa?"

The only alcohol I usually drank was red wine and that was

rare. "I'll have what you have."

The waitress left and returned with our margaritas. We chatted about nothing in half-shouts above the din around us. I hardly noticed how quickly our glasses emptied.

"We must have been thirsty." Brad signaled the waitress. "Let's order another round."

"And some appetizers," I suggested. I hadn't had much of a lunch, just some crackers and a cup of soup. I wasn't about to follow in my mother's footsteps by becoming drunk.

The moments flew by as we sipped drinks and picked at the flat bread pizza we'd ordered.

"Anything more happening with New Hope?" Brad asked.

I shook my head. "I tried to Google some information, but didn't come up with anything new. I've been too busy at work to put much time into it but, Brad, I'm not going to let it drop."

"Just be careful, Marissa. Like Aunt Doris told you, sometimes it's better to just leave things alone."

"You guys ready for the check?" the waitress asked, interrupting us.

"Ready to go?" Brad said.

"I guess so," I said, realizing the appetizers we'd eaten had done little to counterbalance the effect of the margaritas .

As we stepped outside, everything seemed to swim in the bright lights around me. I swayed on my feet. "Uh, Brad, I'm not sure I can drive home. I'm not used to drinking that much."

He stared at me thoughtfully and glanced around. "I noticed a Ritz Carlton hotel not far from here. We could walk there. Make it a special night."

My eyes widened with surprise. *The Ritz? Could we?* I thought of Lady. I'd fed her and took her outside just before I left for the airport. She'd be fine. But the Ritz Carlton was expensive and the thought of being in a hotel with him increased the whirling in my head.

"I'll be okay after we walk around a bit." The sidewalk took another spin.

He reached out to steady me. "Are you sure?"

I gazed up at him in a daze. "Maybe we'd better go to the hotel. There's no way I can drive."

"Let's go get my stuff," he murmured and offered me his hand.

We made our way to the car, grabbed his suitcase and walked hand in hand down the block to the hotel.

Brad registered us at the front desk. A bellman walked us to our room and explained the various functions of the room and the amenities of the hotel. I fidgeted, waiting for the man to get through his practiced spiel.

After the bellman left, Brad grinned at me. "You okay?"

"Sure," I mumbled and plopped down on the couch.

Brad sat next to me, kicked off his loafers and wiggled his toes. He leaned back, put his arm around me and settled me against him. Having his lean, muscular arms around me seemed right. The feel of his thigh, pressing against mine through his khaki pants, was solid, manly, and not frightening at all. I snuggled up against him. His hand drew caressing circles on my back. It felt so good.

Brad lowered his lips onto mine, demanding a response I was only too glad to give. When we broke apart, Brad searched my face.

"Should we go to bed?" he whispered hoarsely.

"Yes." I held out my arms to him, my inhibitions gone. "It's what I want too."

He picked me up and carried me over to the king-sized bed. His eyes never left mine as he took hold of the corner of the spread and whipped it back before settling me on the smooth silky sheets.

He lifted his shirt over his head, giving me a moment to study him. His bare chest was broad with a sprinkling of light brown hairs, his waist tapered above his hips. The bulge below his waist was obvious.

I took off my clothes, crawled into bed and pulled up the sheet.

Brad lay beside me and took me in his arms. "I want you, Marissa."

"Me too." I chuckled drunkenly. "I mean I want you too." My eyes closed against the spinning in my head.

"Marissa?"

"Yeah?"

"We'd better wait. You're falling asleep. We'll try again tomorrow."

I rolled over, letting sleep overtake me.

Later, I rose from the bed and stood beside the window, a shadow to anyone looking up from below. Watching lights in the city, I drew a deep breath. Once again, I'd disappointed Brad. And myself.

"Marissa?" Brad mumbled, patting the empty space next to him groggily.

I moved quickly to his side. "I'm here," I whispered.

He smiled in his sleep and rolled over, and I climbed in beside him, hugging him close.

The next morning I was awakened by the sensation of butterfly wings beating against my cheeks, my neck, my lips. Startled, my eyes flew open.

Brad's face appeared next to me. He grinned. "I knew you couldn't hold out much longer, sleepyhead."

I smiled at him, and his brown eyes darkened. I glanced at the bedside clock and sat up in alarm. "Brad! It's almost ten o'clock. I have to get home to Lady. The poor dog must be miserable."

I stumbled out of bed.

We quickly dressed and checked out of the hotel. At a nearby deli, we grabbed cups of coffee, raced to the car and headed up Georgia 400 toward home. Thankfully, the Saturday morning traffic was light and we made it to Cumming in record time.

I pulled into the driveway of the rental house and turned to Brad. "I'll get Lady."

When I opened the kitchen door, Lady wiggled a welcome and hurried past me. She squatted on the lawn, and seeing Brad, greeted him with her welcoming bark.

Brad pulled his suitcase out of the car. Lady bounded over to him, wagged her tail, and gave him a canine smile that brought a grin to his face. He gave her several pats on the head and murmured hello in a low, soothing voice.

"Come in."

He stood in the middle of the living room. "Nice. Where should I put this?" He indicated his suitcase.

"My bedroom is straight ahead. But I made up the pull-out couch in case you want to sleep there."

His eyes sparkled with mischief. "Think again."

Lady trotted to my bedroom, as if by leading Brad there, she was approving the arrangement. Brad and I exchanged smiles and followed her.

We spent the afternoon listening to music and watching a movie, curled up on the couch together. Lady lay sleeping beside the couch. It seemed so natural to have Brad's arm around me and to rest our feet on the coffee table, like a comfortable old couple.

I smiled up at him. "I'm so happy you're here."

"Me, too," he said and lowered his lips to mine.

The movie ended, and I rose. "What sounds good for dinner?"

Brad patted his stomach. "How about cooking something outside? I'm pretty good at that."

"That would be great, but my gas grill has been leaking. I wasn't sure how to fix it."

"No problem. Lead me to it." After inspecting it, he took a wrench and tightened a few connections of the hoses leading from the tank to the grill itself.

"Think that'll do it," he said, standing back.

I gave him a quick kiss on the cheek. "For that, you get a nice steak."

He laughed. "Deal. Need anything else fixed?"

"Well, since you asked, I need to replace a light bulb in the ceiling fixture in the front hall. It means getting the ladder out."

He gave me a little salute and went to the garage for a ladder. Delighted, I watched him work. I'd dreamed of doing simple ordinary things together. I took tenderloin steaks out of the refrigerator, placed them in a dish and poured a mixture of olive oil and minced garlic over them, letting them marinate while the stuffed potatoes baked. After setting out a plate of cheese and crackers, I handed Brad a bottle of pinot noir to open. Brad poured each of us a glass of the red wine, and we headed outside.

It was perfect. The early September evening still held warmth and the wooden deck in back of the house gave us a perfect view of the changing colors in the sky as dusk set in.

Brad heated up the grill and Lady lay down next to his chair.

I studied him, loving the curve of his cheek, the slight indentation in his chin, the jaw line of dark whiskers.

Brad looked over at me and his eyes darkened. He rose

from the chair and came over to me. Brushing aside a strand of hair away from my face, he bent down and kissed me.

I reached up for him and then started when the buzzer on the stove sounded, shattering the moment.

We tended to dinner, but seated at the small table in the kitchen, the air between us hummed with sexual tension. I could only make a pretense of digging into the meal. There was something more compelling on both our minds. After what seemed an endless exercise of pushing my food around my plate, I rose.

Brad gave me a questioning look and I took his hand.

We stopped outside my bedroom door. "Are you sure this is what you want, Marissa?" Brad said.

"Yes." I wanted it more than anything. This need to give myself to him was a feeling within me as strong as the pulsing desire in my core. It thrummed through me, awakening new persistent feelings.

Inside my room, he took me in his arms. "I love you, Marissa. It's happened quickly, but it feels right." He helped me ease my shirt over my head and then began to undress.

I took off my jeans and stood in my underwear, momentarily fighting an impulse to cover my body with my arms. My gaze slid over his body, seeing Brad in a different light. He wasn't any man; he was the man who knew me well enough to be patient. Patient and kind.

I shut the door on Lady and we lay down on my bed, taking our time to get acquainted, moving comfortably close to one another, removing the last of our clothing.

Brad stroked my body. "You're beautiful, Marissa. All of you."

I thought of his need, and mine grew. He pressed against me even closer. I reached up and caressed his cheek, understanding that by thinking of what might please him, I was setting aside what might hurt me.

His hands continued to move across my body, tantalizing it. Old images melted away under the heat of something pure and real as he began to show me what true lovemaking was all about, demonstrating so wonderfully what I'd missed for so many years.

"I'll go gently," whispered Brad, over me now. "Let me know if it's too much."

He stroked and kissed me until I begged for more. And then he entered me.

I tensed at the pain.

"Easy," said Brad. "It'll get better." He leaned down and kissed my ear, and I wondered at his endurance as he moved slowly, letting me get used to the feel of him inside me. Soon the need for something more returned, and all discomfort vanished as I was lost in the rising tide of passion. We moved in pounding rhythm until I cried out in sheer release.

Brad followed with a cry of his own, and I discovered the joy of giving him as much pleasure as he'd given me.

Tears stung my eyes and overflowed.

Brad pulled away. "What's the matter? Did I hurt you?"

I shook my head. "No, it's just that I'm so happy."

He gently wiped the tears from my cheeks. "You have a funny way of showing it," he said, his words soft, tender.

"You don't understand," I whispered. "I'm free now."

His lips met mine and I pulled him to me.

I awoke the next morning to find the bed empty. For a brief moment, I wondered if I'd dreamed of having Brad here with me. Then I heard Lady bark outside and realized Brad must have let her out. I stretched happily. He was not a figment of an overactive, aroused imagination, after all.

Barefoot and wearing a purple silk nightshirt, I padded into the kitchen and gratefully inhaled the aroma of freshly brewed coffee.

"Ha! The princess awakens!" Brad teased, handing me a mug filled with coffee.

I took a sip, then yawned and stretched again, like a contented cream-fed cat.

Brad embraced me and kissed my neck. "It's a nice day. Let's do something, go somewhere."

I gazed at the sunny skies outside and smiled at him. "Dahlonega is a pretty little town not too far from here. There's white water rafting in the area, too."

"Sounds good. We'd better get going. My flight is at seven."

At the mention of Brad's departure, sharp disappointment stabbed me. I hated the idea of his leaving.

Brad grabbed his cup of coffee. "I'm going to take a shower." He wiggled his eyebrows. "Join me?"

A cold chill spread through my body, catching me off guard. I braced for the backlash of bad memories and waved him on, forcing a smile I didn't feel. "You go ahead."

Shaking off the bad memories of my youth, I felt stronger. I took a steadying sip of coffee and headed for the bathroom. I'd take a shower with him, after all.

"So, where are we going?"

I smiled at Brad from behind the wheel of my car. "Dahlonega. It's a small town in the Blue Ridge Mountains of North Georgia. I discovered it not long after I moved to Atlanta. I think you'll like it. And it'll give you a chance to see some of the countryside."

The drive up into the mountains didn't take long or maybe I felt that way because I was so happy to be with Brad. The thought of him leaving seemed to make each minute sprint by. We parked in the middle of town and walked around the square, holding hands as we peeked into shop windows and pointed out things we liked or thought ugly.

Brad's stomach growled. "I'm starving. 'Looks like a good restaurant over there. A line of people is waiting to get in."

"That's The Smith House. Their food is great, all southern-style. Sound good?"

He patted his stomach. "Sounds perfect."

We walked across the street to the large, two-story, tan clapboard building. Rocking chairs lined the wide porch like obedient school children. Many were filled with a variety of people, sitting and rocking, observing the crowd outside.

We stood in line, holding hands. His fingers around mine felt good.

Inside, we took places at a long table with mostly older couples. They looked at us and smiled.

"Newlyweds?" the gray-haired woman sitting next to me asked.

Heat roared to my cheeks. "No, just dating."

She winked at me. "Could've fooled me. Enjoy the day with your young man. Time goes by so fast." She sent a loving look to the white-haired man sitting beside her.

I had no idea where my relationship with Brad was going, but I hoped I'd enjoy a lasting   relationship like hers. The outing with Brad today had proved we were compatible in ordinary ways outside the bedroom.

The waitress brought out fresh platters of food and I laughed at the way Brad's eyes lit up when he saw the mounds of mashed potatoes, butter beans, biscuits, and all things Southern. The platter of crispy chicken kept his gaze.

Later, as we left the restaurant, Brad said, "Now that's what I call fried chicken! You can give that to me anytime."

I smiled. "What shall we do next?"

Color deepened in Brad's eyes. He sent a silent, hungry message, and a thread of anticipation wove through me. We strolled back to the car, hand in hand.

I gave Brad the car keys. "You can drive. You know where you're going."

He looked at me with a troubled expression. "Do I, Marissa?"

I knew what Brad was really asking, but I couldn't answer. Everything was happening so fast. And there was the problem of him living in Barnham.

Brad cupped my cheeks in his strong fingers. I kissed him. For now, that's all the assurance I could give him.

I drove Brad to the airport. Silence hung heavy, a gray cloud of unhappiness in my car. Three short days had changed my life forever. I wanted to thank him but didn't know how to put my feelings into words. He'd opened a door to a future I'd dreamed of for a long time, never quite believing it could happen to me. But so many things stood in our way.

"Will you come to Barnham for a long weekend?" Brad asked.

I hesitated. Going back to Barnham was like taking three giant steps backward. Did I want that?

Expectation brightened his features.

After what we'd experienced together, it would be foolish, I realized, to let bad memories prevent me from going there. Besides, I didn't want to disappoint him. "How about Columbus Day weekend?"

He grinned. "Okay, see you then."

His good-bye kiss at the curb of the airport terminal was sweet and tender. I closed my eyes, storing the taste of him, the feel of him, the smell of him in my mind.

He walked inside the terminal, leaving behind a gaping hole in my heart.

"Hey, Lady, move your car!" A policeman waved me away from the curb, and the magic of the weekend evaporated in a cacophony of blaring horns.

CHAPTER NINE

My boss announced he was putting together a huge seminar for leaders in the telecom industry. I juggled my schedule at MacTel to work on one PowerPoint project after another and to coordinate the meeting for eighty-five attendees at the Hilton downtown. But as I sat at my computer or talked on the phone memories of Brad filled my thoughts. He'd called several times over the past few days. Each time we talked, I imagined him with me once more.

One night, after a late meeting at work, I drove into my driveway, exhausted. A huge brown box sat at the back door. Curious, I climbed out of the car and went over to it. The return address said The Olde Port Gallery in Portland, Maine. I checked the address label. My name was typed onto it. A bizarre idea struck me but was immediately dismissed. Hunter Hartwell was a mere acquaintance; there was no real connection between us. But the fact remained, he was the only person I knew who lived in Portland, Maine.

I hoisted the box inside while Lady wiggled past me, barking as if the delivery person were still there. About four feet tall, the box was fairly thin. I loved packages, and eagerly grabbed a sharp knife and slit open the taped end of the box. A wrapped parcel lay inside. My fingers tugged on the wrapping until they touched a wooden edge, perhaps a heavy, ornate frame of some kind. A painting?

I lifted it out of the box and laid the package on the floor to rip open the remaining protective paper. The paper came off in bunches, exhibiting piecemeal, tantalizing portions of what appeared to be a portrait. When the last corner of the painting was freed of its wrapping, I set it against a kitchen cupboard and stood back, shaking. The portrait was of me.

Gripping the back of a kitchen chair for balance, I took a deep breath, completely undone. Me? How could that have happened? I looked closer and drew in a raspy breath. The white blazer was the same one that had belonged to my mother. My thoughts whirled in sickening circles.

I knelt in front of the portrait. It was my mother. Good God, she looked young and innocent, hopeful and happy—unlike the woman I'd known and had half-loved, half-hated.

"Mom?" Tracing her face with a shaking finger, I imagined she gave me a slight nod, and scrambled to my feet, frantic now. Who in hell had sent this to me?

I grabbed the box and looked inside, but saw no note or letter. I ruffled through the bits of paper I'd torn off the portrait, but, again, found nothing to indicate who'd sent it. In desperation, I picked up the painting and turned it around.

A creamy envelope hung on the back, held in place by a strand of scotch tape. I peeled it off with trembling hands and noted the fine quality of the heavy paper stock. Opening the envelope, my mouth grew dry. In crisp black, block letters, the name Arinthia C. Hartwell, bold and commanding in its script, marched across the top of the card inside. One hand-written sentence stared up at me, simple but powerful enough to force me to cry out.

"Granddaughter, come home."

Stunned, I propped the portrait back against the cupboard and slowly lowered myself to the floor, not trusting my legs to hold me. I'd always wondered who I was, where I came from. Now I knew, and it was scarier than I'd ever imagined it could be.

The phone rang. I heard it as if from a distance and

remained seated on the floor, too absorbed in the startling news to respond to the sound. Eventually, the phone stopped ringing and Lady's barking brought me to my feet. The whole world felt as if it had shifted and I was not in Atlanta anymore but in some unfamiliar place between Atlanta and Maine.

Come home. What did that mean? I had made a home of my own, safe and secure, in Atlanta, a far better one than what I'd called home as a child. What was home to Arinthia Hartwell? A beautiful place, I knew, but why had my mother left it? My thoughts spun as I went about fixing Lady's meal. I'd desperately wanted a "real" family. Now that one had been plopped in my lap, I shook with uncertainty, imagining possibilities that might not be so wonderful.

I poured myself a glass of wine from a bottle leftover from the weekend with Brad and took a deep sip to steady my nerves. Picking up the brief note from the woman I now knew must be my grandmother, I wrote down the phone number I'd noticed at the bottom. There wasn't any question as to whether I would obey the implied command to call her. There was so much I had to know. I paced the kitchen, waiting until my nerves quieted. So many questions came to mind. How did Arinthia determine I was her granddaughter, besides the obvious similarity between me and the woman in the portrait? There had to be other factors. Did she know who my father was? What would Hunter and his sisters say when they found out? Arinthia my grandmother? I didn't know whether to laugh or cry. The idea was so preposterous.

I checked my watch. Seven o'clock. Surely Arinthia would have eaten by now. I picked up the phone with stiff, cold fingers. Simone answered the phone. When she heard my voice, she said simply, "You got the package, then?"

"I don't know what to say. Is it possible to speak to Arinthia?"

"Yes, she'd like to talk to you and then I'll be happy to answer any questions you may have."

I waited to hear Arinthia's voice, wondering if her speech therapy had helped and how much I'd be able to understand. I clutched the phone to my ear, not wanting to miss any nuance.

"M'rissa, grnddotter. Thea's gurrl."

"Hello ... Arin... Grandmother," I said, floundering over the word.

"Come," Arinthia spoke with more vigor. "Come."

"I don't know when I can ..." I began.

"Come," she said, even louder.

Simone got on the phone. "Marissa, it's very important that you come to Maine as soon as possible. Arinthia has a great deal to tell you and show you. Imagine how Arinthia feels to discover you after all these years. We had DNA testing done on the glass of iced tea you drank from when you were here and there's no doubt you are who we say you are."

DNA testing? Weird. "But she talks about Thea. My mother's name was Margaret Cole."

"Thea was named after her mother, using the last part of Arinthia's name. Her middle name was Margaret and she must have used Arinthia's middle name, Cole, after she ran away."

"Ran away?" My body turned cold. Clyde's words came back to me. She had worked for cash so nobody could find her. Why?

"I think you'd better come home as soon as possible, Marissa, and when you do, plan to spend a long time here. We need you."

"But my home is here ..."

"Not anymore, Marissa. Your real home is here, with your grandmother and family." Simone's tone was insistent, causing me to hesitate.

"I'll have to think about it. It's all such a shock to me."

Simone's voice softened. "Of course, dear. But think of the life you can have as a Hartwell. Everything will be provided for you."

I glanced around at my simple surroundings. I had gone without, saved money and scoured garage sales for each item in the room. It would be wonderful not to have to worry about the smallest expense, but I was proud of all I'd accomplished.

"I have a dog. Her name is Lady. She'd have to come, too."

"Hold on," said Simone. I couldn't make out the mumbling in the background but when Simone came back on the phone, her voice was cheerful. "Arinthia says to bring her along. She likes dogs."

"I'll call you tomorrow and let you know what I decide. I'd have to get permission from work to leave for a couple of weeks."

Simone chortled. "My dear, you'll never have to ask permission or work again. Wait until you see what Arinthia has in store for you."

I hung up with a promise to call the next day with details of my visit.

Lady looked up at me with tawny eyes full of curiosity.

I shook my head, incredulous at what changes lay ahead. "Lady, I'm not sure, but I think I'm going to have a family after all."

She barked and wagged her tail, a sure sign of approval.

The phone rang as I was washing dishes. I jumped and checked the ID number. Brad. I picked up the phone, eager to share the news.

"Hey, Sweetheart, how's it going? I've missed you," he said.

"Me, too," I managed to say, though my throat clogged with unexpected emotion. My life had been thrown into turmoil, and I wasn't sure where my relationship with Brad would fit in.

"What's wrong? Miss me that much?" Brad teased.

I gulped, uncertain how to begin. "You won't believe what happened today," I said it as if it was the beginning of an everyday story, but it wasn't. And I couldn't decide whether a tragedy or a comedy was about to unfold before me.

Brad listened to me without saying a word. When I got to the part about going to Maine at my grandmother's request, he said, "Is that what you're going to do? Live in Maine?"

"Oh, Brad, I just don't know. I'm so worried. I still don't know why my mother left. Simone, Arinthia's companion, said she ran away. But Arinthia wants me in Maine. She says my real home is with her."

"Do you want me to come with you?"

I hesitated. Brad would make me feel so much more secure as I faced the family I never knew I had, but I sensed I had to go alone, to face them all with a matching strong will.

"No, thanks," I said regretfully. "This is something I need to do on my own."

A pulsing silence filled my ears.

"Guess this means you're not coming to Barnham like we planned."

"At least not now, I feel terrible about letting you down, but I have to be truthful. It's going to take some time to get everything straightened out. Brad? I don't want this to hurt our relationship in any way."

"I understand. I'm happy for you, I really am, but just a word of warning. Beware of getting what you thought you've always wanted. Things don't always turn out the way you want them to."

"Brad? I'm sorry. I didn't know this was going to happen. I'll give you a call as soon as I know anything..."

"Good luck," Brad said softly as he hung up, leaving behind a disturbing buzzing in my ear.

Overwhelmed by all that had happened, I drew in a shaky breath and burst into tears.

As I walked into MacTel, about to ask for a leave of absence, the enormity of realizing my whole life had changed struck me all over again. I'd talked to Doris after hanging up with Brad. Her words of encouragement helped me decide that I owed it to myself to learn the answers to questions that had haunted me all my life.

When I told him the situation, my boss was understanding. He promised to write a letter to the company's Human Resources, recommending the time off, considering the uniqueness of the problem. He advised me to allow myself several weeks to come to a final decision about moving and compared my request to maternity leave.

Leaving his office, I felt like a solitary person standing at the edge of the ocean, trying to imagine life in an unknown land well beyond the sandy spot beneath my feet. What would I find in New Hope, Maine? The question pounded at me, filling me with an excitement and an equal amount of worry.

My landlord wasn't so accommodating when he heard the news. A relative of his had wanted to rent the house for some time and he'd been waiting until my lease was up to tell me. He requested that I empty the house of my belongings as soon as possible.

I spent my hours off from work, sorting through my things, amazed at what I'd accumulated over the last eight years in which I rented a house—years of being on my own, independent, able to make my own decisions. I wondered if that would change. I hoped not.

I secured a storage area not far from the house and made several trips to it, borrowing a truck from a neighbor whose son was eager to help me for the money I promised. Seeing the things I'd worked so hard for, sitting in storage, awaiting my return, I felt better. I still had choices. Whether Arinthia's house in Maine would really become my home was yet to be determined. I knew from experience a house wasn't a home unless love and kindness were there.

CHAPTER TEN

Two days later, I drove up to the gate at Briar Cliff and got out of the car to open it. Lady bounded out onto the grassy verge and stared at the house, quivering.

I knew how she felt. "New and pretty scary, huh?" My voice shook. I worried the old me was about to be buried in an unmarked grave.

Lady wagged her tail at me and went about her business while I swung the iron gate back against the stone pillars beside the driveway. Lady took off toward the house and stopped as if waiting for me, before taking off again. I was left to follow her into the future.

I parked by the front entrance and grabbed one of the suitcases from the car and headed around the house toward the front , wanting a look at the calming water.

Arinthia was dozing in one of the white wicker chairs scattered along the wide swath of porch. I stood a moment, studying her. *Grandmother.* I was of her flesh and blood. A shiver crept across my shoulders. It was so surreal.

She opened her eyes. The blue in them lighted when she saw me and she gave me a lop-sided smile. "Rissa..."

"Hello, Arinthia ... Grandmother ..." The strange word momentarily paralyzed my tongue.

"Glad ... here." Arinthia said in a surprisingly clear voice and struggled to her feet, holding onto the arms of the chair for support.

"You're doing much better," I commented, awed by her improvement.

Her lips twisted into a half-smile. "Had to."

Simone emerged through the front door. "I thought I heard voices out here. Welcome, Marissa. Let me take your bag. Surely you have more."

"I do but …"

"I'll have Henry bring them in."

I raised my eyebrows.

"Henry Cantwell has been handyman here for years," Simone said. "We rely on him for many things, don't we, Arinthia?"

Arinthia nodded and held my hand, indicating with a toss of her head that she wanted to go inside.

We took our time entering the house, each step she took measured. Now that I knew I was going to live here for a while, the size of the house seemed even more overwhelming.

"Let's go into the sunroom," Simone suggested. "I've set up refreshments there since we've been expecting you."

I heard Lady barking outside. "My dog. I've got to get her."

"Ah, yes," said Simone, taking Arinthia's arm. "Bring her along. Arinthia and I will meet you there."

I went out to the front porch and called for Lady. She came running around the corner of the house, tongue lolling, a happy expression on her furry face. I smiled at the sight of her, grateful for her familiar company. She followed me inside the house and I led her to the sunroom, curious to see her reaction to the two women.

"Come," ordered Arinthia. She held out a hand to Lady and clucked a greeting.

Wagging her tail, Lady went over to her and, after a quick sniff, moved away.

"Here," said Simone. "Come here, Lady."

The dog looked up at me as if to say, "Do I have to?" I gave her no response, waiting to see what she would do on her own.

Lady moved in Simone's direction and sat down just beyond her reach, her gaze never leaving Simone. For several moments, the two stared, taking the measure of one another. Then Lady lay down next to me, facing Simone.

I fidgeted as Simone served tea for us, and wondered when the subject of my mother and my relationship to Arinthia would come up.

"Arinthia's made good progress, don't you think?" Simone handed me a cup of tea.

"Very much so," I replied politely.

"She's one stubborn woman, I can tell you," said Simone. A note of admiration rang in her voice.

"How long have you been with Arinthia?" I asked, helping myself to a small piece of cake from the silver plate in front of me.

Simone exchanged a look of affection with Arinthia. "For over fifty years. Funny, it doesn't seem that long. I was hired as a personal secretary, but, as you can see, it's evolved into much more than that."

Arinthia nodded. "Frnds." She held out a bite-sized chunk of cake to Lady. Lady slowly rose, accepted it from her and settled herself at my feet, munching happily.

"Then you must have known my mother."

Simone stiffened, glanced at Arinthia, and turned back to me. "Yes, but your mother hadn't been born yet when I came here."

"You told me Thea was too young to be gone, insinuating she'd died at an early age. Why did you tell me that?" It had been bothering me for some time.

"Had to," Arinthia answered for her, her cheeks flushing. She waved her good arm in the air and tried to speak again but her words became garbled in her agitation.

Simone held up her hands, halting my questions. "It's okay,

Arinthia. Marissa and I will talk about it later. Let's not ruin the welcome of your granddaughter after all this time."

"Grndduter ... help ... me," said Arinthia. Her sharp eyes pierced mine, and I saw steely determination in them.

"What is it you want me to do?" I asked, my throat gone dry, not sure I'd like the answer to my question.

"Later," said Arinthia. "Papers."

Simone spoke up. "After you relax a bit and get unpacked, I've got some papers for you to read through. You'll find them interesting. They have to do with family history and the business that's in the family."

"Is that what I'm here to do? Something about the family business?"

Arinthia lifted her good right arm and smacked it down on the armrest of the chair. The sharp sound of it echoed in the air like a roll of thunder. "Yes. You."

At that moment, a man who I assumed was Henry Cantwell, walked into the room, carrying the portrait of my mother.

"Where should I put this, Miz Hartwell? Do you want me to mount it in the hallway with the others?"

Arinthia shook her head. "Never."

Even if her word hadn't been clear, her response was. My mother wasn't going to be part of the household, even now. What, I wondered, had happened between my mother and my grandmother to conjure up such bitterness? Whatever the cause, it was clearly far from over.

Henry paused and stared at me. "You sure do look like her, Miss. That you do."

Tears glistened in Arinthia's eyes but she sat rigidly upright in her chair, a forbidding figure, warning away sentimentality.

Simone stood. "When you're ready, Marissa, I'll show you to your room."

I took that as a signal to leave Arinthia and rose to my feet, unsettled by all I'd seen and heard.

Following Simone up the winding staircase, I was pretty certain which room would be mine. Simone confirmed my suspicion by leading me to the end of the hallway, farthest away from Arinthia, to the pink and white room I now knew had belonged to my mother. I stood at the threshold, seeing the room in a new light, trying to imagine my mother there.

A white four-poster bed with a crisp white canopy was offset by a pink gingham spread and flounced pink dust ruffle. A white rocking chair held a pink-and-green-plaid seat cushion and sat atop a colorful braid rug in front of a small, brick fireplace. The color scheme continued in the floral wallpaper, sprouting rose buds and greenery. In other homes, perhaps, the theme might have seemed overdone. In Arinthia's house, the scene was tasteful, with enough variety in patterns and fabrics to be interesting. Still, I could never remember my mother wearing pink. It just didn't seem her color.

"It must feel strange, you being here in your mother's room," said Simone, sensing my uncertainty.

"A little ..."

Simone's expression grew dreamy, and I knew she was visiting the past. "She was such a willful child. What a shame. No one, but no one, defies Arinthia Hartwell." She waved her hand in the air as if to brush away the memory, and resumed her usual crisp manner. "I'm sure you want to get settled. I'll be back with the papers. We eat promptly at six thirty. If you care for a cocktail before dinner, come to the sunroom at six."

I watched Simone walk down the hallway, feeling as I had before, that life at Briar Cliff was something out of the past, where time was regulated according to the dictates of the master or mistress of the house.

"Well, Lady," I murmured, "it's a whole different world. I wonder if I'll ever get used to it."

She nudged my hand and ran her nose under it. I gave her a pat on the head. Lady needed comforting too.

It didn't take long to unpack my suitcases. I lay my clothes in the bureau drawers or hung them in the closet, realizing how sparse my wardrobe was. In these surroundings, they looked like what they were—bargain basement items bought on sale. I loved them anyway.

"You ready for some reading material?"

I whipped around, wondering how Simone had slipped into my room so quietly.

She smiled pleasantly at me. "Or you might want to investigate the house a bit first and get a little more comfortable."

I returned her smile. "Good idea. I have to feed Lady."

"Well, then, come along with me," said Simone. "I'll introduce you to Henry's wife, Becky. She comes in and prepares dinner for us. I'm not a cook, you see."

"It seems you're kept pretty busy with Arinthia."

"Before her stroke, we took weekly trips to Riverton, checking up on various Rivers Papers' activities. Not that we had to, mind you, we merely wanted to be sure we knew what was going on in the business. Now, we're just as happy to stay here at home." Simone dropped her voice to a whisper. "I imagine Arinthia will keep going, doing what she's doing until she drops. As much as she doesn't want to admit it, it's getting harder and harder for her. She needs you here to help her with the business." She turned to leave.

I stopped Simone in the hallway. "Hunter thinks he's going to get the business, and it will be turned over to the men in the family at last."

A fire came into Simone's eyes, lighting them with a resolve that would warn even the most robust soul.

"He and his father are waiting for Arinthia to die. They're just like circling buzzards. I tell you, they couldn't hide the fact they were disappointed when Arinthia pulled through her stroke. But with you here, the whole family is going to get the surprise of their lives. And I, for one, can't wait to see the expressions on their greedy faces."

A sense of dread washed over me. Hunter, Samantha, and Allison would make formidable enemies in a fight that wasn't really mine. Daunted by the prospect, I wasn't at all sure I wanted to stay at Briar Cliff, as part of the Hartwell family, let alone helping Arinthia with a business I knew nothing about.

Simone shook a finger at me. "Don't say a word to Arinthia about the other Hartwells. She's no fool. She knows they want her out of the picture. That's what makes your arrival so wonderful." Her lips curved into a smile that sent another wave of uneasiness through me.

I followed Simone down the stairs, into the large, well-equipped kitchen. A short, round-faced woman glanced up at us from behind a wide, marble counter. "So you're the daughter. Yep, Henry said you looked like her."

"Becky, I'd like you to meet Marissa Cole," said Simone, assuming a quiet, authoritative voice.

Becky wiped her hands on her white apron and held one out to me. I took it and gazed into sparkling green eyes which immediately drew me in with their openness.

"Nice to meet you," she said and patted Lady on the head.

Lady wagged her tail and leaned against Becky's wide legs, clearly enjoying the attention Becky was giving her.

"We used to have a couple of dogs at home." Becky rubbed Lady's ears. "It'll be good to have a little more life here in the house."

"I'd better get back to Arinthia," Simone said. She turned

to me. "Why don't you meet us in the sunroom when you're through here?"

It wasn't really a question but an order couched in polite conversation. It struck me then, as I watched her briskly walk away, that the person running the household wasn't Arinthia as much as Simone.

Becky showed me where she'd stored the cans of dog food I'd brought for Lady. Lady's bowls sat on the floor beside her bed in the butler's pantry next to the kitchen. Later, I decided, I'd move the bed upstairs. I wasn't about to give up the comfort of having Lady sleep close by.

"You knew my mother?" I asked Becky as I scooped dog food into Lady's bowl.

Becky shook her head. "Never even met her. I'm Henry's second wife, you see. His first wife died not long after they were married. Cancer, don'tcha know."

Puzzled, I asked, "Then how do you know what my mother looked like?"

Becky chortled. "That's easy. Henry keeps a photograph of your mother and your uncle on his bureau. They were the children he never had. We couldn't have any children of our own. And, I've heard it said that Thea, especially, had a real way of making Henry and every other man around here fall in love with her. She was the apple of her father's eye."

"My grandfather?"

"Yep," Becky said. She lowered her voice and leaned closer. "Heard, too, that it made the mother very jealous. It happens sometimes."

I wondered how that had played a part in my mother's life at Briar Cliff. Maybe reading the family history Simone had talked about would give me some clues.

At five minutes after six, Lady and I strolled into the sunroom, ready to relax after what had been a grueling couple of days of packing and closing the house.

"Late." Arinthia gave me a look of disapproval as I sat down opposite her.

I looked over at Simone in confusion. "Didn't you say to come at six if I wanted a cocktail? I don't."

"Arinthia likes her cocktails promptly at six."

"Even with the medication she must be on?"

"Do ... damn well ... please," said Arinthia with an aggressive tone I hadn't heard before.

Simone flashed me a silent plea and I immediately switched the conversation to the details of my trip north. As I talked, the tension in the room dissipated. Arinthia continued to drink one drink after another. That, I figured, was pretty much how most evenings were spent at Briar Cliff. I vowed I would not be trapped into following Arinthia's pattern. I'd seen the damage it could do. It had brought my mother down to a miserable level.

Dinner was a grim affair—three single women seated at a table which was too large, in a dining room too formal to be comfortable. I missed the little pine table in my tiny kitchen in Atlanta. And watching Arinthia disintegrate into a blubbering woman, uttering angry words, reminded me too much of my childhood. True, the physical surroundings were very different, but the behavior pattern was painfully similar. I excused myself as soon as I could.

Simone gave me an understanding look and bid me goodnight.

As I left the room, I felt like a prisoner temporarily freed on parole, and I couldn't help wondering about Simone's extraordinary devotion.

I rose early, and Lady and I slipped out of the quiet house

unnoticed. Pink fingers of sunrise spread in the indigo sky, creating a rosy promise of a nice day. I strolled along the beach in the early morning chill, finding it hard to believe I was back in Maine under these strange circumstances.

I huddled under a fleece jacket and worked up some body heat by jogging along the sand. It felt good to stretch my muscles after tossing restlessly in a bedroom that encouraged too many memories.

After a twenty-minute run, I made my way to the kitchen to give Lady her morning treat. The aroma of freshly brewed coffee wafted from the room and I wondered who else had risen at such an early hour.

Simone smiled at me as I entered the room. "Coffee?"

I gratefully accepted the dainty cup she handed me. "You're up early,"

"I've always been an early riser,"

I studied her a moment. She had to be fairly close to Arinthia in age but the difference between them was dramatic. Her dark brown eyes contained mystery and her dark hair, sprinkled with gray, was pulled back in a neat bun that gave her an air of authority.

"Is something the matter?" Simone asked. "You're frowning."

"Nothing that another cup of coffee won't cure." I shook off the nasty notion that Simone had taken advantage of my grandmother's illness by completely taking over the household. Or had it always been that way? If so, what was the story between them?

"Have you read the family papers I prepared for you?" Simone asked. "If you're to understand the situation today, it's important for you to know about the family background."

"I started to read them last night but fell asleep. I'll get to it this morning," I assured her, and went upstairs to change.

I picked up the typed pages Simone had put together for me and studied them a moment. Every family had its skeletons. I wondered what I'd find in this one.

I settled in the rocking chair and soon became engrossed in the Hartwell history.

William Hartwell, my great-grandfather, and his brother Edward were young visionaries of a sort when they'd discovered the un-harnessed water power available at falls in the Kennebec River.

Quietly they began to buy up land around the falls and soon built a dam above the fifty-foot drop to supply water for the pulp and paper mills they began to operate a few years later. The business continued to grow, with the building of dams, penstocks, and hydroelectric generating facilities slightly upriver from the paper mill. During World War II, the Hartwell Paper Mills sold its paper production to the United States government.

I read through the dry facts eagerly, but my interest heightened when I read that in 1908, William married a young girl named Florence Sullivan and in 1910 they had a son, my grandfather, whom they named Herbert. Fifteen years later, after many miscarriages, they finally had another son, whom they named George—my great-uncle and the father of Hunter and his sisters, from a late second marriage.

I lay the papers down in my lap and gazed around the room my mother had once occupied. It seemed surreal to go from no family to layers of them.

Curious, I read more. Some time after his marriage, my great-grandfather William and Edward had a parting of ways. A bitter fight between them ensued, and William ended up with the business while Edward tried his luck in the oil business out West. Throughout the following years, William's company and another joined forces and developed a method of coating paper. At the time of my grandfather Herbert's death in 1980, the company was sold to Rivers Papers, a large paper conglomerate, with the written agreement that a Board position would be eternally reserved for a Hartwell family member and an annual stipend given for retaining the seat. The battle between Arinthia and George for control of the family's seat began.

The typewritten report ended and handwriting, which I assumed was Simone's, followed. "We thought your mother's brother Timothy would grow into that position and, to protect it, Arinthia would secure the seat until such time as he was ready to take over. You must remember, it is important for this side of the family to continue to hold onto the seat on the Board so that the income and prestige associated with it not be turned over to Hunter Hartwell. George has continued his struggle for the position and will do anything he can to take the business back and manipulate the Board. That's why you, Marissa, are so important to us."

I stopped rocking. As if the papers they held were icy with a premonition, my hands turned cold. What in hell had I gotten myself into?

CHAPTER ELEVEN

I needed to talk to Simone about the challenge of becoming part of the family business. Downstairs, I found Arinthia in the kitchen, slowly feeding herself. She set down her spoon and pointed a finger at me. A frown of disapproval creased her face, making it appear even more twisted than normal.

"Wha rr ... warring?"

Confused, I looked down at my running bra and my exercise tights.

"What am I wearing? It's my jogging outfit. Why?"

Arinthia shook her head, her features coming together in sharp lines. "... like 'horrr."

Whore? I stepped back, feeling as if she'd slapped me. My God, is that why my mother had used that word so easily with me? Had her own mother taunted her with it as Arinthia was doing to me now? My temper flared. I was not about to accept treatment like that from anyone ever again.

"Grandmother, it's the twenty-first century. Women dress like this all the time. There's nothing wrong with it."

She shook her head, defiantly. "No Har...well."

My stomach churned. I couldn't let her get away with it. "Don't talk to me that way and don't judge me by the way you live. My God, you and Simone carry on as if you were still young girls living in the thirties. Women have come a long way since then."

"Thea?" Wild-eyed, Arinthia gripped the table. She stared in my direction but did not see me.

My heart sank. My mother must have had similar

arguments with Arinthia. I knelt beside her chair and took hold of her hand.

"Grandmother? It's Marissa. I'm sorry if I upset you."

She shook her head as if to clear the memory. The horrified expression disappeared from her face. She focused her attention on me. "Course ... rissa. I know." She patted me awkwardly on the back.

Simone came into the room and gave me a questioning look. "Everything all right?"

I shrugged, still shaken by the episode. "I guess so."

"Have you read the papers I gave you?"

"That's why I came downstairs. I wanted to talk to you about it."

She waved her hand in dismissal. "It's too late. We don't have much time. You need to go up and change your clothes right now. Hunter and his father, George, are due to arrive in fifteen minutes. It seems Hunter saw your car parked here and George called me, furious. We've got to get ready for them." Simone's expression was serious, even a little frightened.

"Why? What do they want?"

Her lips thinned. "What do they want? Any excuse to take over the seat on the Rivers Papers executive board so they can place Hunter inside the business." She gave me a little push. "Go along and get ready, dear. We want to present you in your best light."

Letting out a noisy breath, I rose and left the kitchen. I hadn't been here a full day and already I was so frustrated I could taste its sourness.

I climbed the stairs and headed for the shower, and wondered for the umpteenth time why the whole atmosphere at Briar Cliff seemed like something out of a nineteenth century novel.

I dressed carefully, more for my own satisfaction than

Simone's. If what I'd read in the family history was correct, George and my grandfather had fought bitterly, following in the footsteps of their father. Maybe, I thought whimsically, Hunter and I could break tradition.

I emerged from my bedroom to the sound of voices in the front hall. Curious, I peeked around the corner at the top of the stairs. Hunter stood next to a tall man with snow white hair and the same chiseled features I'd admired in him. I descended the stairway in black tailored slacks and a white blouse just slightly wrinkled from being packed. I wore the pearl earrings I'd worn to dinner with Hunter. My hair was held back with a couple of clips and cascaded down to my shoulders in bright, loose curls. It was the best I could do under the hurried circumstances.

The man I assumed was George looked at me with haughty suspicion as if I'd weaseled my way inside the house through what used to be the servant's back entrance. My hands turned cold. I fought to regain my self-confidence. As I drew closer, I gained strength. I was, after all, Arinthia's granddaughter.

"Hello ... cousin." Hunter's brow furrowed in contempt. "Who knew?"

"Not me." I looked him squarely in the eye. "My mother never talked about Briar Cliff or Arinthia. I had no idea I even had a family."

Simone spoke up, interrupting the tension building between us. "Marissa, you already know Hunter Hartwell. I'd like you to meet his father, your great-uncle, George."

Her formality prompted me to hold out a hand to him. His blue eyes were as cold as I imagined the waters outside would be this winter. I suppressed a shiver.

"My pleasure, Mr. Hartwell."

He shook my hand without comment and turned to Simone. "Perhaps we'd better meet with Arinthia."

Simone signaled him to follow her, and they headed toward the sunroom.

Hunter halted me. "You really had me fooled, you know."

"I had no idea. Honest. I'm as surprised as you are to find myself here, a member of this family. When my mother died she asked me to bring her ashes to a place called Briar Cliff in New Hope, Maine. I didn't understand why. She'd never mentioned Briar Cliff or New Hope before."

Hunter lowered his voice. "My father is really pissed. He thought everything was in place for me to take over."

"Is that what you want?"

Hunter's gaze moved into the distance as if he couldn't face me—or a truthful answer.

"I don't know what's going to happen," I said, frankly. "I don't know what to expect."

"I do. Those two old lesbians are going to make sure you represent the family at Rivers Papers, not me." Hunter's voice was bitter. "You're an answer to their prayers."

Lesbians?

George appeared at the entrance to the hall. "Coming, Hunter?"

Hunter's expression changed, lost its aggressiveness. I almost laughed out loud at the suddenness of it and then realized how much dominance George had over his son. The cockiness that had added a swagger to Hunter's step when I'd first seen him disappeared.

I followed them into the sunroom, still wondering about the relationship between Arinthia and Simone. Was it possible they were lovers? It would explain Simone's devotion.

The furious expression Simone wore and the heightened color on Arinthia's face signaled their stress. I settled in a seat on the couch beside Arinthia, next to Simone's chair, unconsciously placing myself on their team.

"It seems that George thinks we've got an impostor in you," said Simone, crisply. "Even though we've had a number of things in your past checked out, a DNA test performed, and your likeness to your mother is unmistakable, he thinks there is a reason to challenge us—in court."

I swallowed my surprise, thinking fast. "I don't know what to say. I can only tell you the truth. I grew up not knowing anything about my mother's family or my father."

"Who is your father, young lady?" George crossed his arms in a challenge to me.

My mouth grew dry. "I always thought Tim Hartwell was."

George's guffaw was nasty. "Not likely."

Tears formed in Arinthia's eyes. Simone gripped her hand.

Anger boiled within me. Her son was dead. His memory didn't need to be shredded by jealous greed.

George pressed his case. "Can you prove your relationship to us? Simone says a DNA test proves it, but I haven't seen those results."

I glanced down at the gold ring I'd found in my mother's drawers and twisted it on my finger. The initials M.C. and B.B. would only encourage George to believe I wasn't who these two old women wanted me to be.

"Just a minute, I'll be back shortly."

I raced up to my room, took the clips out of my hair, changed into a black blouse and lifted the white blazer off its hanger. Slipping it on, I tried to remember every detail of my mother's face in the portrait I'd studied night after night.

Smiling, I posed in front of the mirror, striking the same pose she'd assumed in the painting, pulling my hair into a similar style. Satisfied, I returned to the sunroom, determined to prove to George that I was Thea's daughter.

All talk ceased as I entered the sunroom. I paused, head

cocked to one side, and smiled, like my mother in the portrait.

"My god!" said Simone, her eyes wide. "It's her!"

"Thea! Coat!" Arinthia garbled.

"I found this blazer in my mother's closet. I had no idea where it came from or what it meant until I saw the portrait."

"Anybody can purchase a blazer. It doesn't prove a thing," George scoffed.

"Pocket," said Arinthia.

Simone stood. "I remember now. Let's see the jacket, Marissa."

I took off the jacket and placed it in her outstretched hands. She lay the inside open and pulled away the fabric of the interior pocket.

"They're here. Take a look."

I leaned over. The initials T.H. were sewn inside, deep enough that I hadn't noticed them.

"Let's see," said George.

"This proves it," said Simone triumphantly.

"Yes," said Arinthia. Her twisted smile was every bit as powerful as her flashing blue eyes.

Observing the negative energy between George and Arinthia, it occurred to me that these two had been sparring for a long time.

"Things dif...rent now," Arinthia managed to get out brokenly.

"Well," said George, his tone sharp. "It isn't over, Arinthia. You and I had an agreement, and this is one agreement you won't break. I'll see to it."

He signaled to Hunter, and Hunter followed his father out of the room with a backward glance at me.

Arinthia collapsed in her chair. Gasping, she lay her head against the back cushion and closed her eyes.

"Take deep breaths, Arinthia. It's over. He's gone. You just relax for a while," said Simone in a soothing voice.

"Is she all right?" I was alarmed by the lack of color in her face.

"We'll let her rest quietly. Come with me. We can talk outside. It's such a beautiful fall day."

I stepped onto the porch and took a deep breath of fresh air, invigorated by the early October weather. The family confrontation had frazzled me. *Are all families like this?*

Lady lumbered to her feet from her spot in the sun and wagged her tail. At her doggie smile, my mood lightened. I patted her and took a seat in one of the rocking chairs that lined the front porch.

Simone joined me and let out a sigh.

"Is it always that way between Arinthia and George?" I asked.

"Their love/hate relationship goes back a long way."

I gave her a puzzled look.

"Years ago, George and Arinthia were engaged to be married," she continued. "When his older brother Herbert came home to meet the bride, Arinthia chose him instead. I don't think George has ever forgiven her. He claims she did it so she could get the business."

"Is that true?"

Simone shrugged. "Arinthia's always been a very practical woman." Admiration coated her words.

Listening to her, I had a flash of revelation, and could well imagine she was speaking about herself as well.

"What happened to George? Did he just step aside?"

Simone shook her head. "George married the daughter of a well-known lawyer in Boston and settled down to practice law. The marriage was an unhappy one, as you might imagine, and lasted only a few years. He returned to Maine, set up an office in Portland, and became well-known in his own right, handling cases for paper mills. He was quite the man around town, footloose and fancy-free, as they say. That all ended when he met Hunter's mother, Adrienne, in his late forties."

"What is Hunter's mother like? I've met his sisters and I'm curious about all of them."

Simone sighed. "All in all, Adrienne is a nice lady—much too nice and too young for the likes of George, if you ask me. He is a dominating man, even at his age."

"Was my grandfather the same way?"

A smile softened Simone's features. In that brief moment, I caught a glimpse of how beautiful Simone must have been as a young woman.

"Your grandfather loved people and loved life." Her face filled with a luminous expression I recognized. *Why, she loved him!* I thought with surprise. It was something I'd have to sort out later.

"Did...did he love my mother?"

Simone glanced at me, eyes wide. "Of course! She was the light of his life. She could do no wrong. He adored her."

I was still puzzled. "But, why did she run away?"

Simone caught her lip. "Thea was only ten when Herbert died. She turned willful after that. Her father had spoiled her all those years and Arinthia was not about to put up with it. There was always tension between the two of them. Even as a young child, Thea knew how to turn the tables on Arinthia to get her own way."

The image of my mother enduring Clyde's drunken tirades was so in contrast to the strong, willful person Simone described, I couldn't help but say, "Did something happen to change her?"

"I think being sent away to school broke her of some of her bad behavior, but it made her harder. She became determined to show Arinthia that she didn't care about her family anymore. They'd hurt her, so she'd hurt them back. That kind of thing."

"Where was she sent? To St. Andrews?"

"Yes," Simone said softly. "I tried to tell Arinthia at the time that it was a mistake ..." Her words drifted away. She straightened and gave me a warning look. "None of this is to be mentioned to Arinthia. It would only upset her."

"Tell me about St. Andrews."

Simone rocked back and forth in the wicker rocking chair while I waited for her to speak.

"St. Andrews was the wrong place for your mother—a girls' school for the rich. Thea went from being willful to out-of-control. Drugs and the whole scene. How do I know? I was the one who handled all the calls home. Arinthia refused to deal with the fact that she'd made a mistake. In the end, it cost her dearly."

Henry Cantwell appeared at the front door. "Simone? Miz Hartwell wants to see you. And then Becky needs to talk to you about dinner."

Guilt washed across Simone's face. She jumped to her feet and gave me an apologetic look.

Henry held the door open for Simone and turned to go.

"Wait. Can I talk to you a minute?"

Henry paused. "Uh, yup."

He stood in front of me, leaning back against the white, wooden porch railing. His skin was tanned and weathered. His gray hair wreathed around his bald head like a halo.

"Henry," I began awkwardly, "Becky told me you were close to my mother." There was something so wholesome about him that I understood why he'd apparently been the person my mother had turned to after her own father died.

He looked at me, listening.

"I want to know more about her. I need to know why she

ran away." I gulped nervously, knowing the answer without his affirming it. "It was because of me, wasn't it?" She'd been just eighteen when I was born.

"Maybe," said Henry. "But more than that." He turned and pointed to the large maple tree in the yard at the corner of the house where my bedroom was situated. "See that tree? We called it the Talking Tree. It's where we'd meet when things were going bad for her."

The blood drained from my face. *My mother had a Talking Tree?* Feeling sick to my stomach, I clutched my middle. *My God! My God!*

"Miss? You all right?"

Tears came from the depth of me, clawing their way to the surface, shredding the bitterness I'd built up over the years.

I glanced up at Henry, letting the tears flow freely. "My mother ... Did her father ... secretly ... harm her? Is that why she needed the Talking Tree?"

Henry shook his head, staring intently at me. "It were the mother causing her trouble. It were just a way for Thea to get the anger out."

I wiped the tears off my face with a broad stroke of my hand. "Did my grandmother hate my mother? Is that it?"

Henry looked down at the wooden flooring of the porch and kicked at it aimlessly with a boot. When he looked up, his thinned lips told of his anger.

"Sometimes it did seem that way."

He continued to stare at me, and the expression on his face became soft and tender as if he understood that I had endured the same kind of thing. He held his arms out.

Knowing how much Henry had loved my mother, how much he'd guessed about my own difficult childhood, I rose and fell into them.

"There, now," he murmured, patting me on the back, and I

knew then he must have done this countless times for my mother.

Calmer now, I took a deep breath and stepped back. "Who named the tree?"

"Why, I did," Henry said. "'Thought it might be a good thing for her."

I nodded, not quite ready to tell him that I had a Talking Tree of my own. It had always been called that. I realized now that my mother must have named it and wondered if she'd secretly used it too.

CHAPTER TWELVE

With Lady at my side, I sat with Arinthia and Simone in the sunroom. Arinthia sipped her cocktail at a much slower pace than she had the evening before.

"Good news," said Simone. "While you were out walking the dog, Adrienne Hartwell called. She'd like to host a welcome luncheon for you at the country club on Friday. I told her that would be fine."

I bristled. She hadn't discussed this with me before accepting.

Simone noticed my pique. "It's a good opportunity for you. This social occasion or something like it was bound to happen sooner or later. Better to get your introduction to the community over with."

Drawing a deep breath, I told myself to let it go. Somehow I'd maintain my independence in the face of what now seemed ironically like too much family and too much intrigue.

Arinthia pointed a finger at me. "New c...coze."

New clothes? I straightened in my chair and then let my shoulders relax. Arinthia was right. The pink dress I'd worn to dinner with Hunter was much too summery for our current weather, and I had no viable choice for cool weather.

Simone leaned over and patted my knee. "Things are different now. As a representative of the Herbert Hartwell family, you need suitable attire. Arinthia and I talked about it and we've decided to give you a whole new wardrobe."

"Got to show 'em." She smiled slyly.

The few clothes I had hanging in the upstairs closet were

getting pretty tired, but I worried I'd be more indebted to these two ladies.

"Allison Hartwell has agreed to take you shopping," said Simone. "She'll pick you up tomorrow morning at ten o'clock."

My enthusiasm evaporated. More family. More decisions without my input. "Why Allison?"

Simone glanced over at Arinthia and back to me. "Of the Hartwell children, Allison is the most likely to be friendly. She's made it clear from the beginning she wanted no part of the business."

"Sam wants...bad," Arinthia mumbled.

"Samantha is a different story," Simone explained. "You said you met her already?"

"At Harry's, in town."

Simone shook her head. "Harry's. That's a bad sign. Samantha is a bright girl, but she hasn't learned that she's blowing her whole future by not dealing with her drinking problem. Of George Hartwell's children, she's the one who's the brightest and has the most business sense. Ah, well. I tried to talk to her about it one time but she wouldn't listen."

"Hunter told me she's very angry that her father refuses to even consider her talents because she's not a male."

"He's an old-fashioned, domineering father. It can't have been easy for Sam, being the oldest, knowing no matter what she did, she'd never measure up."

Stroking Lady's head absent-mindedly, I studied Simone. Her figure was trim, her eyes bright and aware, her mind mentally sharp. It occurred to me that were it not for Simone's oversight, Arinthia might have been uprooted from her financially rewarding seat on the Board of Directors of Rivers Papers.

###

I paced the backyard and checked my watch for the third time. Ten-thirty. As much as I was reluctant to spend the whole day with Allison, I found myself annoyed by her tardiness. When she arrived fifteen minutes later, a cheery smile on her face, I softened my stance. She probably had been given little choice about escorting me into Boston.

"Sorry I'm late," she said. "I had to convince Mother not to go with us. Not today." She rolled her eyes. A prick of jealousy stabbed me. I couldn't remember a single time when my mother and I had gone shopping for clothes together, just for the fun of it.

I went inside to tell Simone that Allison and I were ready to go. She handed me a bank debit card and said, "Use whatever you want to buy yourself some decent clothes. Allison will help you select them. She'll know what you need."

Her words stung. I had always prided myself on being selective at the thrift stores I'd frequented. I liked nice things; I just couldn't afford to buy them at the regular price. Trying to control my resentment, I followed Allison to her SUV and climbed in.

We pulled onto the road, and Allison and I chatted about the crisp, gray day, searching for pleasant conversation to keep us on common ground. I discovered Allison worked part-time in a local bank, did a lot of volunteer work for the Junior League and had a wicked forehand cross-court shot in tennis.

"At Harry's last summer, I heard you say you hated your job. What's up with that?"

An unladylike snort was Allison's reply. "It's just to keep me busy until the right man comes along. Or so my father thinks. He believes that crap, you know? He thinks that any daughter of his should marry well and be happy she's got a husband." She shrugged. "The hell with it. I've played his game and it wasn't much fun. I'm tired of the whole charade.

In fact, I'm thinking of striking out on my own, maybe moving to California where no one gives a damn about a paper mill in Maine."

I was surprised by her vehemence. eager for a straightforward answer, I asked, "What do you think of Arinthia? And Simone?"

Allison laughed. "Those two old ladies? They're the shrewdest women I know. Who cares if they're lesbians, as some people say. I'm not so sure, not that I care. Even though they've been challenged many times through the years, they've managed to hang onto a very lucrative situation."

"Your father would like to see them booted off the board."

Allison let out a noisy sigh. "This business about putting Hunter on the board of Rivers Papers is consuming him. Father's got the idea that if he can do that, he'll have an inroad into getting control of a few of the board members and making some big changes."

"For revenge?"

Allison's gaze locked on mine before she turned back to the highway. "You know about Arinthia and my father?"

"Simone told me. But I knew something was going on. The tension between them was unbelievable."

"I've always wondered, if he's still in love with her," Allison said softly.

"I'd call it more like hate from the looks he gave her."

Allison was quiet, and I let the subject drop.

We arrived in Boston an hour later. I peered out of the car window and admired the beautiful, old brick apartments and condos along Storrow Drive as Allison headed into what she called the Back Bay.

"Where are we going to shop?"

Allison grinned. "There are a couple of little stores on Newberry and Boylston Streets that I want you to see. As long as money is no object, it should be fun."

I kept quiet, though it bothered me that I'd be spending someone else's money. I worried it was bribery for me to continue to do what those two wily women wanted.

We pulled into a parking garage. The air had turned warm, making it seem more like early September than October. Excitement building, I trailed after Allison. No matter what concerns I might have about the situation, I loved nice clothes.

An hour later, my enthusiasm had dimmed. I'd tried on dresses, skirts, slacks and jackets in two different shops. Most seemed acceptable, but my practical mind balked at the outrageous prices. As it was, I bought a plain, black dress, a pair of gray slacks with a matching cashmere sweater, a black skirt, and a brown leather jacket.

Allison was becoming annoyed with me, and I, with her.

"Let's get lunch," she said, as we left *Francoise's Boutique*. "I need a glass of wine."

We stowed the purchases in the car and stopped at a little sidewalk café. "Grab a table out here," Allison said. "I'm going inside to the ladies room. Order me a glass of chardonnay."

I sat at a small round table covered with crisp white linen. A waiter, looking slightly bored, approached.

"May I help you?" he asked.

"A chardonnay for my friend," I responded. "And a glass of water for me."

His eyebrows lifted. "No wine?"

What the hell, I thought, contemplating a few more hours with Allison. "As a matter of fact, a glass of chardonnay will be just fine."

He smiled with satisfaction and left to place the order.

The sun was warm on my face as I lifted it to the sky. Puffy white clouds skittered across the blue background. A playful breeze tugged on a variety of colorful banners and awnings that dressed up storefronts along the street. People hurried by, carrying intriguing packages. At this escape from my normal routine, pleasure flowed through me. I wondered if this is how the rich lived.

"Sorry to take so much time." Allison slipped into the seat opposite me. "One of my old boyfriends called me on my cell. He wanted to take me to dinner." She smiled. "I told him no. He thinks he can just come and go as he wishes."

I thought of Brad. I hoped my going to Maine wouldn't hurt our relationship. As much as I cared for him, I had to know about my family. Even thinking the word *family* sent shivers of delight through me.

"So? You got anybody special in your life?" Allison leaned forward eagerly. "Good thing Hunter got nowhere with you. It would have turned out to be a little awkward what with you surprising us by actually being our cousin and all."

My cheeks grew hot. "Let's get something straight. My mother never told me anything about her family. I had no idea who or what was in New Hope when I carried out her wishes for her ashes to be scattered here."

Allison studied me a moment and leaned back in her chair. "Sometimes my sense of humor gets out of hand. Sorry if I offended you."

I let out a breath of relief. Allison was someone who told it like it was. I needed her as a friend and ally.

"So? Do you have anyone special in your life?" she asked.

I tried to hide behind a nonchalant nod. "His name is Brad. He and I grew up in the same town in New York."

"Is he hot?" Allison asked, giving me a sly smile.

I grinned. "*I* think so."

"You're blushing. He must be. Seriously, how long are you going to stay in Maine? And are you going to take over for Arinthia?"

The waiter brought our glasses of chardonnay to the table. I took a sip of mine, gathering my thoughts. *Was* I going to take over for Arinthia?

"I don't know. I've no idea what it involves. Both Simone and Arinthia have everything planned out, but I'm not sure about a number of things. I've never even seen a paper mill."

Allison shrugged. "It's not that exciting. Mostly high-tech now, with big machines and guys running around making sure they're working properly. Not like the stories my father tells of men sluicing logs downstream to the mill and handling them."

I listened, impressed. "I guess you grew up hearing a lot about it."

Allison grimaced. "Sam was the one who always wanted to be a part of it. She loves the idea that our ancestors were among the first to establish mills in Maine. She's really pissed that she's been pre-empted out of the business because she's a woman."

"Is that why she drinks so much?"

"That's part of it. I suspect her wild behavior is a way to get my father's attention." She smiled. "Guess I sound like an amateur psychologist."

I pressed on. "Isn't there some way she can participate in the business?"

Allison shook her head. "You don't know Sam. It's all or nothing with her."

Satisfying our hovering waiter, who kept checking his watch, we ordered Chicken Caesar salads.

"Tell me about your mother. What was she like?"

Allison's question popped my balloon of happiness. I stiffened.

"Not a good scene, huh?" said Allison.

I shook my head, unwilling to talk about her.

Our salads came, and we dug into them.

In the silence, I tried to imagine my mother living the good life in New Hope with Arinthia and Simone. She'd been a spoiled child and then a rebellious one. I'd known her as a weak woman. What had happened to her? Did it have something to do with my father? Who was he, anyway?

"What do you know about my mother?" I asked Allison.

"Not much has ever been said in the family about Thea. She was way older than I and was long gone by the time I even realized I had a cousin like her. After Thea ran away, Arinthia refused to let anyone even mention her name."

My thoughts turned to Arinthia. How cruel Allison's words made her seem. Then I remembered Arinthia's tears at the mention of Thea's name and knew the story was more complicated than that.

"It's hard for me to think of my mother as Thea and coming from a place like this. I've always known her as Margaret Cole."

"Families can be really difficult. Father was fifty-four when I was born. I always thought of him as a grandfather, not a father. He was so removed from us kids. Not like a lot of fathers today."

"Well," I commiserated, "you know what they say. You can choose your friends, but you can't choose your family."

"You got that right."

In the past, it had been difficult for me to make friends—because of my situation and the fact that I didn't trust most people. Time for another change. I cleared my throat. "Do you think we can learn to be friends, Allison?"

She studied me for a minute. "Yeah. As I said, I have no interest in the business. We can be friends, but, Marissa, I'm not sure about Sam. Hers is a different story. And Hunter won't come to your aid."

I smiled at her. I'd take what I could get and work on the rest later.

Allison placed her napkin on top of the table and picked up the tab. "Shall we get going? We've still got a lot to do."

I decided to be frank with her. "You know what? I don't want to shop in this section of Boston anymore. I want to go to the Boston Bargain Basement. That's more my style."

Allison whooped with laughter. "All right! Maybe we'll have better luck there. They just advertised that a big new shipment of designer stuff has arrived, so it's a good time to go."

We paid the waiter and headed out.

Inside the store known for designer discounts, the aisles were filled with people pawing through the racks.

"You ready?" said Allison, giving me a challenging smile.

I grinned happily and pushed into the fray, much more at home among these bargain shoppers than I'd been in the elegant shops we'd gone to earlier.

The time flew by as I sought out the clothing and shoes I needed. With good nature, Allison accepted a pile of things I placed in her arms. We left a couple of hours later, laden down with huge shopping bags filled with pants, sweaters, skirts, shoes and even underwear I'd bought at bargain prices. Allison, too, had added considerably to her wardrobe. By the time we hauled our purchases back to the parking garage, we were chatting like old friends.

"Why haven't you ever married?" I asked. The men at Harry's bar had circled her, hanging onto her every word.

She cocked an eyebrow at me. "Oh, but I have been married. For less than a year. It turns out that Willard Jackson the third was not the devoted husband I thought he'd be. He was much more interested in screwing his boss's secretary than me. An old girlfriend of his."

"Oh," I gasped, "that ... that ..."

"Sucks," finished Allison, with a wry look.

We looked at one another and laughed so hard we had to stop and put down our packages. I held onto Allison as laughter rolled out of me in high notes. She whooped musically beside me.

"God, that felt good," Allison said when we'd both calmed down. "I was so damn humiliated. Believe me, I have no intention of getting caught again. Besides, I'm having too much fun playing the field and driving my parents crazy."

The drive home seemed to take no time at all. More comfortable with one another, we talked about my work, her tennis friends, and other harmless topics.

Still chatting, we pulled into Briar Cliff's driveway. Lady trotted out to meet us, wagging her tail. With Allison on friendly terms with me, I felt as if this whole thing might work. Thinking I might become part of a real family, after all, I said good-bye, grabbed my bags and walked toward my new home.

CHAPTER THIRTEEN

B efore dinner, I put on a fashion show for Simone and Arinthia. I swished back and forth in a filmy skirt, worn with a complementary sweater. Not wanting to take advantage of them, I'd been practical but had picked out a few fun items too.

"Head high," Arinthia commented brokenly. "Like Hartwells."

I lifted my nose in the air with exaggeration and paraded in front of her, making her laugh softly.

Warmed by my success, I gathered everything together and took my purchases upstairs. The sound of the antique clock in the living room chiming the six o'clock hour caught my attention. Brad should be winding down his day at the office.

I settled in the rocking chair in my room and punched in his number on my cell.

At his crisp "hello," my heartbeat sped up.

"It's me, I've been thinking about you."

"Ah," he said, and in his voice, I could sense his smile. "I've been thinking about you, too. How are things Down East?"

"Brad, you won't believe it! Arinthia bought me new clothes and my cousin Allison and I are becoming friends. Even Lady is getting used to everything even though she still hasn't caught the pesky squirrel that constantly teases her."

Brad chuckled. "Sounds like things are going well."

"I wish you could see Briar Cliff and meet my family." The word "family" tumbled out of my mouth as naturally as I might have dreamed at one time.

"Odd you should mention that," said Brad. "I was thinking about coming to see you. It's been a while."

"Six weeks and two days."

His voice became a sexy whisper. "I've missed you too, Marissa."

"When can you come for a visit?" I asked, not the least bit ashamed of the pleading I heard in my voice. I wanted so much to see him again.

"How about this weekend?"

"Really? Wonderful! I'll let Simone and Arinthia know you're coming and email you directions. Oh, I can't wait to see you!"

My pulse pumped happily as I ended the call. Life, which had seemed so wonderful a short while ago, was so much better.

I all but skipped downstairs and into the sunroom to inform Simone and Arinthia that Brad was coming for the weekend. Instead of the nods of agreement I expected, Simone and Arinthia wore identical frowns.

"This isn't a serious thing, is it?" Simone asked.

I blinked in surprise. "We've been seeing one another a short time ..."

"Good," she said. "We don't want anything to divert you from taking over for us. Your job here is too important."

I looked at her in confusion.

"Silly girl." She gave me a smile I didn't trust. "I told you, we'd take care of everything for you as long as you were part of our plans."

The happiness I'd experienced moments ago evaporated. I was definitely being bought, and I still didn't know exactly what was expected of me.

"What is it you want me to do?"

Simone glanced at Arinthia and back to me. "We want you

to learn about the business so you can take over the seat on the Board. We need you to handle our shares of the business as well as other investments. If we lose the seat to George, we lose a lot of money and, more importantly, he wins back for his family what rightfully belongs to us." It sounded as bad as the feud between the Hatfields and McCoys.

"Grrrn..dotter," Arinthia mumbled and I heard her clearly. I, as her only blood relative, was expected to carry on this battle for her. At eighty-eight, Arinthia was in poor health and knew, undoubtedly, that even though she'd made admirable strides in recovering, the time left to her was limited. She was not about to let George best her. And I was the pawn in this unusual game of chess.

"It's an interesting business," said Simone in a conciliatory tone. "Fascinating, really. I've arranged for Hunter to show you the mills. He'll pick you up tomorrow morning."

I gritted my teeth. Simone had done it again—planned my time without including me.

She sensed my frustration. "It's for the best. You'll see," she said in a conciliatory tone. "I've also put together some information on the business for you to read."

I told myself to remain calm, that learning about Rivers Papers would be interesting and was a small price to pay for a family. But inside, I wanted to rebel against my loss of freedom.

After dinner, I lugged the notebooks Simone had put together up to my room, still resentful that my life had been taken over by two elderly women determined to control it.

I stood inside my bedroom, noting the richness of it, and wondered if the price for being part of this family would prove to be too high. Resigned to learning more about a business I may or may not become involved in, I lay down on the bed and opened the top notebook.

In moments, I was caught up in the history of Rivers Papers. Like so many other mills in Maine, they had initially depended on manual labor. Now high-tech operations ran it.

Back in the beginning, when the mills were starting up in the late 1890s and early 1900s, developers of mills were required to build dams, railroads and even housing for the workers who ran the operation. Today, I read, automated roll-wrapping systems were in place and some of the more modern paper machines could produce 420 tons of paper per day—a staggering amount.

I pored through the pages as if I were studying for a college exam. One of the aspects that interested me most was the discussion of dioxin. In 1996, all of the paper mills had signed onto an agreement with the goal of eliminating the discharge of dioxins which, admittedly, were a danger—a danger with horrifying results.

Reading about the side effects in detailed medical terms, my eyelids began to flutter.

I awoke to the sound of rain slanting against the windows in a steady rhythm. I snuggled under the covers, content to laze in my warm, comfortable bed.

Lady gave me a questioning look. I patted her on the head. "Not yet, girl."

She thumped back down on the floor, as satisfied as I to remain indoors.

A few moments later, a knock on my door jarred me out of my sleepy doze. I lifted to my elbow. "Yes?"

Simone swung the door open with a banging sound that reverberated in the room. Dressed in a plaid robe, her hair hung loosely in graying trails down her back. The look on her face left no doubt that something was wrong.

Alarmed, I sat up. "What is it? What's the matter?"

Simone clasped her hands together. "It's Arinthia. She's not feeling well. She'd like to see you. Right away."

I jumped out of bed, hurrying to catch up to Simone, who'd already moved half-way down the hall.

Inside Arinthia's room, my body turned icy. Arinthia's mouth hung open and her skin had a gray look to it that spelled trouble. Her eyes searched mine as I approached her.

"Gr...n dotter," she mumbled and reached for my hand.

I took her cold hand in mine and squeezed it gently.

"Need talk." She waved Simone away. "Go."

Hurt flashed across Simone's face. She glanced from Arinthia to me and gave a little bow. "If you need me, I'll be right outside."

Lady stood by the door, studying us with a liquid brown gaze.

"I'll let the dog out," Simone added, "and then come back upstairs."

"Thanks," I said, grateful for her thoughtfulness.

"Riss...ah."

I turned back to Arinthia and gazed into her pleading eyes. I perched on the edge of the bed, careful not to disturb her, sensing she needed me near. "What is it, Grandmother?"

Tears rolled down her cheeks. "Sorree. Thee-a."

"Yes, I understand," I said softly, hoping to soothe her.

"No, don't!" Her expression became fierce. "No!" She half rose from her pillows and slumped back down again.

I gulped nervously as she closed her eyes and lay quietly. I found my feet and rose on shaky legs. This wasn't just a case of not feeling well. Arinthia was dying, and we both knew it.

Heart pumping furiously, I stroked her wrinkled cheek, not knowing what else I should do. She continued to lay still, her eyes closed. At her continued stillness, panic exploded inside me. I ran out of the room to find Simone.

She met me on the stairway.

"This is bad. Have you sent for a doctor?" I asked.

Tears glistened in Simone's eyes. "I can't. Arinthia doesn't want any doctors called. No ambulance, nothing. I promised her."

Gulping nervously, I grabbed her hand. "C'mon, let's get back to her."

We hurried into Arinthia's room and stopped. Arinthia lay on the bed motionless, her face waxy in death. An expression of peace softened the harsh lines of her face, changing her whole demeanor. She looked almost ... happy. Funny how actions can blur or enhance one's features, I mused. Alive, she'd seemed so uncompromising, so determined.

The sound of crying brought me out of my reverie. Simone's face was buried in her hands. In the large, cold room that now served as a temporary tomb, her body shook with sobs which echoed her heartbreak.

I turned to Simone and held her in my arms. I didn't know what kind of relationship she'd shared with my grandmother, but I was certain she'd truly cared for her.

Simone straightened and said in a business-like tone, "I'll call the funeral home. They'll take care of everything."

She left to use the phone and I gave a last look at the woman who'd appeared in my life out of the blue, claimed me for her own, and then left me before I really got to know her. Regret seeped through me like unshed tears.

Feeling an overwhelming sense of loss, I closed the door to her room and wandered downstairs. I twisted my mother's gold ring on my right hand absently, wondering what was to become of me.

Becky Cantwell, still wearing her coat, greeted me with flushed cheeks. "Simone called me. I got here as soon as I could. Is everything all right? She said Arinthia wasn't feeling well."

"She's dead," I answered woodenly. "It just happened. Simone is calling the funeral home now."

"Poor dear." Becky gathered me in her arms.

Her abundant body was comforting. I lay my head on her shoulder, my mind awhirl. Arinthia had shouted "no" at me with such strength it was frightening as if she were telling me I knew nothing. What didn't I understand? What had happened between my mother and grandmother? Was it a matter of one horrible moment between them or many? I had so many questions.

I stepped back and managed a shaky smile. "Thanks, Becky. Maybe you'd better check on Simone."

Becky shook her head. "Let her be. I suspect she needs time to herself. I'll put on some coffee. It's still early and we'll be having company."

I sat at the kitchen table sipping coffee and nibbling on the granola Becky had placed before me.

Simone appeared, dressed in black slacks and a black and white sweater, her hair now neatly styled in her usual French twist. Her eyes were red-rimmed but her manner was brisk and business-like.

"The men from the funeral home will be here any moment. Go upstairs and get dressed, Marissa."

I pulled my T-shirt closer around me and took a last bite of my breakfast. Simone was right. It was time for me to get ready for whatever faced me.

When I emerged from my shower, I could hear the murmur of noises below. I dressed slowly, not wanting to see the men from the funeral home or observe Arinthia being carried from the house. Following Simone's example, I dressed in black, donning some of the clothes I had so eagerly shown to

Arinthia and Simone not long ago.

Descending the stairway, I followed the sound of voices and entered the living room, surprised to find George Hartwell there. He and Simone stopped talking when they saw me.

"George is here to see you," said Simone. Round red spots of color were centered on each cheek.

"Me? Why?"

In the living room, he motioned me to a chair opposite his place on the couch. Wary, I sat on the edge of the overstuffed chair, alert to the tension in the room.

"Now that Arinthia is gone, you will, no doubt, be taking over for her as she planned."

My eyebrows shot up. I gave Simone an inquiring glance. She nodded.

"I didn't know ... I wasn't sure ..."

George waved my uncertainty aside. "Once Arinthia had an idea in her mind, it was a foregone conclusion she'd bring it to fruition. Very few people got away with defying her."

My thoughts immediately swung to my mother.

"I've come up with a plan." George placed his hands on his knees and leaned forward, his blue eyes bright beneath a shock of white hair. "A plan to protect our investments in the mills." He waved a finger at me. "Arinthia wasn't the only one who had a large stake in Rivers Papers. I've been buying up its stock for some time."

At my silence, he continued. "I think there's a way we can divide the duties involved in Arinthia's special arrangement with Rivers. By sharing those duties with Hunter, you'll have a better chance to acquaint yourself with the business on a timely basis and we can be sure that nothing foolish will be done to destroy the power the Hartwells have always enjoyed."

Out of the corner of my eye, I saw Simone fidget, but I didn't need her to send me warning signals. I knew exactly what George was doing and it wasn't going to work. Sharing power with Hunter would mean eventually giving him license to take over.

Smiling pleasantly, I played dumb. "No decisions along that line can be made until I understand exactly how I fit into the picture. I have no idea what Arinthia planned ..." My voice shook with regret. "In my short time here, we never really talked about it. It's all so new to me."

He rose stiffly. "I don't have the details of Arinthia's will. She never permitted me to handle that part of her affairs. If, after meeting with her lawyer, you have any questions, call me. Adrienne and the girls will come over later today. They'll want to help in any way they can."

Simone's eyes shimmered with tears as she stood before him. "Thank you, George. Despite what differences you and Arinthia had, she respected you."

Grief momentarily changed George's features, drew them downward. He nodded and straightened as if he hadn't allowed his emotions to show for a moment. "Arinthia was her own woman. I'll give her that." The tenderness in his voice made me wonder if Allison was right, that he'd loved Arinthia all along.

I followed Simone and George to the door. The rain had stopped, but droplets of water, sparkling like diamonds in the emerging sun, clung to the leaves of the rhododendrons flanking the entrance. They reminded me of all I'd suddenly been given and my hands began to tremble. Nothing in life is free. I knew that lesson very well.

We watched George climb into his Land Rover, parked next to my tired little Honda. He gave a quick nod of his head and drove away.

"We'd better talk," said Simone. "Come with me now."

She led me to a room off the kitchen, whose doors had remained closed to me. Filled with curiosity, I watched as she unlocked the door and entered. Inside, over-crowded book shelves lined two walls. A third wall held a small brick fireplace, flanked by two burgundy leather wing-back chairs. Looking right at home, Simone walked over and took a seat behind a large mahogany desk and indicated a chair in front of her.

I lowered myself onto it, observing the change in her demeanor. There was nothing submissive about her. This was *her* room and she was used to controlling much more beyond it.

She cleared her throat. "While you were shopping with Allison yesterday, Arinthia changed her will. Looking back, I wonder if she knew she was about to die. She was most insistent about it."

Simone tapped her pen against the surface of the desk. The skin around her eyes turned red and I realized she was close to crying. "The gist of the will is that you are to get all the Rivers Papers stock she owns, along with the house and its contents. You'll maintain the seat on the Board. I'm to have the use of this house for as long as I wish, with all household expenses financed by the interest of a separate trust she established for such purposes. When I die, the trust will revert to you, as well."

I gasped. "I had no idea ..."

"Nor, I." Simone's nostrils flared. "It's not what Arinthia and I had agreed would happen." She averted her eyes as if she couldn't stand the sight of me. "I realize I'll have to treat you well, that it's in your best interest not to have me around. As you can tell, I'm ... "

"Stop! Don't say that." I went to her and gave her an

awkward hug. "I can't imagine anyone being that greedy."

"Oh, but I can." Simone's lip curled, and the murderous look she gave me made me cringe.

My knees felt weak under her bold stare. I sat again, overwhelmed by all I'd been told. "How am I going to be able to take an active role in serving on the Board of Rivers Papers? I've never even seen a paper mill."

Simone drew herself up, composed once more. "After things calm down, I'll make sure you get a good introduction to it. But first, we have to give Arinthia her due. We'll have a small service for her on Saturday. She didn't want anything elaborate, just a quiet, simple remembrance."

"Okay. Brad was planning to come this weekend so the timing will be good."

Simone cocked an eyebrow at me. "You won't be distracted by him?"

I fought back a flare of temper. My relationship with Brad was none of her business. "He's very important to me, Simone."

"Yes, I suppose so," she said slowly as if realizing such a thing might be possible. "But it's important ..."

I rose. "If you don't need me, I'm going to go call him."

"Go." She waved me away absent-mindedly and, with a look of dejection, picked up a document from her desk.

CHAPTER FOURTEEN

Friday morning, Brad pulled into the driveway. Lady barked a frenzied greeting and galloped across the lawn to reach him. I followed close behind and ran into his open arms. His lips touched mine and, as his arms tightened around me, the brisk, cold air around me disappeared in a rush of warmth. He looked down at me and grinned.

"I'm so glad you're here," I said, eager to fill him in on all that had happened. "Everything has happened so quickly. I thought I'd have time to get to know Arinthia and find out what went wrong between her and my mother. Now, I'm left to carry on for her in a business I don't even know."

"You'll do fine." Brad kept hold of my hand as we turned to go inside. He glanced at the house. "Nice place."

"I can't believe my grandmother left it to me." After living in the tiny, unkempt house in Barnham, Briar Cliff seemed like a brown-shingled palace.

I led him through the back door and into the large, homey kitchen where Becky was busily preparing food.

"This your man?" She wiped her floured hands on her apron and beamed at Brad. "We've been waiting for you."

Brad grinned and shook her hand. "Something smells great."

"Pumpkin bread." She handed him a small slice. "Don't let Henry know I gave you some. I told him he couldn't sneak a piece, don't cha know."

"Mmmm," Brad rolled his eyes in appreciation.

I laughed at the look of triumph on Becky's face and led Brad to the front hall.

"Leave your suitcase here at the bottom of the stairs. I want you to meet Simone."

My throat grew dry as we headed to the sunroom. Foolish as it seemed, I desperately wanted her to approve of Brad.

We entered the room and Simone's gaze swept over us. A polite smile formed on her face. She rose to her feet and moved toward us with a briskness that belied her age. Her austere demeanor suited the cold elegance of her simple black cashmere sweater and subtly-checked black and white pants. Today, large diamond earrings winked at her ears, a bequeathed gift from Arinthia.

"Simone, this is my friend Brad." I eagerly waited for a response from her.

Brad greeted her with soft-spoken politeness and I sensed he, too, was somewhat in awe of this woman who seemed to take up the whole room now that Arinthia was gone and could no longer detract from her.

"You're here just for the weekend?" she asked with a brittleness that was anything but inviting.

"I have to be back to work on Monday. We're working on an important case."

"Good," Simone said. "Marissa is going to be very busy for the next few weeks."

Irritation flared inside me. I clamped my teeth shut.

Though he smiled pleasantly, Brad's tone of voice hinted at defiance. "It's not so far that weekend visits are impossible."

Two tiny dots of red appeared on Simone's cheeks. I was already well acquainted with those signs of her anger.

"If you need anything for your *short* stay, please let me know," she said, continuing a verbal dance with him.

"Thanks." Brad put his arm around me. I leaned into him,

thrilled he was here with me during this difficult transition.

Simone turned to me. "You won't forget that George and Adrienne and the children are coming here for dinner tonight? Becky's made a special meal."

"We'll be here." I turned to Brad. "C'mon. We'd better get your things upstairs. Then, I want to show you the beach. We can walk to town and have lunch there."

As we climbed the stairs, Brad murmured, "Is Simone the dragon lady I think she is?"

I glanced behind me and answered softly. "Even with Arinthia alive, she was the one who seemed to run the show. Some people say they were lovers. I don't know."

"She sure didn't like me."

I wanted to assure him otherwise, but I knew it was true.

We reached the guest room at the far end of the hall away from my room. "Here it is. We chose a room facing the ocean." I went over to the window. "Look! Isn't it beautiful?"

Brad came up behind me. "*You're* beautiful." His warm breath on my neck sent a shiver of delight down my spine.

I leaned back against him, loving the feel of his arms encircling me. "I've missed you."

He turned me so that we were facing one another and his lips met mine. I embraced him without hesitation, filled with a deep satisfaction. I *could* love a man, want him, need him. My heart pounded as I became caught up in his kiss, the smooth touch of his lips, the taste of his tongue.

"Marissa?"

I jumped away from Brad.

Simone stood by the door, her face a mask of disapproval. "Samantha is here to see you."

"Sam?" I frowned, wondering what she wanted with me. We hadn't spoken since she stomped away from me at Harry's Bar last summer. And Allison had warned me that she and I wouldn't easily become friends.

Following Simone down the winding stairway, I stared at her rigid back, wondering why she was so displeased with me for loving Brad. At some point, I'd have to challenge her on it but now wasn't the time. Hunter's sister, Sam, walked into the front hallway and gave us all a smile.

I stared at her in amazement. She was so ... so ... different. I studied her. She was every bit as beautiful as she had been last summer. Maybe more so. Then it struck me. The unsettling, stormy hue to her gray eyes had been replaced by a sparkle that brightened her whole face.

"You look wonderful!" I exclaimed sincerely.

"Thanks." She gave me a sheepish look and swallowed the last of her pumpkin bread. "Now that I'm no longer drinking, I can't stay away from sweets."

I introduced her to Brad, careful to stick to her nickname.

"Come, we can go into the sunroom," said Simone, looking on with interest.

Sam shook her head. "No, thanks. I've come to take Marissa to lunch. I want to make amends for last summer. Brad can come too, of course."

"Sounds wonderful. I'll grab my jacket."

We left through the front entrance just as Henry was crossing the lawn toward us. I introduced Brad to him and climbed into the back of Sam's Volvo. Brad settled in the front, and we took off.

"What's with Simone?" Sam asked. "She was hovering like a mother hen."

I sighed. "She's been like that ever since Arinthia died. It's as if she's afraid to let me out of her sight, and I don't know why. She keeps telling me I have to stay here and do my duty."

"She certainly doesn't like me in the picture," commented Brad.

"True. She made that very apparent."

Sam turned the car toward town. "There's something I want to say to you, and I didn't want to do it in front of Simone." She glanced at Brad. "Perhaps now is not a good time..."

"Feel free to say anything you want in front of Brad."

Sam continued to stare straight ahead but her hands gripped the steering wheel so tightly her knuckles turned white.

"First of all, I want to apologize for my inexcusable behavior last summer. It's one of the reasons I decided to give up alcohol completely. It's been over ten weeks now. I'm in a good counseling group and determined to beat this addiction because, for the first time, I truly understand how much I can help others."

I drew in a breath, impressed by the change in her. "Thank you, Sam. Your apology means a lot to me."

She took a moment to pull into a parking space downtown and turned to me. "I'm starting my own consulting business. One of the men in my group suggested it and it makes all the sense in the world. With my MBA and some of the connections I have through Harvard Law, I can help women get grants from private sources and help them complete paperwork for government loans. I've already got my first customer. The sister of one of the women I've met."

"It sounds good, Sam."

"It's taken me a long time, but I finally get it, and I'm happier than I've ever been."

"I'm glad," I said simply, meaning it wholeheartedly.

We got out of the car, and I filled with affection watching Brad inhale the salt air in deep, satisfying breaths. He turned to me with a grin. "Nothing like the smell of the sea."

"How about lunch at The Lobster Trap—one of my favorite

seafood places in town. Have you been there?" said Sam.

"Not yet. Sounds good to me."

We were seated at a table by the window, where we could enjoy the view of the harbor. Pleasure boats had been removed from the water, stored for the winter months. Sturdy fishing boats still in the harbor were moored here and there, bobbing on the water like life-sized bathtub toys. The number of tourists had dwindled since summer, though late "leaf-peepers" wandered through town, carrying shopping bags of treasures dug from the interiors of the numerous shops lining the street.

After we had placed our orders, Sam talked quietly about some of the ideas she had for helping women in business.

My mind spun. Perhaps she would help me. I pushed forward with my idea, hoping it wouldn't erase the baby steps we'd taken toward friendship.

"Any chance I could be one of your clients by giving me advice as I begin to learn about Rivers Papers?"

A series of emotions crossed Sam's face, and I tensed. Her smile was hard-edged and then she let out a sigh, softening her expression.

"At one time I would've told you to go to hell for daring to ask. I've wanted your position for as long as I can remember. I've learned with the help of others in my group that I need to drop the whole idea. I thought the only way to prove myself to my father was to learn the business and claim it for my family. Dumb, huh?"

I shook my head. I knew what it was like to try to be something different to gain approval.

Brad caught my hand and gave it a squeeze. I turned to him and smiled.

"How long have you two known one another?" Sam asked, grinning at us.

"Just a short time..." I said as Brad piped up, "Forever..."

"We grew up together in Barnham, New York," I explained, laughing softly.

"Yeah, I've known her since she was a girl," added Brad. "She lived next door to my aunt."

Sam leaned closer. "Barnham, New York. It's so strange. You never knew about Thea? Us? Arinthia?"

I shook my head. "My mother was known as Margaret Cole. She said she had no family. I'd heard the name, Tim Hartwell. He was an Army buddy of Clyde Breeden's, the man who lived with my mother and me." Just saying Clyde's name sent a shiver skittering across my shoulders.

"Thea was fifteen years older than I," said Sam. "It's hard to believe she's ended her life and I'm just beginning mine."

After lunch, Sam drove Brad and me back to the house. As I started to climb out of the car, she pulled me back and took a deep breath.

"I'll help you out as long as you understand I'm doing this to keep my father and Hunter from overpowering you. You deserve a chance to succeed, like any other woman in business."

"Thanks." I knew that Sam would be a tough teacher, but I wanted the best. I didn't like the idea of George Hartwell and his son taking my place any more than she did.

That evening, the whole Hartwell family came for dinner, and I had the opportunity to spend some quality time with my great-aunt Adrienne. At sixty, she was a soft-spoken, warm person who perfectly counter-balanced George-—her inflexible, elderly husband. Admiring her classical features, I knew immediately where the girls got their beauty. I observed the obvious affection between Adrienne and her daughters, and a lump formed in my throat. Even Hunter, I noticed, was careful to be gentle with his mother, teasing her in a loving way for needing her glasses to read an article in the Boston *Globe* about Arinthia's upcoming funeral.

When she finished reading it aloud, Adrienne playfully poked fun at Hunter, sitting next to her in the sunroom. "You'd better hope Bettina has a good sense of humor. She's going to need it when she realizes what a slob you are." Adrienne turned to me with a twinkle in her eye. "It's official. The wedding has been set for a year from June. After trying for years to domesticate this child, I've given up. Bettina can take over."

Sam and Allison made faces at Hunter, and we all laughed. Even Simone.

I loved being part of this family. It seemed so real, so nice. Smiling at Brad, I imagined having my own family.

George spoke up. "Laugh all you want. Marriage with Bettina Browning is a good thing. With her father's business interests and ours, it's a perfect match."

"Father, that's so archaic," complained Allison. "You tried matchmaking once with me and it didn't work."

George's penetrating stare, directed at his daughter, made my stomach curl. But Allison looked him squarely in the eye. "You know it's true."

Adrienne interceded. "Of course, darling, but yours was a unique situation. Let's not unearth any skeletons. What's done is done. We're looking forward to welcoming another daughter into the family. Right, George?"

He hesitated a moment, then glanced at me and nodded.

My admiration for Adrienne grew. She was a natural peacemaker. No wonder everyone seemed to get along.

Much later, after everyone had left and Simone had gone upstairs, Brad and I bundled in warm coats and went outside for a walk. Lady trotted at our heels. Though the evening was crisp, the moon hung in the dark sky. Its glow cast shimmering light on the water rolling in and backing away, highlighting the sandy stretch of beach in front of us.

"Your family is very interesting," Brad commented, clasping my hand as we strolled along the hard crust of beach at the water's edge. "I really like Adrienne. Allison and Sam, too. But I got the distinct feeling that George is someone for you to watch. Hunter, as well."

"No doubt about it, George Hartwell would love for me to turn the business over to Hunter and be done with it. He went on and on about having a true Hartwell at the helm, as he put it. His talk bothered Simone no end."

"Dragon Lady was not happy," Brad agreed. "What's the story with Hunter? He didn't look happy, either."

"I met Bettina last summer. Hunter told me then that they were engaged to be engaged, that sort of thing. He wasn't upset by it but he didn't seem to be in love with her, either."

Brad stopped and drew me close. "Like us?"

I nodded and gazed up at him. In the moonlight the angular features of his face were pronounced, giving him an added dimension of strength. I wasn't sure where our relationship was going, not with the unexpected complications in my life, but I knew I would always love Brad for giving me the chance to be free from Clyde's cruelty.

"So, how sound a sleeper is Simone?" Brad murmured. "Should I tiptoe past her door to get to your room tonight?"

I smiled, my heart beating in little leaps of anticipation. His lips met mine in a kiss filled with urgency.

I grew ready for more, then, stepped back. "Oh, hell ... I'm sorry ... Simone ..."

"Guess it's not going to happen, huh?" Brad gazed into my eyes, sensing my disappointment. "Dragon Lady would spit fire if she caught us together in your room or mine. Right?"

"It'll have to wait until we're alone. Really alone."

He grabbed hold of my hand and I was as frustrated as he when we went inside to our separate rooms.

CHAPTER FIFTEEN

Saturday was another "high sparkler"—crisp and clear. Promptly at four, the two limousines we'd ordered for the funeral service drew up to the small chapel atop a hill on the far side of town, overlooking the distant harbor.

Aware Arinthia had been somewhat of a recluse over the years, I was surprised to see other cars in the parking lot. The waitress at the coffee shop had said many in town didn't like her.

Brad helped me out of the limousine. I paused and observed George Hartwell emerge from another limo. He greeted a number of men who came forward to say hello to him, and I realized then that the people here for the funeral were business associates of the Hartwells, not beloved friends of Arinthia.

George stood in their group and talked to them for several minutes. I couldn't hear what he was saying, but the men clustered around him turned and stared at me. I lifted my chin and turned to Brad and Simone.

"Shall we go inside?"

Brad offered an arm to me and the other to Simone, and we walked to the chapel's entrance like royalty.

The chapel was a white, clapboard, building, like those you typically see in picture postcards of New England. I stepped inside the vestibule and immediately noticed a brass plaque mounted on the wall, stating the chapel was built in 1764. Inside, white pews stretched in rows alongside the wine-colored carpeting of the main aisle. A simple wooden cross, unadorned, hung above a plain, wooden table.

Brad led Simone and me to the front row. The hard wooden bench was softened by a wine-colored cushion that most assuredly was absent in colonial times. Squirming to get comfortable against the hard, straight back of the pew, I could well imagine children of long ago twitching and praying the church services would end.

The minister walked over to the plain, white-painted pulpit, and I was surprised to see how young he was. No doubt he hadn't known Arinthia well, or even at all. He proved it when he spoke about the love of family Arinthia had always demonstrated. I thought of my mother's ashes floating in the waters in front of the home she hadn't seen for many years and knew his words weren't true. He spoke of forgiveness as a part of loving. I hoped I could do that for my mother one day. I was still wrestling with that thought when Brad leaned over and whispered, "Ready to go?"

Startled, I looked around and realized others had risen to the sound of soft music and were making their way out the door.

"Your mind was a long way from here," Brad smiled tenderly.

I nodded, convinced that until I found out about my mother's past, I wouldn't be able to plan my future.

When I stepped out into the sunshine, I was surrounded by the same group of men who'd earlier formed a ring around George. Hunter stood at my side as I was introduced to lawyers, the CEO of Rivers Papers, and assorted Board Members. Though the names became confusing, their intent did not. They, like George, appeared to want me to turn my seat on the Board over to Hunter.

Seething inside, I smiled sweetly. "I know I have a lot to learn about the business, but I'm going to do what's right; I'm going to honor my grandmother's wishes and assume her position."

Though they'd murmured words of welcome, disappointment coated their faces. I couldn't decide if it was because I was female or there were other, deeper reasons for wanting me off the Board.

Only a few of the attendees at the funeral came back to the house for the small reception we'd planned. Bettina Browning and her parents were among them. Hunter introduced Brad and me to them and walked away to get a glass of white wine for Bettina.

After he left, Bettina waved her hand in front of me, smiling proudly. "Did you see my diamond? Hunter really did me proud." The white, emerald-cut diamond set in a platinum diamond-encrusted band was enormous.

"Very nice," I remarked, wondering if she and her parents realized that Hunter would not be taking over the Arinthia Hartwell estate as they'd once thought.

Adrienne appeared at my side and talked about the forthcoming wedding plans. Grateful for the diversion, I slipped away.

Brad found me in the kitchen.

"Hey! What are you doing in here? You should be out front, greeting everyone."

I let out a long sigh. "I feel like a fraud, some kind of interloper. These people all know one another, like one another, have their own ideas about how things should be done. The only reason I'm here is through some freak coincidence."

Brad sat opposite me at the kitchen table and gave me a hard stare. "You sure it was just a coincidence? Maybe your mother was giving something back to you, something she couldn't do on her own. Don't you think you owe it to yourself to stand your ground?"

I rose to my feet. He was right. I'd been handed an opportunity not many people had. No matter how uncomfortable this new mantle of responsibility felt around my shoulders I'd handle it—maybe not the way everyone thought I should, but I'd do the best I could. I hadn't made it on my own for so many years without sheer determination.

I followed Brad into the living room with new purpose.

Allison came over to me. "Guess what? My old roommate from college called me out of the blue last night, asking if I'd be interested in working with her in California. She owns a small gallery along the coast and is looking for a partner. I'm going to think seriously about it."

I smiled. "That's wonderful, Allison. That's what you wanted."

"Funny how things work out," she commented, giving me an impish grin. "Take a look at you! One day you're working in Georgia, the next you're some big-wig in a small town in Maine."

"I've only just begun to fight," I said, much more comfortable with the idea.

Allison grinned. "You know, Marissa, I'm glad I met you. I think you might be just what this family needs."

I glanced over at George and Hunter, heads together, and knew from the furtive looks cast in my direction that they were talking about me. A chill spread through my body.

The morning was foggy and gray. It matched my drooping spirits as Brad lifted his suitcase into his SUV and turned to me, an enigmatic expression on his face.

Breakfast had been a tense affair. Simone made a point of ignoring Brad and he continued to talk to me as if she wasn't in the room with us. I wondered as I had all morning, what was going on.

"Will you tell me what you and Simone are fighting about?"

Brad's lips drew together in an angry line. "After you went to bed last night, Simone asked if she could speak openly to me. She made it very clear that if I had any feelings for you at all, I'd stay out of your way. She told me you had an obligation to the family to stay here and protect their interests. She said you could live well for the first time in your life and I had no business destroying your chance to better yourself."

I felt as if my stomach had dropped to the tops of my shoes. "What did you say to her?"

"Nothing. And after thinking about it all night, I've decided to leave it up to you, Marissa. I really care about you, but a relationship between us would never work if I forced you away from here. I tried that once with Amber. Remember? And I can't just up and leave the law firm I've worked hard to develop with my father."

Realization struck me like a blow to the belly. My pulse pounded. He hadn't told Simone to go to hell. He was willing to walk away. Feeling like an idiot for thinking what we had was special, I blinked back tears with fierce resolve.

"You'd just walk away?"

"She's right, you know." He gave me an uneasy look. "You deserve a chance to have the family you've always wanted. God knows it isn't easy for me to admit, but I have to be realistic. You'd be better off without me."

"Oh, Brad, that's so unfair. I've waited all my life to have roots and history and real family members. I have to stay right here. They need me. I can't leave."

The minute I said the words, I wished I could swallow them. Pain flashed across Brad's face. He didn't move an inch but I felt as if he'd leaped backward behind the wall I'd just thrown up between us.

"I didn't mean it quite that way ..." I began.

"Forget it, Marissa. I've learned that truth sometimes comes out when we least expect it." He turned and climbed into his SUV.

I watched helplessly. "Brad, wait!"

He rolled down his window. "Look, Marissa. You have a lot to think about. As you said, you now have a family. I don't want to come between you and them. What you do with your life is up to you."

I understood Brad didn't want to go through another major emotional upheaval, but it didn't make my pain any less when he gave me a quick wave and drove away without looking back.

I stomped into the house in a rage. Simone had interfered in my life again.

She was sitting at her desk in the small office by the kitchen.

"You!" I slammed the door behind me. "What right did you have to speak to Brad, to tell him to walk away from me? You've ruined my life!"

An angry gleam lit Simone's eyes. She rose from behind her desk, stiff-backed and haughty, her lips drawn into a thin line. "So you are your mother's daughter, after all. I wondered when that temperamental, selfish side of her would show up in you."

Shame was quickly counter-balanced by the deep anger I felt toward her. "Ever since I arrived here, you've been trying to control me as if I were a puppet at the end of a string. You may have gotten away with that with Arinthia, but I'm not going to be a part of your big plan, whatever that is."

Shock and something like fear changed Simone's expression, brought a pleading look to her eyes.

"I'm sorry, Marissa," she said quietly. "You don't understand ..."

"Don't you think it's about time you explained a few things to me?" I pounded a fist on her desk in frustration.

"It hasn't been easy taking care of Arinthia, living my life under the roof of someone else..."

I wanted to sympathize with Simone, but I couldn't. She'd made choices in her life and had obviously been rewarded for them. Being someone's companion didn't always mean living a life of luxury. Yet, as far as I could tell, that's exactly what Simone had been given.

We glared at one another.

"What do you mean I'm Thea's daughter? Did you try to control her, too?"

Simone waved my question away with a swipe of her hand. "No one could control Thea. We tried to make her understand what was required of each of us, but she wouldn't listen."

"Do you know who my father is?"

Simone's expression changed once more, became a look of defeat. She shook her head. "Thea had a special allure about her. Boys and men alike were drawn to her in a way that was almost frightening. Your father could have been one of any number of people she attracted. God knows, Arinthia and I tried to find out. After Thea ran away, Arinthia didn't seem to care anymore. She washed her hands completely of Thea and anything to do with her, calling her nothing but a whore."

I sat down, weak-kneed. "Then why was Arinthia ... I mean ... Grandmother ... so happy to find me?"

"She had her first stroke almost a year ago. We thought she wasn't going to make it. It scared us both. She wasn't happy about the prospect of turning Rivers Papers over to George's family. That got her to thinking and wondering about Thea. We hired someone to try to trace her, but any leads from years ago had long since dried up. Fate brought you to us. Now, whether you like it or not, you must follow through. As I told you before, you'll be amply rewarded."

I narrowed my eyes. "What's in it for you?"

She blinked in surprise and a slow smile spread across her face. "Good, you're tough. That's what we need. You see, I don't want to die knowing my life has been a waste. I want my commitment to Arinthia to have long-lasting meaning. If the business goes to George and his family, it will mean that I've failed. I can't let that happen."

Why had Simone made it seem like it was her purpose in life? She was just Arinthia's companion. What wasn't she telling me? "Why aren't there any pictures of Tim Hartwell around? I understand about Thea, but why not Tim?"

Simone's eyes filled with tears. "Such a sweet, sweet boy. But he, too, disobeyed us, went ahead and joined the army. We tried to talk him out of it but he would hear nothing of it. I think he wanted to prove himself a capable leader or some such thing."

"Because he was gay?"

Glaring at me, she rose to her feet. "Why would you say such a thing?"

"I ... I ... heard it in town ..." I stammered, surprised by her anger.

Simone pounded a fist into the palm of her other hand. "Vicious, vicious people. Can you understand why Arinthia and I have kept to ourselves through the years? One never knows what foul rumors are generated by envious people."

She stared into space, her lips quivering. "Timothy was the most perfect of sons. No mother could have asked for more. Arinthia adored him."

"But my mother wasn't adored, was she?"

Simone focused on me and shook her head. "Thea? No,

even under the best of circumstances, she and Arinthia never got along."

A pang shot through me. I knew what it was like to yearn for a mother's affection, to feel desperate to know you were loved, no matter what.

"Tell me about St. Andrews. Is it far from here?" My mind whirled with possibilities. It might hold clues for me.

Simone frowned. "Don't waste your time. It's not a small girls' school anymore. It's a coed private school for troubled teens."

I bit my tongue to keep from snapping at Simone. She was trying to control me again. "Simone, I'll do what I have to and find answers on my own."

She shrugged, brushing aside my words, but I knew I'd annoyed her. "Be careful what you wish for, Marissa. Life takes sudden twists and turns when you least expect it."

I left Simone's office more determined than ever. Life for me had become like a winding mountain road through uncharted territory. I needed to map out a plan of my own. The devil with fate!

I went to the quiet of my room and sank into the rocking chair, thinking about Brad. It'd hurt that he'd been so willing to walk away. He couched it in noble terms, his wanting me to have a chance at my new life, but what I'd desperately wanted to hear him say was that he'd told Simone to go to hell with her ideas, that he had ideas of his own—ideas that included me.

My rocking grew faster and faster as I thought back to the tension of our parting conversation. He'd said the truth sometimes came out unexpectedly. He was right. Now that I had a family, a history and yes, money and power, I didn't want to walk away from it. But it didn't mean I didn't want him, too.

CHAPTER SIXTEEN

A re you ready?" Simone called up to me from the bottom of the stairs.

I patted my hair one more time, trying to tame the curls that threatened to pull away from the no-nonsense knot at the back of my head. The black pants and crisp white shirt I'd chosen to wear were simple and business-like, perfect for my first visit to Rivers Papers.

I descended the stairway, hiding my jumpy nerves. Simone would consider it a sign of weakness. "What time did you arrange for Hunter to pick me up?" I asked her, checking my watch. He was to introduce me to the staff at the mill.

Simone frowned. "He promised he'd be here before eight o'clock. He knows it takes over two hours to get to the mill. It would be just like him to try and ruin your first appearance."

A car horn blared. I grabbed my purse and coat from the kitchen counter and gave Simone a quick wave. "See you sometime this afternoon."

"Good luck!" said Simone. "And remember to take notes!"

I let out a sigh. Over the past few days, Simone and I had gradually arrived at acceptable boundaries between us, but it took a lot of diplomacy on my part. She still liked to order me about.

I hurried outside and stopped. Samantha's Volvo waited in the driveway.

"Surprise!" said Sam, as I opened the car door and climbed in.

"Where's Hunter?"

The smile on her face evaporated. "He's sleeping it off. He and Bettina went into Boston last night. Apparently, they got into a fight and he got even by getting drunk as a skunk."

"You don't mind taking me up to the mill?"

Sam shook her head. "Not at all. I said I'd help you and I will." She lifted a shoulder and let it drop. "The irony is that Hunter isn't really interested in the business and I've loved it all my life."

"What would he want to do if he wasn't being forced into the paper business?"

She held up a hand. "Don't laugh. He'd like to open a restaurant. He's always been interested in cooking and food, but my father would not pay for him to go to Cornell or one of the other hotel schools. He vowed his only son was going to fulfill a family destiny." She grimaced. "I know. He's so out of touch with things. He's an old man who's never lost sight of his goal of representing his side of the family at the mills."

We headed to Riverton, a town on the Kennebec River north of Madison. On this crisp November day, the warmth inside the car was comforting. I'd lived in Atlanta long enough to find the colder temperatures in Maine hard to get used to.

After driving for some time, Sam spoke. "Allison told me you and your mother didn't get along. What was she like?"

I hesitated and decided to be open with Samantha about my mother's drinking. After all, Sam was working very hard to overcome the same disease.

"She was an alcoholic and drug addict who lived with a man who abused her verbally and emotionally, Not a good scene."

She shot me a knowing look. "He ever torment you?"

I took a deep breath and studied the bare-branched trees that stood in a line along the roadside like an honor guard. The anger I'd thought I'd conquered made my voice low, my words knife-edged.

"Clyde Breeden was a sonuvabitch. He was a bitter, angry man who loved to get his kicks by making lewd comments and grabbing me whenever he could. It's taken years of counseling to put it behind me."

"I knew it had to be something like that. The pitying way you treated me when we first met really annoyed the crap out of me. Later, when I'd sobered up and was getting help, I realized you obviously knew something about alcoholics. It was written all over your face."

"Really? I haven't mentioned any of this to Simone or anyone else in the family. My mother left home for a reason I don't yet know. Until I understand her better, I don't think it's fair to say too much." Remembering Doris's reproach, I added, "She worked hard at her job."

"Oh? What did she do?"

"She cleaned houses. For one woman, in particular."

Samantha was silent.

"Clyde said she did that kind of work for cash so people couldn't trace her. I wonder why."

Samantha shrugged. "Hard to say. Family history paints her as a very head-strong young woman. In that respect, she was exactly like Aunt Arinthia. Perhaps that's why they never got along." The corner of her mouth lifted in a curl of derision. "Did you know Arinthia and my father were engaged to be married? Can you imagine if that had happened?"

At the look of horror on her face, I couldn't help laughing

Samantha's grin evaporated. "There's always been an underlying tension between the families. My mother is the one who has kept the two families together. She smiles and pretends the ugliness simply doesn't exist."

"Did Arinthia choose Herbert over your father for the money, like some people think?"

"Could be," said Samantha. "She was one tough woman—

determined to hold her own, have her own way, no matter what it took."

Unexpected sympathy for my mother filled me.

The town of Riverton, Maine looked like a more rural, wintry version of Barnham, New York. Brick storefronts, edged with wooden trim painted in various colors, lined the main street. A brick church with a towering steeple captured one corner of the central city block and was opposed by an unimaginative painted cinder-block building that, according to the white sign posted on the lawn in front of it, housed city hall offices.

"Not much to look at, is it?" commented Samantha. "Wait 'til you see the mill."

Steam rose from a stack down the street. I was surprised that Rivers Papers was right in the middle of town. Samantha turned left before the approach to the bridge that spanned the Kennebec River and we drove up to a gated entrance to the mill.

Through the chain-link fence, I studied the surprisingly modern mill. The sleek white metal buildings were in stark contrast to the faded brick outbuildings on the property.

We passed through the gate and parked. I got out of the car and stood a moment, inhaling a rich, piney smell that reminded me of the upcoming Christmas holidays.

"Pretty, huh?" said Samantha. "But don't get fooled. The pleasant smell is really airborne resin that will coat the lungs if someone is over-exposed to it. Think black lung disease."

I could barely concentrate on what Sam was saying because I was distracted by a steady low humming noise.

She pointed to the roof of the building. "Huge fans help direct the heat and steam away from the mills."

Overwhelmed by the massive structures in front of me. I was awed to think that my great-grandfather had begun with a simple mill years ago and I was now standing in front of the major enterprise it had become.

"Cool, huh?" Sam grinned. "Pretty impressive. Wait until you see the inside."

We were met at the entrance to the building by a guard who checked our shoes. "Sorry, Miss Hartwell, you know the rules." He pointed to my feet. "Steel-toed shoes are required."

Sam pulled an extra pair of boots out of a canvas bag she carried and handed them to me. I slipped them on and stood up the guard handed each of us a yellow hard hat and safety glasses. Feeling like a near-sighted alien, I turned as I heard a voice calling my name.

A tall, thin gray-haired man wearing slacks and a sport coat, along with the required gear, approached and held out a hand.

"Miz Cole? I'm Jake Weatherbee, Vice President and a member of the board. Glad to see you here. Samantha, what a surprise! We were expecting Hunter. The meeting is going to start shortly. Care for some coffee?"

I shook my head at the offer and held out my hand. "I'd like to see the inside operation before going into the meeting. I've never been to a paper mill before."

His eyebrows lifted in surprise. "I suppose I could show you around."

"Thanks, anyway," Samantha said. "Jonesy can show us. He's the one I usually see."

"As you wish," said Jake pleasantly, but I detected a trace of annoyance. Curious, I followed Samantha into an alcove outside a huge metal door.

"It's noisy inside the room," she explained. "The workers wear OSHA-approved ear muffs to protect their hearing.

Conversation is difficult, but once we're inside the supervisor's office, we'll be able to talk more freely."

She opened the door and I was lost in the sights and sounds of a major paper operation. The long, air-conditioned room contained a huge, self-enclosed machine.

Samantha pointed from it to the flat screen on the wall. The inside workings of the mammoth machine were represented on what was a three-dimensional display that dominated one wall like a huge television screen.

We reached a glass-enclosed office and stepped inside. Immediately the sounds from the main room were muted.

A round, pleasant-looking man rose from behind his desk and opened his arms.

Samantha rushed into them. "Hi, Jonesy." She gave him a warm hug. "Long time, no see."

He tipped her chin up. "You doin' okay now?"

Samantha grinned. "It's been ninety-two days."

"Good." Jonesy eyed me curiously. "One day at a time. That's the way."

Samantha turned to me. "This is the long-lost cousin I was telling you about. Marissa Cole. She's taking over for Aunt Arinthia."

I held out my hand. "Glad to meet you, Mr. Jones."

His blue eyes twinkled, and with his whitish-gray hair and trimmed white beard, I was reminded once more of Christmas holidays.

"Now don't go callin' me Mr. Jones," he said. "I've been Jonesy ever since I started here and that was over thirty years ago." He grinned at Samantha. "'Bout the time this one and her sister were out of diapers and Hunter was in 'em."

Samantha's smile lit her face. "You can see why I've always loved coming to the mill."

Jonesy flushed and jabbed a finger in Samantha's

direction. "This one was full of questions from the time she could talk. Always loved this business." He spoke gruffly but his affection for Samantha was clear.

"Can you give Marissa a quick overview of what's happening out there?" said Samantha. "The meeting is going to start shortly."

"Where's Hunter?" Jonesy asked. "'Thought he'd be the one bringing her to the meeting."

Samantha shrugged. "He couldn't make it, so I brought Marissa here in his place."

"You gonna like this business?" Jonesy asked me bluntly. His blue eyes penetrated mine.

"I don't know much about it," I answered truthfully.

He slapped a hand on my shoulder and drew me toward the window. "Okay, here it is in a nutshell. That massive machine you see is fully enclosed to help regulate heat and moisture and, believe it or not, noise. Can't imagine what it would be without it. That sucker has a 280-inch width and is putting out 3,500 feet of paper a minute."

At my astonished gasp, he continued. "The secret to running it is that big electronic model on the wall. It tells us what is happening inside that machine. At every critical point, there is a warning light that tells the operators if there is a problem so they can check it out on their computers. Each man stationed alongside it is responsible for a different part of the machine. They have to keep their eyes on it to watch for warning lights indicating any problems before or as they happen."

"It's like they're working in virtual reality," said Samantha enthusiastically. "They have to see what's inside by looking at their computer screens. Cool, huh?"

"Yeah," said Jonesy. "We don't want no break happening. That's a disaster no one forgets."

"That's not the only machine, is it? What are some of the others?" I asked Jonesy.

"Gawd, we got a lot. Hydro pulpers, grinders, winders and slitters, super calendars... you name it, we got it. Rivers Papers is up-to-date. That we are." Jonesy's voice echoed with pride.

"You love this work, don't you?"

Jonesy cast a glance at Samantha. "Most of the time, I do."

Samantha checked her watch. "C'mon. We'd better go find the others. The meeting is about to start."

Although I had the feeling I was being rushed away from a potentially enlightening conversation, I followed Samantha's advice, said good-bye to Jonesy, and hurried out of his office.

The board meeting was to take place in the conference room of one of the brick outbuildings that overlooked the river. A large mahogany table, surrounded by brown leather swivel chairs dominated the room. The outside view drew my attention. I stood and gazed out the window. The river below us was more than a picturesque ribbon of blue wending its way through the town, I realized. It was the essence of Rivers Papers' strength. Without it, the mill would never have been developed.

Jake Weatherbee came up beside me. "See the dam down here? Note the inflatable "flashboards". We can raise or lower the water by a few feet. We use them for flood control in times of high water or in times of low water. Raising the "boards" allows the generation plant to maintain head pressure, or the surge of the river, to turn the generators. Doesn't sound like much, but it's a significant deal economically when we can increase electrical output. Lot to learn, isn't there?"

"There is, I'm sure." William Hartwell and his brother Edward had been farsighted. I wondered if they'd ever imagined how extensive their small business would become.

Waiting for the room to fill, I took a seat. Samantha sat at my side. The looks we received were not encouraging. They ranged from outright curiosity to barely- veiled hostility. My hands grew cold at the thought of speaking in front of such well-known, well-versed business execs. I hunkered down in my chair, awaiting the arrival of Theodore Beers, Chief Financial Officer. His private jet had been delayed leaving Newark Airport, causing him to be late landing in Waterville.

"Here he comes now," said Jake Weatherbee, rising to his feet, and all but saluting.

A young, broad-shouldered man strode into the room as if he owned it. A buzz immediately filled the air as men greeted him enthusiastically. He dismissed the commotion with a quick nod and a wave of his hand and focused green eyes on me.

"I'm Ted Beers. You must be Marissa Cole."

His curtness caught me off guard. "Yes, and this is ... He stopped me. "I know Samantha. What is *she* doing here?"

I could feel Samantha tense beside me and reached out a hand to still her. "Samantha has agreed to help me get organized and up to speed on the business. She's to be my consultant. I want her to stay."

Ted frowned and glanced around the room.

Jake shrugged. "Nothing in the by-laws says she can't stay. She just cannot speak or participate in any way."

"Agreed?" Ted asked the others. At their nods, he said, "Okay, she can stay. But no comments. Understood?" He glared at Samantha, making me question their past history.

The meeting progressed in a crisp, clear fashion that defied all my earlier concepts of what a boring board meeting would be like. Ted Beers was a no-nonsense man whose arrogance annoyed me, but he kept the meeting moving.

I studied him. His trim body showed every sign of careful attention to detail, from his manicured nails to the perfect styling of his coffee-colored hair. His clothing was impeccable. He asked questions and opinions of others, but never indicated in any way that I was a part of the board, new member or not. Any significant issues were quickly assigned to various other individuals to follow up, with a reminder that no discussion would take place until further information was gathered, preventing me from asking too many questions.

Lunch was brought in, and the meeting continued non-stop while we chewed quietly on sandwiches and salads and sipped soft drinks or water.

Ted wrapped up the meeting at two o'clock. "That's it for now. Remember, all issues are to be brought to my attention as soon as you have any items of worth." He checked his watch. "I've got to get back to New York for an early evening meeting. See you in January."

Without looking at me, he left as quickly as he'd arrived, in control of himself and everyone else, it seemed. His rudeness stung. The men in the room chatted among themselves and I rose, determined to fare better in the future. Ted Beers may not like the idea but I was a member of the board. An important one.

Samantha and I exchanged glances of frustration and we headed to the door. At the last moment, I stopped and cleared my throat.

"Gentlemen, it was very interesting to meet you and to learn how this board is run. Until next time, safe travels." Though I was seething inside at their treatment of us, I forced a smile.

During the surprised silence that followed, Samantha and I made our escape.

"Ted Beers is one of the most egotistical men I've ever met," said Samantha, shaking her head. "Be careful. He'll make trouble for you."

I swallowed hard. I had a lot to learn—about the business and the men who ran it.

Outside in the parking lot, we were hailed by Jonesy. "Samantha, just needed to know if anything came up in the board meeting I should know about."

She glanced at me and back to him. "No changes of any kind. Ted ran the meeting in his usual way. Jake and the others let him get away with it." Disgust coated her words.

"Thanks for the information," Jonesy said. "And make it ninety-three days, hear?"

"What was that all about?" I asked as we got into her car.

"He's just encouraging me to keep going with my program," she said with a nonchalance that didn't convince me there was nothing more.

My frustration with the meeting and now being put off by Samantha rubbed me the wrong way. "Sam, that's not what I'm talking about, and you know it."

Samantha gave me a sheepish look. "There are things going on here that some people are not comfortable with—Jonesy, especially. I'm not privy to all the information, but it has something to do with a rumor about some changes in plans and land deals. I promised Jonesy I'd give him any news if it was brought up at the meeting. That's one reason I was glad to be the one to bring you here. He and I have been talking a lot over the past several weeks, about my drinking, among other things. Jonesy has been sober for almost twenty years now and has been a wonderful support to me." Her voice shook with emotion.

I realized how difficult it must be for her. "I'm sorry, Sam. It's none of my business."

"Oh, but it is." Samantha's eyes sparked with an internal fire. "I think Ted is trying to hide something. But I'll be damned if I know what."

"Have you and Ted known one another for long?"

The corner of her lip lifted in a lopsided grimace. "He and I dated a couple of times when he was elected to the board a few years ago. It didn't work out. As you may have noticed, he's not an easy person. Capable? Yes. Warm and fuzzy? No effing way. And not very good at even that."

I blinked in surprise and burst into laughter at the wicked smile that crossed Samantha's face. Both my female cousins were beautiful, bright and outspoken—strong women in their own right. I hoped the Hartwell side of me would hold up to their standards. I was going to need every bit of strength I had to make a place for myself in the family business.

CHAPTER SEVENTEEN

For the first time in my memory, I wasn't dreading the holidays. I had family around me and a greater sense of who I was.

We celebrated Thanksgiving at Adrienne and George's home—a large, beautifully restored, white colonial house set amid a grove of trees off a country road outside the city of Portland. Viewing it in the car with Simone it was, I decided, the northern equivalent of Tara, the famous fictional Southern plantation in *Gone with the Wind*. Though very different in structure, it seemed to me to be equal in elegance as I drove up to it.

"Did you and my grandmother come here often?" I asked Simone.

She shook her head. "Holidays only. You saw how it was between her and George. But Adrienne is a nice woman and we all try to please her during these family times."

Adrienne greeted us at the door and gave us each a quick embrace. "I'm so happy you could join us this year, Marissa."

"Thank you," I said, touched by her warmth. At moments like this, I was tempted to pinch myself to make sure I wasn't dreaming.

"Here, I'll take your coats," said Hunter, as we stepped into the house. I smiled at the way he looked at his mother for approval as he helped me off with my wrap and then turned to help Simone.

Adrienne led us into the living room. A cheery fire blazed in a large brick-faced fireplace, adding warmth to the room.

George rose from the couch and looked at us with a slight smile. "Greetings. What can I get you to drink? Wine? Sherry?"

Still chilled from the outside air, I accepted a glass of red wine while Simone chose sherry. At a wooden, game table off to the side, Allison and Sam were working on a jigsaw puzzle. I went over to them. "Hi, Happy Thanksgiving. What's this?"

Allison looked up at me and smiled. "It's a holiday tradition. We put together the puzzle, which serves as an advent calendar. You'll see what I mean when we're finished."

Sam nudged her sister. "If we ever get finished."

"Stop talking," Allison playfully scolded. "It's your turn."

Hunter came over to us, a beer in hand. "I get to finish the puzzle after the two of them get stumped. Happens every time."

"Get out of here, little brother." Allison pushed him away. "It's not your turn yet."

I laughed at the interplay between them. Growing up the way I had, I'd missed so much. My thoughts shifted to Brad and I wondered what he was doing. It hurt to think he hadn't cared enough to call.

Adrienne left us to go to the kitchen. Turning down my offer to help, Allison and Sam soon joined her, Left on my own, I took over an empty chair and stared at the puzzle pieces, trying to see what went where.

Hunter came over and took the other empty seat. I took the opportunity to speak softly to him, away from George and Simone. "Look, I don't want any hard feelings between us."

He shrugged. "Okay by me. But it won't be so easy with my father. Watch out, Marissa."

I swallowed hard, grateful for the warning.

Adrienne was a perfect hostess as she oversaw the traditional Thanksgiving meal laid out on the large dining room table where her teasing, boisterous children sat. Even Uncle George, grumpily admonishing his grown children from time to time, seemed gentler than usual.

After the last of the turkey and vegetables were taken away, Adrienne offered a choice of pumpkin or pecan pie. We all laughed when Hunter said, "I'll take both."

As we lingered over coffee, Simone spoke up. "I've decided to go to my sister's for Christmas. It's been years since I've been able to do that."

I straightened in my chair. "Sister? I didn't know you had a sister."

Simone's lips drew into a narrow line. "Arinthia's state of health has kept me close these past few years. But surely you didn't think I had no one else."

At the irritation in her voice, I looked away.

Adrienne leaned over and patted my arm. "You wouldn't have known. Simone doesn't talk much about her family."

Crestfallen at Simone's news, I sat back. I'd imagined a cheery Christmas morning at Briar Cliff, fixing breakfast for the two of us, building a cozy fire in the living room just like an old-fashioned Christmas scene. Not that Simone and I were all that close. She continued to find fault with me every chance she got. I understood how disappointed she was by the last-minute changes to Arinthia's will and gave her some leeway but still it hurt.

Allison rose and tapped me on the shoulder. "You want to go outside with us? Sam wants to grab a cigarette."

I followed Allison and Samantha out to the screened-in porch at the back of the house. It had turned milder as the afternoon wore on, but I was glad for the heavy sweater I wore over my wool slacks.

"Simone can be a pain in the butt," Allison said, eying me steadily.

"Brad called her the Dragon Lady."

We all laughed.

"So, what do you know about her?" I asked. "Obviously, she hasn't talked about her family to me."

"My mother said she was just a young girl when she came to work for Arinthia and Herbert," said Sam. "Simone was one of a large French-Canadian family with thirteen children and had been sent out into the world to find work to help support her siblings. I guess they were dirt poor."

I thought back to Simone's anger at Arinthia for changing her will and realized how much Simone had wanted the house, the money, everything. They were things she'd worked for her whole life.

Allison poked me. A mischievous grin crossed her face. "Brad's a real hottie. Is he coming for Christmas?"

I took a deep breath. "Probably not. Simone basically told him to leave me alone, that I had more important things in my life, that I had to take over for Arinthia."

"No way." Allison's eyes were wide with disbelief.

Samantha shook her head. "Just because Simone has devoted her whole life to Arinthia and the business, it doesn't mean you have to. If I were you, I'd get that man up here ASAP. He seemed like a really good guy."

I kept quiet, but my mind spun with possibility. Brad hadn't called and I'd made no effort to be in touch with him. Maybe it was time I called him.

With the Christmas holiday fast approaching, I decided to do some Christmas shopping. I eagerly headed outside to my old Honda, climbed in the car and turned the key. An ominous wheezing sound came from under the hood. I tried again. This time, the car didn't even produce an unhealthy cough.

I went inside to the kitchen to see Becky. "My car died. Who should I call?"

"Why don't you take the Cadillac?" she said. "It's yours now. Arinthia kept it in perfect running order. It's not what you young people would consider the right image, but it still runs. Or better yet, you've got enough money and credit now to just go buy a new one."

I sank into a kitchen chair, literally knocked off my feet by the reality that I was now able to do such a thing. Becky was right. I could buy a new car without the usual financial worries. In fact, I could buy several, if I wanted to. I jumped to my feet.

"Where's Henry? I think I'm going to need his help."

Becky looked up from an open cookbook and gave me a wink. "He was out in the garage a few minutes ago. Go for it, honey."

When I found him, Henry was bent over his workbench, sharpening a saw. I grinned. "Henry, can you help me? My old Honda is on its last legs. I need to find something else."

Smiling, he put down his wrench and wiped his hands on his pants. "Well, now, I can do that. Yep."

Later that day I drove my new, silver, Toyota SUV through the stone gates of Briar Cliff. No matter how long I lived, I would remember this day. There'd been no waiting and worrying about credit. The bank knew my name, assured the dealership that the money was good, and, with comparatively few strokes of the pen, I had a new car.

At dinner, I happily recited the story to Simone.

She gave me a warning look that knotted my stomach. "The Hartwell name and your position at the paper mill made that possible. You've been given a great opportunity, Marissa. Don't fail."

We ate in silence until Simone said, "My sister has asked

me to come early, so I'm flying down to Florida the week before Christmas."

Unwilling to let her see my disappointment that, yet again, I would be alone for the holidays, I swallowed the last of my meal and pushed my plate away. Henry and Becky had announced they were planning to visit a niece in Pennsylvania.

A trace of bitterness entered Simone's voice. "I'm sure you'll do just fine in your new home."

The next afternoon, I was sitting in the sunroom, leafing through a coffee table book on Maine, when my cell phone broke into song. I picked it up and checked the screen.

Brad.

My pulse raced. I hit the talk button. "Brad! How are you?"

"Just wondering the same about you."

"I'm ... I'm ... okay. Still trying to get used to everything. How... how about you?" My throat had turned so dry I could barely get the words out. Waves of longing washed over me.

"I'm all right." He paused. "No, that's not true. I've missed you, Marissa. I want to see you."

My heart stopped and then sprinted forward in happy beats. I'd never stopped wanting him, loving him. He'd invaded my thoughts constantly, especially at night when my body remembered how comfortable, how wild, how soothed, how hot, he'd made me feel.

"Brad? I've missed you, too."

"I don't want some old biddy to keep us apart. She doesn't know what it's like between us."

"I'm going to be alone over the holidays. Do you want to come here?" My pulse pounded as I waited for his answer.

"Let's give us another chance, see where it takes us."

Tears of happiness stung my eyes. "Then you'll come?"

"Yeah, I'll be there. Look, a client just walked in. I'll call you later with the details."

I hung up and drifted out to the kitchen, floating on a sea of happiness.

"Do we have any Christmas decorations?" I asked Simone.

"They're stored in the attic," she replied, giving me a curious look. "They're yours now. Arinthia and I didn't do much celebrating these last couple of years. Seemed like too much work."

I climbed the attic stairs. Bare light bulbs illuminated the chilly room, exposing an array of boxes and trunks scattered about. A cluster of boxes in one corner had the word *Xmas* scrawled across them. I walked over and knelt beside them.

Taking a deep breath, I opened the first box, feeling as if I were laying a hand on history. Who knew what might be inside? Gingerly, I pulled aside the tissue paper and discovered an assortment of fragile glass ornaments in different shapes and colors. I carefully lifted a number of them out, wondering if my mother had ever hung them on a tree. They looked that old.

In another box, a red silk shawl was carefully folded. I drew it out and realized it must have been used as a tree skirt.

A separate box contained a breathtakingly beautiful porcelain angel for the top of a tree. I sat back on my heels, staggered that these old family things now belonged to me. I filled with gratitude. Had my grandmother known how much they would mean to me? Or, as Simone had indicated, were they simply neglected reminders of the past. No matter, going forward, I was going to make them part of my life.

"Find everything?" Simone asked when I approached her in her office some time later.

"I can use most of the decorations, but I'll have to replace the lights."

"Some ornaments are very old and, I suppose, quite

valuable. The blown glass ones, especially."

Curious, I settled in a chair in front of her desk. "Did my mother enjoy Christmas here at Briar Cliff?"

Simone's eyes lit with memories. "It was a wonderful time. The children were so excited and the house was always decorated beautifully."

"I wish I'd really known my mother. Uncle Tim, too."

A wave of sadness crossed Simone's features but was quickly overtaken by her usual, composed manner.

"'No use crying over spilt milk,' as they say."

I rose, wishing I could feel warmth for Simone. Each time I thought we might share a friendly moment, she withdrew, ruining the moment.

I covered the mantel in the living room with greens and candles, wrapped a holly rope around the banister leading to the second floor, and placed candles and decorations everywhere I could. At the Rotary Club's Christmas tree lot, I chose the biggest tree I could handle and drove it home on top of my new SUV. I wanted everything to look perfect for Brad's visit.

He called just before the holiday. "Looks like I can make it in time for dinner Christmas Eve. We're closing the office early."

"I can't wait to see you," I said, meaning every word of it. He would be my family for the holidays. And maybe then we'd be able to use the time together to move forward with our relationship. I hoped so. I really did love him.

Simone left for her sister's, and I wandered through the house feeling for the first time as if it were really mine. I rubbed my hand over the cherry dining room table which Becky kept in perfect condition. Observing the antique corner cupboard filled with china and silver pieces, I was awestruck. These treasures were mine now. And because they'd once belonged to family members, they meant so much more to me than just nice things.

Upstairs I approached Arinthia's room. I opened the door and peered inside, half-expecting to see Arinthia's looming presence.

"Grandmother?" I whispered, but the only answer was the echo of my words.

I stepped over the threshold. Weeks before, Simone and I had gone through Arinthia's jewelry, choosing the pieces we wished to keep. But I hadn't wanted to do the same with her clothing. Simone had willingly taken on the task of seeing that my grandmother's personal things were distributed to the right charities. The closet was empty of everything but pretty pink fabric hangers lined up evenly along the closet rod. Her initialed silver brush and mirror sat on top of her mahogany chest. I opened the bureau drawers. They, too, were empty.

Simone had done an admirable job. I closed the last drawer, feeling as empty as the room. I twisted my mother's gold ring around on my finger. As soon as the holidays were over, I'd go to St. Andrews school to see what I could learn about either of my parents.

The ring slipped off my finger and fell to the floor with a clanging noise. Bending down to retrieve it, I noticed the corner of a photograph peeking out from under the chest of drawers. I picked it up and gazed at it. In the picture, Simone and my grandmother, both looking very young, sat on the front porch steps of Briar Cliff, squinting into the camera.

Arinthia sat tall and straight, looking somber and every bit the self-contained matron she was. Simone wore a wide smile and held her hands in front of her rounded stomach. My heart began to pound. I studied her closer. Simone was pregnant!

Questions assaulted me in rapid-fire succession. Had she lost a baby? Whose baby was it?

I sat back on my heels. No wonder Simone had talked so lovingly of Thea and Tim. They must have seemed like her own children. With new respect for her, I tucked the photograph in my pocket. When Simone returned, I'd try to find a gentle way to ask her questions about it.

Lady barked, and I heard Becky call out, "Marissa? I'm here."

I went downstairs to greet her, happy for the sound of her voice.

Days seemed to drag as I awaited Brad's arrival. I kept busy, going through the mountain of information I'd been given on the paper mill—checking numbers, learning who our customers and suppliers were, and the various steps of processing. But at night, alone in my bed, the memory of Brad's arms holding me close spun other, more intimate thoughts through my mind.

Christmas Eve morning, I sang along with the radio as I wrapped stocking gifts for Brad. "*Chestnuts roasting on an open fire ...*" I warbled. Lady's ears perked at my squeaky notes. She whined. "Okay I'll stop," I laughed. "But I'm so excited! Brad's coming here, Lady!"

The phone rang. I ran to answer it. Brad said he'd let me know when he was on his way.

"Marissa? Brad, here. Bad news. My father has had a mild heart attack. I'm at the hospital with my mother and Aunt Doris. They say he's going to be fine, but I promised to stay here for a day or two to make sure everything is okay. Can you postpone Christmas one day for me? I'll get there as soon as I can."

Disappointment weighed me down, but I fought to keep upbeat. "Of course. We'll celebrate whenever you get here. I'm so sorry about your father. Please tell your parents I'm thinking of them."

"Thanks. I'll call you later," Brad said and hung up.

"Well, Lady, so much for a romantic day." Deflated, I plopped down on the couch and decided I'd take up Adrienne's offer to join them for Christmas dinner. In the meantime, Lady and I would share Christmas Eve like we usually did. Alone.

That night, after dinner, I listened to Christmas music and wandered through the house, admiring the decorations, wondering what other Christmases here might have been like. Each decoration, each room surely held secrets of happier or perhaps sadder times. If only they could talk!

I called Brad to wish him Merry Christmas and was forced to leave a message. Slipping into bed, I hugged my pillow close to me, wishing it were him.

Christmas at Adrienne and George's house was a replay of Thanksgiving—lots of food, laughter, and teasing. Hunter had accepted a dinner invitation from Bettina's family, but his sisters carried on as if he were there— talking about him and teasing one another.

I watched them, thinking of all the gifts that I could have been given, this gathering was the best. It wasn't until dessert was served that I had reason to think otherwise.

George cleared his throat, gave Adrienne an apologetic look and turned to me. "Sorry to bring up business on an occasion like this, Marissa, but I thought you ought to know that Ted Beers phoned me yesterday. He would be a lot more comfortable having Hunter on the board, considering that you want Samantha, here, to consult with you, as you put it."

Surprised, I glanced over at Samantha. She stared stonily at her father, and I knew beneath that hard look was a lot of pain.

"George," reprimanded Adrienne. "You are not to ruin this time together with any such talk. I'll not have it."

I rose. "I'm not going to discuss this now or in the future, Uncle George. Samantha and I are working together."

George glared at me and turned to Samantha as if to say something.

"C'mon." Allison tapped Samantha on the shoulder. "Time for a fresh air break."

I followed Allison and Samantha out of the room, furious that George was still trying to undermine my position with Rivers Papers.

Out on the porch, Samantha paced back and forth in angry strides. "What do I have to do to make him respect me?" she wailed in a pitiful tone. "Every time I seem to be going forward, he holds me back."

"Unh, unh," said Allison, shaking a finger at her. "You hold yourself back. The hell with what Father thinks. You and everyone else know Hunter can't hold a candle to you, business-wise. Nobody can beat you down, but yourself."

"What's going on with Ted and Hunter and your father?" I asked. "Why are they communicating about me? It doesn't seem right."

Sam stopped her pacing and stared at me. A slow, sly smile crossed her face. "Marissa, you're right. This smells like a rat or a couple of them, and I'm just the kitty cat who can catch them. Leave it up to me."

Grinning, Samantha and I exchanged a high-five. Our battle was about to begin.

CHAPTER EIGHTEEN

There had been rumors of a nor'easter taking shape, but the suspected storm stayed out to sea. I awoke to a fairy tale landscape. A light layer of snow had fallen during the night, lending a make-believe coating of sugar to the trees in the side yard. The dark brown bare branches, iced with wet snow, reached for the gray skies like bony fingers stretching to touch its velvety surface. In front of the house, the deep blue-gray waters rolled toward the sandy beach and reeled back, leaving their cold, wet frothy kisses behind.

Lady and I took a walk along the beach. Chilled to the bone from the brisk wind, I led her back to the house. Brad had left a text message on my phone, saying he'd left for Maine and should arrive early afternoon. I built a fire in the living room fireplace, eagerly awaiting his arrival.

As the hours wore on, my anticipation grew. At each sound of a car drawing near, I raced to the windows. By the time Brad finally drove his SUV through the gates of Briar Cliff, I mutely stared at him through the frosty window pane as if he were a figment of my imagination.

Lady barked and, realizing he was really there, we burst through the back entrance together, racing to reach him.

He climbed out of the car and, grinning at me, held his arms wide open. I rushed into them and nestled against his warmth.

"God, I'm glad to get here. The traffic was terrible. All those sale shoppers out and about." He hugged me hard.

Lady poked Brad's legs with her nose for attention. He

chuckled, leaned over and obligingly gave her several pats on the head. Watching the two of them together, my heart warmed with affection. I took his hand and tugged him forward.

"Come inside! Christmas has arrived!"

"Hold on!" He grabbed his luggage from the backseat of the car, and we entered the house, eager to begin our special day.

Brad stood in the middle of the downstairs hallway and gazed around him. "Wow! You've really decorated the place."

I gave him a satisfied smile. "Most of the decorations are years old. It's so exciting for me to have family heirlooms."

Brad cocked his head and studied me a moment. "You're really into this family thing, aren't you?"

"I know a little bit more about my mother. Now, I want to find my father. I have a feeling the key to him is through St. Andrews, the private school my mother attended. I plan to go there after the holidays, while Simone is away."

His gaze penetrated mine. "Would you like me to go with you? I know how important it is to you."

"You'd do that for me?" My eyes grew misty at his offer. I took hold of his hand. "I'd love it. I have no idea what I might have to face."

Brad gave my hand a squeeze of encouragement. "We'll do it together."

I gazed up into his face, seeing his kindness, his goodness. He was the one man with whom I could see spending my life. Brad's eyes deepened in color as I gazed at him, full of gratitude for the kind of man he was.

He drew me to him and covered my lips with his. I raised my arms and hugged him to me, welcoming the taste of him. I felt so safe, so wonderful in his embrace. His body reacted , and heat coiled through me. Our kiss deepened. When we finally pulled apart, we smiled at one another. The chemistry between us was definitely there.

Brad glanced down at his suitcase. "Where do you want me to put this?"

"Come with me." I took his hand and led him up the winding stairs. At the door to my room, I stopped, suddenly shy, and waited for some kind of indication from him.

He set down his bag, clasped my face in both hands, and planted his lips on mine with such tenderness, such strength, that no other response was necessary.

Brad pulled away, firmly closed the door against Lady's curiosity and led me to my bed. His face was flushed with desire as he drew me against him. I could feel his arousal press against me but I was unafraid. The special magic we'd shared in the past was still a part of us.

He lifted my sweater over my head and undid my bra, freeing my breasts for his loving touches.

Tugging the shirt out of his pants, I stroked his warm chest, feeling the strong heartbeat beneath. He groaned softly and guided my hand lower. I hesitated and let the passion I felt for him take over.

We moved onto the bed. Naked now, we let our eyes, our hands, then our mouths explore.

Later, as we lay stretched out together on the bed, I uttered a sigh of pure pleasure. Brad's lovemaking was everything I'd remembered and then some.

"That's my Christmas gift, huh?" Brad teased. His eyes sparkled with humor.

"I've got a whole day of pleasure planned."

"Give me a few minutes and I'll be ready," teased Brad, knowing full well that's not what I meant. Laughing, I lay my head on his shoulder.

Later, while Brad napped on my bed, I went downstairs to slide a small tenderloin of beef in the oven for dinner. Then I carried a plate of cheese and crackers to the living room.

Pausing at the entrance, I gazed at the Christmas tree in the corner and inhaled its holiday pine scent. The tree's bright colored lights sparkled like fragments of a shattered rainbow. The glass balls, plumed glass birds, and hand-blown Santa ornaments scattered about the tree had presumably graced other Christmas trees in much earlier times. The thought of my mother and uncle playing beside one like it filled me with a new-found peace. My eyes grew misty. I felt as if I were moving forward into the future for them because they couldn't do it for themselves.

"Penny for your thoughts," said Brad softly, coming up quietly behind me.

I turned to him with a smile. "I was imagining my mother and her brother seeing a similar tree in this room years ago. It gives me a sense of roots."

Brad placed a hand on my shoulder. "I understand but, like the saying goes, you also need wings and a sense of freedom. Don't get too caught up in the past, Marissa."

I remained silent. There was so much I didn't know about the people who lived here.

"Marissa, I just don't want you to get hurt," Brad said.

"I know." I gave him a quick kiss on the cheek. "There's a bottle of wine on the counter in the kitchen. Will you open it while I put on some music?"

Brad brought in the bottle of merlot and poured us each a glass as I finished loading the CDs. We settled on the couch and lifted our glasses.

"Merry Christmas, Brad, I'm so happy you're here with me." In the soft orange glow from the embers in the fireplace, I handed him the Christmas stocking I'd filled with gifts for him. He gave me a similar stocking, filled with intriguingly wrapped gifts.

We'd given one another similar items, CDs, and books. Then Brad handed me a small black velvet jewelry box. Seeing it, my heart pounded with dismay. I loved Brad, but it was too soon to even think of marriage.

"Go ahead. Open it," Brad's eyes shone.

My fingers fumbled as I lifted the top of the box. Small diamonds encircled in gold sparkled up at me. Earrings winked at my foolishness and I let out a nervous laugh.

"Do you like them?"

"They're beautiful," I gasped, taking them out of the box and holding them in my hands. Tears misted my eyes. "I've never received a gift like this."

His look tender, Brad smiled and brushed a strand of hair away from my face. "I don't know where our relationship is going, Marissa, but I hope you'll wear these to remind you of me."

I hurried over to the antique mirror in the hallway and inserted the diamonds in my ears, turning this way and that to catch the brilliant light in them.

Brad looked on with a satisfied smile. "'Looks great with that red hair of yours."

Feeling like a fiery-haired queen, I went over to him and hugged him close.

We stretched out on the couch together and listened to the new CDs. We didn't have to speak; just lying close to one another was enough. The heat from the fire competed with the heat between us.

"Brad, how is your father doing? A heart attack, no matter how mild, is dangerous."

"Yeah, it was pretty scary. You know how my father is, bigger than life. I was shocked to see him lying there in the hospital bed. It makes me realize the law firm is really on my shoulders." He let out a sigh.

"It's nice that you were around to help. How's your Mother doing?"

"She's hanging on but it's changed her, too." He rubbed my back. "To tell you the truth, I was glad to get away."

"When is Simone coming back?" Brad asked. "You okay here by yourself?"

"She won't be back until after New Year's Day. I thought I'd be uneasy living all alone in this big place, but I've been comfortable here."

"Who would have thought all this would have happened to you," Brad commented, indicating the house with a wave of his arm. "It's still a bit of a mystery, isn't it?"

"I've decided to use this holiday break with Simone away to see what I can find out about my father. I'll ask about him at St. Andrews. Maybe he knew her there."

"Simone doesn't know who he is?"

I shook my head. "She says no one does. And I still don't know why my mother ran away."

He looked at me thoughtfully. "It had to be something pretty big to make her leave home at such a young age."

I pulled Brad to his feet. "C'mon, we'd better get some dinner. The beef must be about ready."

Inside the kitchen, I prepared a salad, set the beef on the counter and checked the potato casserole I'd made earlier.

Brad carried the tenderloin into the dining room. I hurried to light the candles in the silver candlestick holders I'd pulled out of the sideboard. Setting the table earlier, I'd gone all out, using my grandmother's silver flatware and her Limoges china. After experiencing years of lonely Christmas holidays, I stared in wonderment at the lovely scene and the very special man before me. Brad held out a chair for me.

Laughing, I took a seat, and he sat next to me.

"Cheers, Marissa." He lifted his glass.

"And to you, Brad." My heart overflowed with happiness. I loved him. It was that simple.

With soft music playing in the background, we ate in companionable silence.

"Thanks for making this a special holiday," Brad said.

"It's the first happy Christmas I can remember."

He grinned. "Even if it's a day late?"

I returned his smile. "Oh, yes. It's been perfect."

After dinner, we took a walk outside with Lady, then Brad and I settled down for the night. The presence of him in my bed felt odd yet comfortable. I reached over to brush a lock of hair off his forehead and burst out laughing.

"What's up?" he asked.

"It's the lacy edging on the pillow, and the pink wallpaper in the background," I giggled. "It's just not you."

He twisted the pillow around so the lace-covered hem hung over his head like an old-fashioned nightcap. I hugged him to me, still laughing softly, thinking how much I liked this big hulk of a man. Someday I'd redecorate the room for him, but I wasn't ready to make those changes yet.

In the morning, I woke and hurried to get dressed. I'd invited Allison and Samantha to brunch.

Downstairs, I quickly started the coffee and set the table.

Brad walked into the kitchen just as a car drove into the driveway.

"Just in time," I said, going to the front door to let them in.

Allison walked inside, carrying a covered plate. Samantha followed, holding a plastic container.

"Mother sent this over. One of her special coffee cakes." Allison set the plate on the counter. "It's still warm."

"And I've got fresh squeezed orange juice," Sam said.

I gave them each a hug and reintroduced them to Brad, who served us mugs of hot coffee.

"Interesting news," Sam said to me. "Ted Beers called my father yesterday, presumably to see if he'd made any progress in getting you off the board. I answered the phone and before he could say anything, I told him how happy I was that you were so interested in the business." She laughed humorlessly. "I could tell he was really pissed."

"What's going on?" Brad looked from Sam to me.

I shook my head. "As you know, if I hadn't shown up unexpectedly, Hunter was set to take Arinthia's place on the board. That's what Ted Beers wanted, and apparently, still does."

"Marissa and I think there might be something shady going on at Rivers Papers," added Sam. "We're going to do a little investigation on our own, behind the scenes."

Brad's brow creased. "I've read news stories about Ted Beers. He's a real cut-throat guy and a very successful businessman. He hasn't achieved either status by being nice."

"Don't worry about Sam," Allison said, waving a hand of dismissal. "She's one smart businesswoman herself. And Marissa seems to be tough."

Sam gave her sister a warm look and smiled at me. "We Hartwell women stick together."

I returned her smile, troubled by what Brad had said.

In the dining room, the four of us ate and chatted comfortably. It was interesting to see the interaction between Brad and my cousins. I could tell they really liked him.

"So what are you two going to do for the rest of the week?" Allison asked.

"Tomorrow we're going to St. Andrews,"

Allison's eyes rounded. "The school that Thea attended?"

"I'm trying to find out who my father is."

"You have no idea?" Sam's eyebrows rose. "No one in the family ever talked about him, but I'd think someone might have known who he was."

I twisted my mother's gold ring off my finger and held it up. "I found this in a dresser drawer in my mother's room when I was clearing out her house. Aside from the plain gold hoops she wore in her ears, she didn't have any other jewelry. I never saw her wear this ring."

Allison took the ring from me. "With its carved flowers and leaves, it's sweet."

"Uh, huh. Look at the initials inside. MC and BB. I figure MC is for Margaret Cole. Now I have to find BB."

Allison handed the ring back to me. "A mystery. How exciting."

"Scary," countered Sam.

Terrifying, I thought to myself.

CHAPTER NINETEEN

St. Andrews School was in the town of Maynard, east of Bangor, about three hours away. Words were not necessary as we traveled north on I-95. Brad was well aware of my tension, and rather than talk endlessly about it, left me to my driving and the thoughts that whirled in my head and played with my mind.

Driving into Maynard, I had a sense of déjà vu. It, even more than the mill town of Riverton, was a close replica of Barnham. Perhaps all small towns in the northeast are like this, I thought, as we passed the boxy, yellow brick post office, an old, white clapboard church with a tall steeple reaching for the sky, and a cluster of red brick storefronts along the main street.

It wasn't until we reached St. Andrews School, perched on a hill overlooking the small valley containing the town, that I understood Maynard represented something much more solid than Barnham. The red brick administrative building was tall and stately, rising four floors. Two huge white pillars flanked the wide front entranceway.

I parked the car in the almost empty parking lot alongside the building, and we got out.

"You sure we'll be able to speak to someone? It looks awfully quiet," said Brad.

"When I called here last week, the secretary told me a few members of the faculty and staff would be holding down the fort." I squeezed my hands together nervously.

Brad took my arm. "Even if you don't learn anything about

your mother or father, you'll have the satisfaction of knowing you tried."

My gut twisted. "There are answers here. I feel it inside."

At the last minute, I took off my winter coat so that the white St. Andrews blazer could easily be seen. Taking a deep breath, I climbed the front stairs, clinging to Brad.

We entered the building and walked down a wide marble-floored hallway, past a small formal sitting room to an office marked *Admissions*.

A pleasant-faced woman looked up from behind her desk, startled to see us. Her gaze traveled from our faces to the emblem on the blazer. The nameplate on her desk read Kathryn Givens. "Can I help you?"

"My mother was once a student here at St. Andrews. Is there any way I can get information about her? Are there school records I can see?"

The woman frowned. "Those old records are stored off campus. Is your mother aware you're doing this?"

"My mother died several months ago. I'm trying to learn more about her time here," I explained. "It's a pilgrimage of sorts for me."

She set down her paperwork. "I'm fairly new here but the assistant headmaster, Roscoe Redding, happens to live on campus. He might be willing to see you. If you'll have a seat, I'll call him. By the way, what was your mother's name?"

"Margaret... I mean Thea Hartwell."

Ms. Given's eyebrows shot up. A look of dismay changed her placid features.

"Are you Arinthia Hartwell's granddaughter?"

"Why, yes, though I've just recently learned that."

Kathryn Givens' lips thinned and her manner became decidedly cooler.

"Is something wrong?"

"Mrs. Hartwell made some inquiries about her daughter last summer, and, I'm afraid it wasn't a pleasant conversation."

"Really? I'm sorry."

A nasty thought occurred to me. Arinthia could hardly talk last summer. It must have been Simone who'd spoken on Arinthia's behalf—another instance of taking over. I turned to Kathryn Givens, pleading for her help.

"You'll call the assistant headmaster?"

She gave me a sheepish look. "Oh, yes, I'm sorry. I should never have said a word about that phone call. Let me try Roscoe now."

She dialed a number and quietly spoke into the phone. Moments later she turned to me with a smile.

"Mr. Redding has agreed to meet with you. However, he asks that you meet at his residence instead of here."

"I'd be happy to." My heart pounded with anticipation.

After being given directions, Brad and I walked across the quadrangle to a small, gray-shingled house tucked between two brick dormitory buildings.

The bespectacled, stoop-shouldered, white-haired man who answered our knock looked every bit a typical teacher. I smiled inwardly at the leather patches on his cardigan sweater and the odor of pipe tobacco that clung to it when he opened the door.

"My goodness." He eyed me carefully. "For a moment I thought you were Thea herself. So you're her daughter?"

"Marissa Cole," I said, holding out my hand. "And this is Brad Crawford."

He shook our hands. "Come in, come in. You'll have to forgive the appearance of my bachelor quarters, but I make a very acceptable pot of coffee. Would you care for some?"

"Thanks. Sounds good to me," said Brad.

"Me, too." I was grateful we'd have this opportunity to spend time here. I observed the stack of books lying beside a large brown leather lounge chair in the living room. More books, upright and lying flat to fit on shelves, filled bookcases on either side of a stone fireplace.

"Sit," Roscoe said. "I'll get the coffee and be right back."

"He knew my mother," I whispered to Brad triumphantly after Roscoe had left the room. Excitement whirled inside me. Perhaps he knew my father, too.

Brad winked and gave me an encouraging pat on the back.

Roscoe returned to the living room, carrying a small tray on which three steaming mugs sat, along with teaspoons, a bowl of sugar and a small pitcher of cream.

My mouth turned dry as I waited for him to finish serving us coffee. Questions were burning inside me. Here, at last, was a man who could possibly answer all of them.

Roscoe took a sip of coffee and studied me intently. "So, Marissa Cole, Kathryn Givens explained you've come to find out what you can about your mother, who died a while ago. Did your mother talk of St. Andrews? I see you've got her blazer." He shook his head. "Haven't seen one of those for many years. St. Andrews is now co-educational and is for students who have a difficult time learning to settle down."

"You've been here all these years?" I asked.

"I came here in my twenties some forty years ago. Thought it would be for a short time, but, as you can see, one thing led to another, and I found a family here that I didn't have on my own."

"You teach English, sir?" Brad asked, indicating the books that filled every nook and cranny.

Roscoe smiled. "Good guess."

I twitched anxiously, eager to be beyond small talk. "You knew my mother?" I blurted out. "Will you tell me about her?"

His blue gaze was steady on me, giving the impression he was gauging my likeness to my mother. "Every once in a while a student comes along that shows so much promise you can hardly wait to have them in class. Thea Hartwell was one of those students. She was bright, popular and eager to learn."

Unexpected pride filled me and then made me want to cry. What in God's name had happened to her?

Roscoe hesitated. "On the surface, Thea was happy-go-lucky, but I knew from the essays she wrote that there was a dark side to her, too. I suspected her family life was not happy. There was a neediness to her that was both charming and disturbing."

"She was very close to her father and never got along with her mother, I'm told." At Roscoe's look of surprise, I explained. "My mother and I didn't get along, either. That's why I don't know much about her. I'm trying to understand."

"She left before finishing her sophomore year," said Roscoe. "That was a major disappointment for me and the school. I've thought of her often during the years, and wondered whatever became of her."

Loyalty to my mother forced me to choose my words carefully. "She changed her name to Margaret Cole and ran away to Barnham, New York. That's where I grew up. It's a nice enough town, but she was not a happy person and our life wasn't easy."

"I suspected as much. When she returned from the mid-year break that year, she was a different person—uncooperative, challenging and defiant. I assumed it was a problem from home and wondered if drugs were playing a part. I tried to talk to her about it, but she refused to discuss it. As a teacher and her guidance counselor, that was another disappointment for me."

Roscoe sat back in his chair and sipped his coffee. "Funny

how some students stand out in your mind, even after all these years."

My body felt cold. "Mr. Redding? I believe she left school because of me. I'm also trying to determine who my father is. Do you have any idea who it might be?"

Roscoe rubbed his chin, lost in thought. When he focused on me again, he said, "Thea was very popular, as I said. When the young ladies had mixers with other schools nearby, she was always surrounded by a group of young men. It would be hard to pick out one in particular."

I took a deep breath. "I believe his initials were B.B."

Roscoe leaned back in his chair.

I held my breath, while he mentally scoured the past for answers.

"Sorry," he said, with a shake of his head. "I can't think who that might be. I wish I had more to tell you, but I don't."

I let out a disappointed sigh. Rising, I offered my hand. "Thank you so much for taking the time to see me. Here's my phone number. If you think of anything else, please give me a call."

"I hope I've helped in some small way." Roscoe got to his feet. "Your mother was an outstanding person in many respects. Maybe those are the things to remember."

At his gentle words, tears came to my eyes.

Brad put a protective arm around me. "Thanks for seeing us."

We exited into the blustery air and I shivered, uncertain whether it was from the cold chill or the knowledge that I might never know who I really was.

"Let's make a dash for it." Brad took my hand.

We'd just begun to sprint when Roscoe Redding's shout stopped us.

I turned around, surprised to see him waving us back.

Hope pounded inside me, matching my hurried steps against the hard surface of the ground as we ran back to him.

"I just thought of something," he said, motioning us up on the porch. "The boy all the girls had a crush on was the custodian's part-time assistant, a boy he and his wife took in. His name was William Carpenter, but the girls all called him Billy Boy."

I gripped my hands together, heart pounding. "Where can I find him?"

He shook his head. "Sadly, he was killed during boot camp in the Army. But the custodian and his wife still live in town. Come on in and I'll give them a call."

I entered the house on the heels of Roscoe, eager as a puppy to get inside. We waited in the living room while he went to the kitchen to make the call. Sitting on the edge of my seat, I twisted my mother's gold ring around and around on a finger that felt frozen. Was Billy Boy the man my mother had loved? If my mother had changed her name to Margaret Cole as a matter of secrecy, perhaps she'd also used the code initials "B.B" for William Carpenter. In a way, it made sense.

Roscoe came into the living room and handed me a piece of paper. "Here's their address and directions. Mary and John French are very anxious to meet you, though they can't promise anything beyond telling you about Billy."

Brad and I exchanged a concerned look. I turned back to Roscoe. "Even if he isn't my father, I want to know about him."

"Good luck, young lady," said Roscoe. "And you, too, young man."

I gave him a big smile. "Thanks for all your help."

Following Roscoe's directions, we drove into the heart of Maynard and pulled up in front of a brown duplex with cream trim. Its neatness stood out in this poorer section of town. Gazing at the house from the car, I noticed cheery Christmas lights blinking on the tree inside, and prayed this visit would provide me with answers to my long-held questions.

"You ready?" Brad's voice was soft with concern.

I took a deep breath. "As ready as I ever will be."

We walked up the front steps to the house together, and then Brad knocked. A short, plump woman with neatly trimmed gray hair answered the door with a friendly smile.

"Come in," she said. "I'm Mary French. You must be Marissa and Brad. My husband John and I are happy to talk to you."

Brad followed me inside. The smell of pine filled the air, and I glanced at the tree, decorated with an assortment of paper ornaments. Charmed, I walked over to the tree for a closer look.

"Aren't they beautiful?" Mary commented. "All handmade. Every one of them. We took in foster children for years, and each child was asked to make a special ornament for the tree. We have the most precious collection anyone could have. Of course, they're just pictures drawn or pasted on paper, but I wouldn't have it any other way. They're from my kids."

"Show her the one from Billy."

I turned around to see who'd spoken. A heavy-set man with a fringe of gray hair smiled up at me from a wide, overstuffed chair in the corner of the room. A walker and cane rested beside him.

"John can't get up to greet you," Mary explained. "His hips aren't so good. He's had one operation already and is due for another."

I went over to greet him. The skin of his hand was rough to the touch but his grip was gentle.

"Pleased to meet you, Mr. French. I'm Marissa Cole and this is Brad Crawford. Mr. Redding explained why we're here?"

"To talk about Billy."

Mary walked over to us and held out a round piece of paper, shaped like a ball ornament. "Take a look."

I accepted the paper from her and drew in a breath of surprise. Billy had drawn an opening in the bulb, like those I especially liked. Inside the opening, in pen and ink, he'd sketched a nativity scene. The minute details of it made the scene come alive.

"Very talented, he was," said Mary proudly.

"Yes, I can see that." I took the gold ring off my finger and handed it to Mary. "This ring was my mother's. It has the initials M.C. and B.B. inscribed inside. My mother called herself Margaret Cole. I wonder if B.B. was for Billy Carpenter. I understand his nickname was Billy Boy." My voice quivered. "Do you think it's possible?"

"Sit down, honey," clucked Mary, handing the ring back to me. "I'm going to bring us some cookies and milk. I can't think on an empty stomach."

John winked at me after Mary left the room. "We had lunch not long ago. Mary just wants to give you a treat, as if you were one of the kids."

I sympathized, but couldn't sit still. She hadn't answered my question.

Mary returned to the room with a heaping plate of cookies and four glasses of milk.

"There now," she said, after serving all of us, "I'll just set this down beside you, Brad, so you can help yourself."

"These sure taste good." Brad finished one cookie and reached for another.

Mary beamed with pleasure, then, grew serious. She sat down beside me on the couch and took one of my hands in hers, which were gnarled with age.

"We'll tell you what we know about Billy. That's all we can

do. Billy came into the system when his mother died of a drug overdose. She was a real hippie type. He was fifteen by the time he came to us." She shook her head. "He was as tough as nails, that one. It took him several months to settle in with our rules. But underneath his toughness, I saw a scared boy. Once he understood that he was part of our family, that we weren't going to desert him, he was one of the best. Billy helped John at St. Andrews after school. He was a good lookin' kid. Tall, dark and handsome, you might say."

"When I took him up to St. Andrews the girls went wild," John chimed in. "He was quiet and tried to stay out of their way. Funny, it just made them want him more."

"Did he ever date any of the girls?"

John shook his head. "My rule was that he couldn't. Mixing with those rich girls would only bring heartache, I told him."

Mary held out her hands in a helpless gesture. "We have no way of knowing for sure whom he saw, but there were times when he was late getting home. And one time he asked me if I knew what real love was. And he mentioned a girl named Margaret in his note to us."

"Mr. Redding said he was killed in the Army," I said softly. "When did that happen?"

Mary's eyes filled with tears.

"I'm sorry ..." I began, remorse eating at me for bringing up a still painful subject.

"It's all right, dear," said Mary. "It's just that, in the end, I feel we failed him. You see, Billy finished his high school courses at the end of the first semester of his senior year. We begged him to stay in school but he said he couldn't stay with us anymore, that he wanted to sign up for the Army, that then people would believe he was a good man, a real man."

"We tried to tell him that he was being foolish, that we already knew what a good person he was." She shook her head sadly. "Somethin' happened to him that winter, somethin' that made him change. I'm sure it had to do with the note he left us when he went away."

I felt the blood drain from my face. "Do you think that something was me? My birthday is in August."

Mary squeezed my hand. "Oh, honey, I know what you're trying to say. I'm just not sure."

"Do you have a picture of Billy?"

Mary and John exchanged glances; Mary rose to her feet. "Let me go find it."

She returned holding a photograph in a gold frame.

My stomach clenched at the possibility the picture was of my father.

Mary handed it to me. "As I said, he was a handsome lad."

The young man who looked out at the camera was indeed handsome, with dark hair that dipped down over a broad brow. He wore a sweater and blue jeans and leaned against the wide trunk of a tree in a casual manner. The guarded expression on his face spoke to me of past hurts but his gaze was clear, direct. I had the impression of an earnest young man who wasn't afraid to look you square in the eye.

Looking for identifying features, my fingers traced the outline of his strong jaw, the way his ears hugged his head and...

My heart beat rapidly with hope. "Did he have a widow's peak?"

Brad looked at me sharply, aware of the excitement in my voice.

Mary answered slowly, "A bit of one, yes. Why?"

I lifted my hair away from my face. "I always wondered where this came from. Maybe it was from him."

Mary's face registered surprise.

"Mother, see if you can find the note," John said. "Maybe

an answer lies there."

Mary left the room again, and I couldn't stop playing with the ring. Billy Carpenter my father? I needed to know.

She returned and handed me a yellowed sheet of tablet paper. The writing in pencil was faded in spots and I imagined how many times it had been held and read.

My eyes skimmed the crudely formed words of farewell until they reached a particular sentence. "I aim to prove I'm able to take care of myself and a family," he'd written. "There's a girl named Margaret. I love her and want to take care of her. My friend Clyde and I are signing up for the Army." The rest of the letter mentioned he'd be in touch and thanked John and Mary for their help.

I set the paper down in my lap and let the tears flow. Margaret Cole and Billy Boy. My parents. It all fit. A chill swept across my shoulders, freezing my insides. My father had known Clyde. That's why my mother had let him stay with us, unwilling or unable to make him leave. I knew it in my soul. Fresh tears streamed down my face. It had all been such a waste.

Mary handed me a Kleenex and dabbed at her own eyes. "The saddest thing of all, the thing that hurts me the most, is I didn't have a chance to say good-bye to him. He packed his bags and left one night, leaving this note behind. He'd gone ahead and enlisted like he said he would. We received one postcard thanking us for everything. The next word about him was from the Army."

Mary kept dabbing at her eyes, though tears slipped through.

"Now, Mother," said John, "no need to blame yourself. We did all we could for that boy. He was a good boy who loved us both."

"And he loved my mother," I added, my voice full of

wonder. I touched the ring on my finger as if to confirm it.

Mary gave me a steady look. "Tell me about her."

"Her real name was Thea Hartwell ..." I began and stopped at John's gasp.

"That's it!" he said. "That's who you remind me of. Uh, yuh. She was one of the special ones. Poor kids. No wonder it never worked out for them. Not with her coming from a family like that." He gave me a sheepish look. "Sorry, I didn't mean that quite the way it sounded."

I held up a hand. "That's okay." I told them what I could about my mother, leaving out some of the grim details, and leaned back in my seat, emotionally drained.

Mary handed me a paper and a pencil. "Give me your address. I'll send you a copy of the photograph and the note. You understand I can't let go of these."

I wrote down the information and handed it to her, overwhelmed by all I'd learned.

Brad sent me a silent signal.

I rose to my feet. "Thank you for seeing us. We appreciate your time."

Mary stood beside me and gave me a hug. "Honey, I know what you're really looking for. Sometimes the answer to finding out about your family is to reach down deep within yourself and bring out the best of who you are."

Though my lips were stiff with the effort of holding back my emotions, I managed to say good-bye.

Brad put his arm around me as we walked to the car. I leaned into him, needing his strength. I'd unraveled part of the mystery of my mother but there was still more to the story.

I had to discover the rest.

CHAPTER TWENTY

New Year's Eve began bright and sunny. I lay in bed, looking out through the window at the beautiful day, basking in the glow of spending more time with Brad.

I planned to make it fun. Simone was due to come home right after the New Year and I'd be back into a routine of studying the paper mill business and my role in it. Ted Beers was not going to get away with dismissing me. I'd be ready for him.

Brad rolled over next to me and sleepily traced my lips with a finger. "Smiling already?"

I laughed softly. "I can't wait to see Ted Beers' expression when Samantha and I go to the next board meeting. In the new few weeks, I'm going to learn all I can about the paper mill business and beat him at his own game."

"Sounds like serious business." Brad rose to a sitting position beside me. His hair formed a tousled crown of brown and his dark whiskers coated the strong jaw I loved to caress. His brow furrowed as he gazed at me.

"Marissa, where are we going with this?"

My heartbeat galloped through me. "What do you mean?"

Brad reached for my hand. "I want you to come to Barnham and see what it would be like to live there again. With me."

Uneasiness gripped me. I'd seen what living with a man had done to my mother—and to me. Brad was very different from Clyde Breeden, but fear of such a commitment coiled deep within me. I gazed into Brad's sweet face, afraid of hurting him.

I stroked his bristly jaw, lovingly. "You know I love you. I wish it were a simple matter of my saying 'yes,' but I can't think of anything like that until I have things settled here. My whole family is counting on me." I nestled closer. "Why don't you trying living here? I'm going to need legal help to deal with all I've been handed."

Regret coated Brad's features. He shook his head. "I can't up and leave my father—especially now. The doctors have put him on a restricted regimen, which means I've got to take care of the bulk of the business."

We stared at one another helplessly. Family commitments had to be met before we could think of a permanent future together. And deep down, I wondered if I could ever leave the family I'd just found.

Knowing Brad had to leave the next day, the evening was bittersweet for me. We turned down an invitation to join Allison and a group of her friends who were going out on the town to celebrate the New Year.

Braving the cold wintry air, Brad grilled chicken outside while I fixed a Caesar salad and made garlic bread. We ate in the dining room where I once more set out Arinthia's...no, my... best china and silver. It seemed so natural, so right, to be dining together. I hoped the day would come when we'd be able to do that for the rest of our lives.

After dinner, we moved into the living room, and I put on some soft music.

Brad held out a hand to me. "Dance?"

I went into his arms eagerly and lay my head against his shoulder. We swayed in time to the music as if in a dream, our bodies caressing one another with each movement. Peace swept over me, and for those precious moments, hope for a future together beat back the nagging fear that I'd lose him forever.

###

After a restless night, I awoke to find Brad's side of the bed empty. I called for him but heard no answer. Slipping on my robe, I went to the window.

Brad and Lady were walking side by side on the beach, heading for the house. Lady trotted close to Brad's side and looked up at him with a pleading expression as if she knew that Brad would soon be gone and the two of us would be left on our own once more.

I hurried downstairs to join them.

Brad smiled when I entered the kitchen. "Lady and I have an understanding. She's to take care of you until we're together again."

Remembering all the times I'd felt so unprotected in the past, so vulnerable, unexpected tears stung my eyes.

Brad hugged me close. "Hey, now, don't cry. Something will work out. I just don't know how. A lot depends on your family."

I swallowed the words I dared not say. How could I live in Barnham when my duty lay here in Maine? After all I'd been given, I wasn't free to go. I understood that. We hadn't talked about it, but his family hadn't seemed all that happy with the idea of Brad dating me. And I didn't want to return to Barnham to stay. I couldn't.

Brad kissed me again, a kiss that already spoke of good-bye. "The car's loaded. Probably best for me to take off now. It's a long drive and I have to prepare for a court appearance in the morning. A land dispute. An important case in Barnham."

I rose up on tiptoes and put my arms around him. Our lips met in a warm embrace of their own. It scared me that I wanted him so much when I didn't see how we could ever resolve the problems we faced. I trailed light fingers across

Brad's brow, smoothing out the lines, wishing it were that easy to erase the uncertainty of our situation.

"I'd better go." Shoulders slumped, Brad let himself out the door and headed for his SUV.

I watched, then grabbed my coat, tugged it on over my robe, and hurried outside to wave good-bye.

From his car, Brad gave a jaunty salute and headed down the driveway.

I returned to the kitchen and stood in its warmth, staring forlornly at the empty driveway. The thrill of having found a family in a lovely seaside mansion evaporated. While it was a beautiful house, it hadn't yet become a home. And it wouldn't. Not without Brad.

I wandered through the empty, quiet rooms until the sound of the phone stopped me. I picked it up, surprised to hear Simone's hello.

"Marissa? I've decided to stay with my sister for a few extra weeks, but I'll be home before the next board meeting at the end of the month. You'll see that Hunter is prevented from taking over like we discussed?"

I bristled at the commanding tone of her voice. "I've already decided to spend the next few weeks doing just that."

"Is Brad Crawford there?"

My lips drew thinned in anger at the way she'd said his name as if he were some sort of loathsome enemy. "He left this morning, Simone."

"Good. Talk to you later, Marissa," she said coolly. "Oh, yes, Happy New Year."

"Happy New Year," I said softly and lay the phone back in its receiver, wondering why Simone and I always ended up sparring with one another. Thinking back to when I first met her, I again had the feeling that Simone, not Arinthia, had been in charge. And for some reason, it made me uneasy.

"Might as well take down the Christmas decorations," I said to Lady. "It's over."

She followed me into the living room. Matching my spirits, the Christmas tree in the corner drooped, its branches hanging low and tired.

Carefully, I dismantled the tree, laying the precious, old ornaments back in the boxes where I'd found them. Had my mother done the same thing, year after year?

I searched in the kitchen for some tape to seal the boxes and found none. Simone's office was the next logical choice. I tested the door. Locked.

Annoyed, I wondered what was so important inside that Simone had to keep it from me or anyone else. Technically, everything was mine now.

I went out to the garage and found what looked like an ice pick in Henry's workbench drawer. Returning to the house, I stood outside the office and set to work on the lock. It wasn't complicated, and after a few moments, I heard a click and the door swung open.

I entered, feeling like an intruder, and tiptoed across the room to the large desk that Simone used.

The roll of scotch tape in the holder on top of the desk was all but empty. I searched for more. The center desk drawer was full of pens, pencils and paper clips, but no tape. I turned to the large drawer on the bottom left and opened it. It was full of files, neatly lined up and identified. Wondering where to look next, I began to roll the drawer closed when a file marked "Real Estate" caught my eye. Aha, I thought, more details about the house I now owned. I pulled the file out and opened it.

In the front of the papers lay a listing of the taxes assessed for Briar Cliff. Waterfront property was very expensive to maintain, I realized, staggered by the taxes and other costs listed there. It still amazed me that I'd become wealthy. The pleasure of having money, however, was tempered by the number of very real responsibilities that went along with it.

I continued to leaf through the papers, impressed by the volume of documents. At the very back, a few sheets of paper were clipped together, topped by a blank one, as if to cover up the contents. I lifted the top sheet and glanced through the document. It was a bill of sale for land between Rivers Papers and Arinthia Hartwell. I checked the date. Nineteen sixty-four.

I tucked the information away in my mind and put the file back. I'd begun a mental list of things I needed to ask Simone when she returned. This would be one of my questions. I shoved the drawer closed and opened the middle drawer on my right, finding a number of office supplies, including extra tape. I lifted a roll of tape out, put it in the dispenser and carried it out of the office, my mind still on the copy of the bill of sale. Jonesy had been concerned about Rivers Papers' real estate. It was something I'd look into.

I'd put the last of the Christmas boxes back in the attic when the phone rang.

"Marissa? It's Samantha. Do you want company this evening? Mother and Daddy are planning another big family dinner and I don't think I can face it. Daddy and Hunter have been watching football together all day, drinking beer. The drinking part of the scene is way too difficult for me. I need a break."

Delighted to have the heavy silence of the house broken by her presence, I smiled. "I'd love it. Tell you what, I'll fix some leftovers for dinner and then let's watch a movie."

"Great," Samantha said, and I realized we'd become friends.

Throughout the rest of the day, my thoughts turned to Brad

again and again. I kept hoping he'd call to say that he'd done a lot of thinking on the drive home and had decided he could move his practice to Maine, after all. Foolish, I know, but I was desperate to believe we'd be able to work things out between us.

My hopes were dashed when he called to say he'd arrived home safely and had begun work on his case. "I miss you already, Marissa. When can you arrange to come here?"

My heart sank. "I don't know. I have no idea what my schedule is. I'm sorry."

"Yeah, well, think about it. Gotta go."

We hung up, and my thoughts began to reel in hopeless circles. How could I give him what he wanted and still do my duty to my family? Looking around at all I'd been given, I was afraid of the price I was about to pay for it.

That evening Samantha burst into the house like a ray of sunshine. She'd become like a sister to me. Smiling, she held a DVD in her hands.

"You ready for *Gone with the Wind*? I even brought my own Kleenex."

"Perfect," I said, needing a good cry.

CHAPTER TWENTY-ONE

With the holidays behind me, I spent as much time as possible studying the paper industry. The copy of the bill of sale between Rivers Papers and Arinthia that I'd discovered in Simone's desk had sparked other questions.

I did some investigation on the internet and learned that early paper mills like the one owned by my great-grandfather had bought up thousands of acres of land throughout the state. The land was valuable and became even more so, not only for its constant supply of raw materials but because, in some cases, the landowners controlled valuable natural resources, such as lakes, rivers, and ponds. This put them in a potentially lucrative position, considering the number of resorts springing up all over the northeast, vying for such locations.

I went back and reread the bill of sale. In 1964, Rivers Papers sold Arinthia Hartwell ten thousand acres of land for $45,000. Even then it was worth ten times as much or more. Why, I wondered, would Herbert Hartwell have done this? Was that land still part of Arinthia's estate? I read through the copy of Arinthia's will her lawyer had given me. Nothing was mentioned about this land, just that all her holdings were left to me.

Over the next few days, I read dozens of old copies of annual reports for Rivers Papers dating back to the early 80's, struggling with them until the numbers and words blurred before my eyes.

I was roused out of my tiresome research by a visit from

Samantha, who bounded into the kitchen with a wide grin.

"Good news, I think." She accepted the cup of coffee I offered her. "I haven't given up on the idea of finding out what Ted Beers may be up to. Jonesy called this morning and told me it would be a good idea if we made another visit to Riverton—incognito. We're to meet him tomorrow at his house. He lives outside of town in a private, wooded area. Sounds like he's got some very interesting information for us."

My body came alive with excitement. After trying to make sense of lingo and numbers, facts and figures, I was eager to get out of the house. I wanted to understand not only the workings of the mills but what had concerned Jonesy. I'd found when I'd worked at MacTel that, however small, rumors generally had a basis in truth.

The next morning, I picked up Samantha at eight o'clock and we headed north.

Samantha turned to me, "You've never told me everything about the visit you and Brad made to St. Andrews School. Did you get the answers you wanted?"

"Yes and no. It seems fairly certain my father is William Carter, a nice kid from a rough background, who was placed in foster care after his mother died of a drug overdose. He was killed in the Army." I lifted the hair away from my face. "He had a widow's peak and so do I. And, Sam, his nickname was Billy Boy."

Her eyes widened. "B.B.? Like the initials on the ring?"

"Uh, huh. And listen to this. In the note he left his foster parents, he said he loved a girl named Margaret. I believe when he found out about me, he enlisted in the army, telling his foster parents it was to prove he was a man. But I think he wanted to provide a living for my mother and me." I waved my hand in protest at the cynical look on Sam's face. "I know, I know. I'm making it sound very romantic, but it makes me feel better to think they really did love one another."

"Why, then, do you think your Mother ran away?"

"I'm convinced when my grandmother found out she was pregnant with me, she told my mother to get out. Then, when Billy was killed, she had no one to depend on except Clyde, a friend of Billy's. In a way, it was all my fault."

"No, no," said Samantha, shaking her head firmly. "You were a consequence of their behavior. That's all."

"Funny, though, if I'm right about this and my mother left her family because of me, she also brought me back to them. Strange, huh?"

"Yes, but I'm glad for you that it happened."

I made a face. "*You* might be, but your father isn't all that happy about it."

A look of resolve settled on Samantha's features. "Something is going on between my father and Ted Beers. I just know it. And, Marissa, you and I are going to find out what it is."

Riverton seemed smaller than when I last saw it—perhaps because the steam rising from the mill's stack by the river swirled above the town and dominated the view.

Past the mill, a couple of miles outside of town, I drove down a long dirt driveway. Icy patches slowed us before we pulled up to a small, one-story white clapboard house.

The front door of the house opened and a large black dog came bounding toward us, barking enthusiastically.

"Beauty, easy girl," said Jonesy, approaching us as we got out of the car. "Glad you could make it. Anybody see you in town?"

"Not that we noticed." Samantha gave him a hug. "Guess what? I've added twenty-four more days of sobriety."

"Thatta girl," said Jonesy. He took hold of her shoulders and looked at her squarely. "I'm real proud of you. It ain't easy. I know."

He turned to me. "Marissa, glad you could come with Sam, here. Thought there might be some things you, especially, should know about." He lowered his voice. "Can't let nobody know about it, though."

Inside, Jonesy indicated seats at a small, square wooden table in the kitchen and poured us mugs of coffee.

"My wife is at work. 'Didn't want her to know nothin' about this. Safer that way."

Unease crept through me. I leaned forward as he took a seat.

"What's going on?" Samantha looked as worried as I felt.

"Okay, here's how it is. I'd heard rumors about changes taking place at the mill." He turned to Samantha. "I told you that."

She nodded, and he continued. "The other day Jake Weatherbee approached me about a hush-hush deal." He turned to me and explained, "Jake's the broker for the company and is always working deals for us with land, soft and hard woods, anything." He took a long draw on his coffee and continued. "So, anyway, he tells me they want me to work on a new project. 'Rivers Papers,' he says, 'is going to operate its own processing plant for kaolin, the filler used in making paper. This plan involves a procedure being patented now—a 'seven-year factor.'"

Samantha nodded knowingly.

"What's a seven-year factor?" I asked.

"Our mill engineers work with manufacturing to work out any new process, designing new equipment for it," Samantha explained. "It's always top-secret stuff. Not only is the new machinery patented, the process is as well. This locks out another paper mill from this technology for years. The patents are usually held by both mill and manufacturer. It's called the seven-year factor because it generally takes that amount of time for another mill or manufacturer to get around the patents and offer a competitive product."

"But isn't it a good thing that Rivers Papers is coming up with something new?"

Both Jonesy and Samantha nodded.

"So what's the problem?"

Jonesy leaned forward. "The problem is where they're going to put it. You know the empty buildings at the far end of our site at the very edge of town? That's where this process should take place. Instead, they want to move it out of town, up to Coldstream."

"Coldstream? Why?" Samantha asked.

Jonesy held up a finger. "That's exactly what I asked. Jake hemmed and hawed and said it would be better for everyone if that's where it was placed. I let it go, but later, I called Sissy Johnson, my cousin who works at the county offices. Guess what she found out for me?" He looked around furtively. "George Hartwell and Ted Beers own adjoining pieces of property in Coldstream—exactly where this plant is going to be located."

"That's it!" said Samantha triumphantly. "I knew they were up to something."

"Wouldn't it cost Rivers Papers a whole lot more to build a new plant in Coldstream than it would to use the buildings they already own?" I asked.

"Oh, yeah. We'll check it out, but I bet they've already set it up so Rivers Papers will pay a small fortune for land they don't really need. It's been done before in this business."

My eyes narrowed as the information sank in. "Your own father would do that to Rivers Papers when he claims he wants

Hunter to be a part of it?"

Samantha's chuckle was bitter. "Why not? He's always felt he was cheated out of the business. And Hunter doesn't give a damn."

"What about Ted Beers?" I asked.

Jonesy shook his head. "Don't trust that guy. He's a real weasel."

"He's always thinking of ways to make money for himself," Samantha said. "I learned that in a hurry."

I turned to Jonesy. "How can I thank you for being so truthful with us?"

He brushed away my question with a wave of his hand. "Don't need to. I've been at the mill for over thirty years. My father worked there before me. Too many changes are taking place at Rivers Papers, all in the name of the almighty buck. Time somebody stood up to the money grabbers. I seen this coming for a while. Couldn't say nothin' til I got the goods on 'em." He turned to Samantha. "This one, she'll know what to do with it, I told myself. She's loved the business since she was just a tot."

"I really appreciate what you've done, I'm new at this but I feel like I've got a real responsibility to do what's right for the company." I glanced at Samantha. "Our great-grandfather founded the original mill that was bought by Rivers Papers."

"And he fought his brother over it," said Samantha.

I gave her a steady look. "It's time you and I worked together to make this right."

"Thing is," said Jonesy. "If money is wasted on shitty deals like this one, they won't pay the workers what was promised to them in the last agreement. Everyone I know will be hurt bad financially, real bad."

"What should we do?" I asked, ready to listen to anything they had to say.

Samantha's eyes flashed. "First off, you and I are going to make a visit to Coldstream."

"Then I want a complete tour of the Rivers Papers property so we can make a comparison of locations."

"Hold on," said Jonesy. "We gotta make sure no one knows where you got the information I gave you. You two drive over to the mill and say you're there to show Marissa, here, around. Then speak to Caleb Clarkson, the head engineer on this project, about any new stuff coming up. You can catch him off guard. Once you sign the confidentiality agreement all of us had to sign before working on this project, he'll have to give you all the information. Get it?"

A slow, sly smile slid across Samantha's face.

"Perfect," I said, returning Samantha's grin.

"I'll ask for you, Jonesy, and act as if I didn't know it was your day off," Samantha said.

We left Jonesy and headed back into town. Once past the gates into the parking lot of the mill, we put on our special boots, met the guard at the entrance and picked up our hard hats and safety glasses.

"Is Jonesy here?" Samantha asked innocently, showing the guard her shoes.

The guard made a call and turned back to us. "He's off today. Did you want to see anyone else, Miss Hartwell?"

"Hmmm," said Samantha, "Maybe we'll go to the engineering department. No need to call ahead. We'll head there on our own. I'm showing Marissa around the mill, now that she's a board member."

The guard looked at me curiously. "Sure thing."

I followed Samantha down the hallway.

We arrived in an office reception area where a number of white drawing boards were mounted on the walls, displaying a variety of sketches and figures. A dark-haired woman looked up from her desk and smiled.

"Samantha! I haven't seen you for a while. My, you look wonderful."

"Thanks, Carole," said Samantha. "You haven't met Marissa Cole, my cousin and a new member of the board of directors. She's taking Arinthia's place."

She smiled, rose from her chair and extended her hand. "Carole Simpson. I've known Samantha since she was a young girl. She used to follow her father and brother around when they'd come on business. She even did a case study on us for her business degree." She gazed at me steadily. "So you're taking over for Arinthia? She was something else— determined to keep an eye on things."

"Yes, well, I'm hoping to learn a lot. But I'll have to work hard to catch up to Samantha."

The three of us laughed politely.

"Is Caleb in?" Samantha asked. "I want Marissa to meet him and learn about this department."

Carole answered *sotto voce*, "He's always in. Poor guy has no life outside this company."

"If you don't mind, we'll knock on his door and go on in," Samantha said.

With a wave of her hand, Carole indicated one of the offices lining the wall.

We knocked on Caleb Clarkson's door and peered inside. When he saw us, he jumped to his feet. He was a short, wiry man with thick glasses, whose gaze never left my face as Samantha made the introductions

He bounced on the balls of his feet as if to make himself taller. "Yup, heard all about you being new to the board and all. But maybe not for long, huh? Something about Hunter Hartwell taking your place?"

My lips thinned. George Hartwell was *not* going to replace

me with Hunter. No way.

"Another one of those nasty rumors," Samantha interjected smoothly. "Not true at all. As a matter of fact, we're here to learn what new projects may be coming up for Rivers Papers."

"Yes," I added. "I want to learn all I can about the mill, especially with another board meeting so close. As I told Ted Beers and the others, I intend to be prepared. Samantha is helping me identify areas of importance."

Caleb looked from me to Samantha uncertainly.

I held my breath. He had to cooperate or we'd be lost.

"W-e-l-l," he said, breathing out the word slowly, "that's different. Samantha, you know the routine. We work on hush-hush projects all the time. Both of you will need to sign confidentiality agreements. Matter of procedure."

"Understood. We want what's best for Rivers Papers."

After the appropriate paperwork had been taken care of, Caleb leaned back in his leather desk chair, his feet hanging inches from the floor. Behind the thick lenses of his glasses, his eyes shone a deep brown.

"We've got a good one going now. We're going to manufacture our own filler. It will mean big savings to Rivers Papers. Yessir, we've been working on it for months."

Samantha nodded eagerly. "Filler? Do you mean kaolin? That's great. I guess you're going to put the plant at the north end of the property, where those old brick buildings are. Right?"

Caleb frowned. "That's where I intended to place it. I even had the renovation drawings almost complete when word came down that the board wanted to move it further north, to Coldstream."

"Why? Do we own property there?" I asked with wide-eyed innocence.

"Not really," Caleb said. He leaned forward, placing his feet on the floor. "I understand Ted Beers and a silent partner of his own some property up there and that's why we're moving it to Coldstream." He waggled a finger at us. "But you didn't hear that from me."

"Tell me, just when did this change of plans come about?"

"Nearly eight months ago."

I quickly did some calculations. Eight months ago Arinthia was incapacitated by her stroke. She must have known about the decision, however, if she kept track of what was happening. Perhaps that's why both she and Simone were so eager for me to take over for her—to keep an eye on Ted Beers and George Hartwell. Neither Ted nor George could be trusted.

Caleb went on to explain how he and his department had designed a machine to process kaolin shipped from Georgia. Listening to him, I could tell how proud he was of his work.

As we rose to leave, Samantha paused. "Caleb? Would it be easy to renovate the buildings on the far end of the site to process the kaolin?"

"Basically, we'd gut the buildings and arrange the space like we needed. Having the process fairly close by would save on hauling expenses. Plus the land in Coldstream requires a lot of site work and the cost of new construction is high." He shrugged. "But then I'm not on the board and don't get to vote."

"Oh, but I do." Satisfaction curved my lips.

He looked at me with surprise.

Coldstream was little more than a strip of road with a few houses, a gas station, and a general store. From that small center, land rolled in all directions in a variety of textures—

open fields, woodlands, and forest. Studying it, I realized how much infrastructure, including roads, would be needed to build anything of any size.

"Doesn't make a bit of sense, does it?" Samantha directed me to stop along the side of the road. "If I'm not mistaken, the land my father and Ted Beers own is off to this side."

"On our way back, let's stop in and see Jonesy's cousin at the county offices."

"Great idea!" said Samantha. "I remember something my father mentioned a while back, and I want to see if the project he was talking about was in Coldstream."

We found our way into the Stevenson County planning and development department. A woman looked up from her desk as we entered the small crowded office.

I hid a grin. She was a female version of Jonesy.

"Hello," Samantha said smoothly. "I'm working with my client here, investigating property for a country home, and I'm wondering if you could give us some information."

Sissy Johnson, as her nameplate indicated, gave a little grunt as she hefted to her feet. "This arthritis of mine is real bad. 'Couple more years and I'm leavin' Coldstream and headin' for Florida. Now, what can I do for you?"

I let Samantha speak. "We'd like to see the maps of Coldstream. It seems like a pretty area, don't you think?"

"There was a big rush for land up there 'bout a year or so ago." Sissy hauled a huge book onto the counter.

We opened the book of plats and leafed through the pages until we found the one that identified the land Ted Beers and my uncle owned.

"Is this a good area?" I asked, tapping my finger on the exact spot. "I see there's a small pond nearby."

Sissy clucked her tongue. "I bet you could get it for a bargain. A bunch of hot shots from the big cities bought up a whole bunch of that land, thinking they were going to put up a fancy resort there. They even had one of those feasibility studies done. Next thing we knew, they were trying to sell it."

"Any other plans for that area?" Samantha asked.

Sissy shook her head. "Not that I know of. Not much happening there. It's off the beaten track."

"Let's think about it before going any further," I said to Samantha. We needed to escape before any information came out about who we were and what we really wanted to know.

We turned to go.

"Wait," said Sissy. "I didn't get your business cards. For my records."

My heart all but stopped.

"We're friends of Joncsy." Samantha grabbed my arm and hurried me out the door. I turned around in time to catch a sly smile spreading across Sissy's face.

CHAPTER TWENTY-TWO

On the way back to New Hope, Samantha and I plotted our next moves.

"I'm going to talk to Caleb," she said. "I want to compare his original budget to the one he had to revise."

"Brad might be able to help us with some of the legal angles. Maybe we can find some way to block this move."

"About a year ago, my father mentioned a resort in Maine. A developer, a friend of Ted Beers, came to him with a plan. He was all excited about the idea, thought he was going to make millions. I haven't heard a thing about it since." Her smile had a touch of sadness. "Now I know why he wanted Hunter on the board so badly. He knew my brother wouldn't question the change in plans—not if it meant easy money in his pocket."

"What about Ted Beers? Are we going to be in danger if we try to squash this thing?"

Samantha frowned. "Possibly. The only way to beat him is to have all our numbers in place and confront him with them. He's a numbers man, after all."

Resolve swept through me. I'd give it everything I had.

After dropping Samantha off for one of her meetings, I pulled into Briar Cliff just before dark. I stood a moment, studying the empty house. It loomed unexpectedly large, and I was glad Henry and Becky would soon return. I rolled my shoulders to loosen the tension of the day and went inside to let Lady out.

Braving the nippy breeze that lifted my hair from my

shoulders, I watched Lady gallop joyfully around the yard. In the distance, the waves of the ocean moved rhythmically, drawing me into a reflective mood. I wondered if my grandmother and Simone suspected George and Ted were going to cheat Rivers Papers stockholders out of money. Perhaps that's why they'd jumped at the opportunity to keep control through me. Shivering, I clasped my arms around my waist and went back inside.

I poured myself a glass of wine and went into Simone's office. I'd spent a lot of time looking at facts and figures for Rivers Papers, but I hadn't begun to go through the files containing my grandmother's personal papers. Now, I thought, was a good time to start.

In a metal file stored in the large closet in the office, I flipped through a number of folders related to Rivers Papers and lifted out a file entitled "Earnings".

Sitting at the desk, leafing through the papers, my skepticism grew. For each monthly meeting Arinthia attended, she was paid ten thousand dollars. Mystified, I shook my head. The amount was a lot less than what it would cost to run this house and maintain her lifestyle. Why would Arinthia be so determined for me to hold onto a position that paid only that?

My fingers drummed a beat on top of the desk. There had to be other income involved. I remembered the bill of sale for the ten thousand acres of land Arinthia owned. Maybe that was part of it. Tomorrow, I'd call Sam and share my suspicions.

In the kitchen, I picked up the phone. It had only been a few days since Brad had left, but it seemed much longer. I needed to hear his voice.

"Marissa, glad you called," he said, cheerfully. "What's up?"

At the welcome in his voice, my heart lifted.

"Sam and I went to see Jonesy in Riverton today. It seems my uncle and Ted Beers have a plan to cash in on some ideas they're promoting at Rivers Papers. We're going to stop them in their tracks."

"Marissa, be careful," he warned. "Ted Beers can be ruthless."

"Don't worry, we'll handle him," I said breezily, and quickly changed the topic. "How's your father?"

"Not great," Brad replied. "He had a slight relapse—did too much too soon. I've been going crazy, trying to take care of everything."

"I'm sorry. I miss you."

"Me, too. Listen, I hate to cut you off, but I've got a town meeting to attend. Talk to you later, okay?"

Disappointed, I hung up the phone. Brad's life in Barnham was full. It was foolish of me to expect that with enough coaxing he would give it up and come to New Hope. And there was no way I could leave. I knew that now. Jonesy had indicated that a lot of people were depending on me to protect their interests. Tears stung my eyes. There was no way Brad and I could make our relationship work.

As soon as I poured my morning coffee, I called Samantha.

"Jake Weatherbee might be able to provide us with some answers," she said after I'd filled her in. "He's the broker for the company and should have some inside information on Arinthia's land. You've found nothing to indicate she sold the land?"

"Not yet. I'm just beginning to sift through her personal files while Simone is away."

"Dragon Lady didn't want you near them?"

I laughed. "Let's just say she was very possessive of her room. But it's time I found out as much as I can about my grandmother's business."

"I agree. See what legal documents you can find regarding the land. We'll go from there."

I hung up the phone and went into the office. Somewhere, among the files, must be the information I sought. I checked the bill of sale once more, carefully scanning the language. It referred to the land as being bound on the west by the central border between New Hampshire and Maine, and the northern and southern boundaries as equidistant from that central point. I found a map of Maine in the library and traced the described area with my finger. Ski resorts like Sunday River were nearby. Not too many miles away lay the Wild River Valley Ski Resort, which enjoyed the reputation as the biggest winter resort in Maine. I'd read earlier about a lot of mill land being sold for resorts and wondered if Arinthia had done that.

My curiosity aroused, I realized there was one person who could easily provide the answer for me. George Hartwell had done legal work for Arinthia in the past. It wasn't until recently, Simone had told me, that my grandmother had changed lawyers so she could change her will. I decided to call George.

He sounded surprised when I told him what I wanted. "A meeting? This afternoon? Let me check my schedule."

I smiled. Well into his eighties, George was a vigorous man who still went into his office every day. But I knew his schedule wasn't heavy.

"Two o'clock should be fine," he said, his manner brisk. "Better be on time. I leave by four."

"Don't worry, I'll be there." Nothing would keep me away.

I hung up and phoned Samantha.

"I'm glad you called," she said. "I've thought about what

Brad said about Ted Beers and I agree he can be dangerous. Let's keep our discoveries in Coldstream to ourselves for the time being. The rest will fall into place after we get more information from Jake."

"Agreed," I said and asked her to accompany me to her father's office.

Samantha and I met at the law offices of Hartwell, Smith, and Lowell. The interior, with its Oriental rugs and dark paneling, reminded me of a colder, more sterile version of Brad's law office in Barnham. Waiting for my uncle to appear, I sat in the reception area with Samantha and couldn't help fidgeting.

George's eyes widened when he walked into the reception area. "Sam? What are you doing here?"

She smiled sweetly. "Marissa hired me to help her learn about Rivers Papers. Remember? I've got my own consulting business now."

He frowned. "We'll be discussing very personal business ..."

Aware of Samantha's growing hurt, I waved away his concern. "There are no secrets between Samantha and me. Anything you might have to say about my grandmother's business holdings or anything else is entirely open to her."

A look of irritation crossed George's features. "Come along, then," he said grumpily.

I exchanged unhappy glances with Samantha and followed him.

His office was impressive in size and furnishings, and, through a large corner window, had a magnificent view of Casco Bay. Once I was seated, my eyes were drawn to the credenza behind his desk. A collection of family pictures—

Adrienne and George and the children grouped together at different ages—were displayed there. A handsome family, I thought. The girls, especially, were strikingly beautiful. I noticed George's hand on Hunter's shoulders in all the pictures, as if he were the chosen one.

George took a seat at his desk. Icy nervousness swept through me. At his advanced age, George Hartwell was still a smart, shrewd man who didn't tolerate fools. His haughtiness made me feel silly just for taking his time.

I lifted a small notebook out of my purse, grateful my questions were already written down.

"Well?" George leaned back in his chair, his hands clasped over his trim stomach. "Just what is it you want to know? I'd have thought Simone would have gleefully told you everything." His blue gaze pierced me.

I swallowed hard. "That's just it. She's given me a lot of general information about the mill but nothing specific about Arinthia's affairs."

Samantha spoke up. "For instance, Father, Marissa has learned that Arinthia was paid ten thousand dollars for each board meeting she attended, but we know her income was substantially higher."

"Right," I added to Samantha's comment. "I also know that she owns or at one time owned ten thousand acres of land in the extreme west-central part of the state. Does she still own it?"

George tapped a finger on the thick file sitting in the middle of his desk, his brow creased. "That's basic information that Simone should have shared with you."

"The land was sold to her in 1964," I said, hoping to impress him with my knowledge.

"In 1968, she sold two thousand acres to a development group. You've heard of Wild River Ski Resort?"

My jaw dropped. "That's on land that belonged to Arinthia?"

"Made a small fortune on that." He pressed his lips together and spoke in a steely tone. "In matters pertaining to money, Arinthia was as shrewd as they come."

His tone spoke of resentment as he continued. "She took that money, invested it wisely and with the wild surge of the stock market in the eighties and nineties, turned a large amount of money into a fortune. You didn't know that?"

I shook my head. "Not specifically. Simone set me up with checking and special savings accounts and said she'd be glad to continue handling things until I was ready to take over."

George's face turned red. He shook an admonishing finger at me. "Foolish girl! You should have insisted on her showing you everything. You're protected in most cases but there's still a large amount of money she could get her hands on if she wanted."

I fidgeted with embarrassment. He was right. I'd felt so guilty about Arinthia changing her will for my benefit I hadn't wanted to appear to pounce on my new-found wealth, especially where Simone was concerned. I'd told the lawyer I wanted things to continue as they were.

"As I said," George continued in a less strident manner, "the land is protected. But you'll want to speak directly to her broker about Arinthia's investments. I should rightfully say *your* investments. Even though she left a large amount of money to Simone, we don't want any confusion about who is now in control of those assets. Simone was given the power of attorney after Arinthia had the stroke, but I thought she understood that she no longer was to be involved, with or without your permission. She should have introduced you to Arinthia's broker and any others who handled business for Arinthia."

I felt ashamed I'd let my guilty feelings override common sense.

"Father, there's something I don't understand," interjected Samantha, giving me time to regain my composure. "What was Arinthia doing with the rest of her land? Just letting it sit?"

George shook his head and rolled his eyes.

I cringed. He treated Samantha as if she didn't know a thing.

"You should know the answer to that, Samantha," he said. "On a rotating basis, it's harvested for soft and hard woods. There's money to be made in selling the assets of the land. And Arinthia, as I mentioned earlier, was no fool when it came to money."

"Was Jake Weatherbee the buyer of the wood?" I asked.

George's look of surprise brought me satisfaction.

"Yes," he answered. "Arinthia sold to Rivers Papers. Why?"

I shrugged. "Just finding out the facts."

George leaned forward, his eyes glaring at me. "I've told you before, Marissa, all of this business with Rivers Papers is better left to Hunter. It's a man's world in the paper business. Turning Arinthia's seat over to Hunter is the logical thing to do. You and Samantha can find something else to do with your time. Leave it alone."

George was protesting too much, I thought warily.

"Father, this business about it being a man's world is so dated," Samantha protested. "Women have doors open to them now."

"Arinthia was a woman and did very well for herself," I added, watching George's face grow redder and redder with agitation. "I'm not about to give up the family position to Hunter. Arinthia trusted me to do better than that."

The jangling of the phone pierced the growing tension in

the room. George picked it up. "George Hartwell ... yes ...no ... I'll call you back, Ted."

"Ted Beers?"

"That, my dear, is none of your business," George said to me. He checked his watch. "It seems as if we've come to an impasse here. Do as I say, Marissa, and make sure Simone is not making any financial decisions for you—decisions that could hurt you."

I rose and stood beside Samantha. "Thank you for your time."

As we turned to leave, George spoke. "For your information, Samantha, where top business is concerned, it will always be a man's world. I've tried to tell you that, to protect you."

Samantha's jaw moved forward and her gray eyes, so like mine in color, flashed. "No, Father, the world has changed, even if you haven't."

We moved through the reception area briskly, smiled at the receptionist, and stepped out into the cool air.

Samantha stood at the top of the marble steps of the building and pounded a fist into her hand. "He makes me so damn mad!"

"How does your mother stand it?" I asked. Adrienne, a good twenty-some years or so younger than her husband, didn't seem like a whimpering wife who would put up with George's ways.

A crafty look spread across Samantha's face. "My mother isn't fazed by my father's attitude. She has her own money, handles all of the household expenses and has more business sense than most men. She's the one who urged me to go to the business school at Harvard."

"What does she think about you starting a business of your own?"

Samantha grinned. "She's very happy about it, tells me how proud she is. It almost makes up for my father's put-downs." She blinked rapidly. "Almost."

A plan formed in my mind. I tugged on her coat sleeve. "C'mon. Let's go see what we can find out about Arinthia's sale of woods. Or, better yet, let's call Jake Weatherbee."

I followed Samantha to George and Adrienne's house. We arrived in time to see Allison loading up the last of her things in a U-Haul trailer.

I got out of my car and dashed over to her. "You're leaving today?"

"I decided to leave earlier than I'd planned. It's time I stopped playing the dutiful daughter home again after her marriage went to pieces. To tell you the truth, I can't wait to get to California and start a whole new life."

I watched as Samantha and Allison embraced. They were both beautiful, but so very different. Allison's blondness was in stark contrast to Samantha's darker looks. The tenderness between them brought a pang. How I'd wished for a sister growing up—a sister who would've protected me from Clyde's taunts and my mother's indifference.

I hugged Allison, sincerely sorry she was leaving. "I'm going to miss you. We were just beginning to know one another."

She grinned. "You'll have to come visit me. But it's a good thing you're here, Marissa. I wasn't sure about you at first, but, now, I am. And keep that man of yours. He's a hunk."

A wave of uneasiness washed over me. Brad hadn't called me back like he said he would.

CHAPTER TWENTY-THREE

Jake Weatherbee agreed to meet me at ten o'clock the next morning at his office in Portland. I entered the office at exactly ten, eager to find out what I could about his role at Rivers Papers and what arrangements he'd had with Arinthia.

Jake shook my hand and motioned me to a seat inside a small conference room off the reception area.

Sizing one another up, we talked about mundane things. When I mentioned how important his position at the mill was to everyone, Jake loosened up. A look of pride crossed his face.

"Yeah, it is important. And it involves a lot of money. I, not the mill, own the equipment for jobbers to do their work, harvesting the woods."

I hid my surprise. "It must be terribly expensive to own and maintain all that equipment. But then, I guess your commissions are pretty big."

"Yep, they can be," he bragged.

That explained the Cadillac Escalade I'd noticed in his parking spot at the mill and the large diamond man's ring sparkling on his right hand.

We chatted for about twenty minutes longer and I left the meeting, my thoughts awhirl.

Back at Briar Cliff, I pored through Arinthia's papers once more, with an eye to finding anything relating to the property she owned. I discovered a folder marked 'Harvests' and leafed through documents relating to various sales of soft and hard woods from Arinthia's land.

Jake Weatherbee was listed as the broker and also the one

performing the original site work on her land in 1970 for future harvests. In 1974, the first harvest was made, bringing in several hundred thousand dollars. Fifteen percent of that amount was given to Jake Weatherbee as a brokerage fee plus a percentage paid to him for the wood harvested from the right-of-way when the logging road was put in.

I sat back in my chair, appalled. Jake had earned a substantial amount of money from my grandmother from the very beginning. And was still doing so. He'd also earned money brokering the sale of the wood he claimed as his to Rivers Papers.

My foot tapped a beat on the carpet. If my grandmother was so shrewd, she wouldn't have let Jake get away with a deal like that. There had to be more to the story.

The phone rang.

"Marissa? This is Simone. I'm arriving in Boston tomorrow at 3:00 P.M. Can you arrange for a limo to pick me up?"

"Sure, Is everything all right? I thought you were staying in Florida until the end of the month."

"I was going to, but George Hartwell called me. It seems he's very unhappy about your situation and wants me out of the picture altogether. You and I need to talk."

"All right."

A gut-wrenching feeling gripped me as I hung up the phone. It could only mean trouble.

I chopped a garlic clove, diced onions, sliced mushrooms and tossed them all into a sauté pan with a little olive oil, preparing my favorite pasta sauce for dinner. I'd tried Brad's cell number, but when the call went to his voicemail, I hung up without leaving a message.

When Brad and I were together, everything was wonderful.

But when he was in Barnham, he was miles and miles away, both physically and emotionally. I added imported marinara sauce to the frying pan, put in a dash of wine and set the mixture to a simmer. Pasta was comfort food to me.

The phone rang, and I hurried to get it.

"Hey, sweetheart. You called?" Brad's voice sent warm tingles of pleasure through me.

"I just wanted to hear your voice, I miss you so much. You seem so far away."

"Yeah, I know. It seems like a long time ago I was there with you."

"I wish I could convince you to be here all the time," I said wistfully. "I really need your help with finances. And legal matters keep cropping up."

"Marissa, you know I can't. You have family things to take care of, and so do I."

Disappointment crawled through me. I'd been foolish to think he'd turn his back on his obligations just because I needed him. I knew how much the security of Barnham and his family meant to him after his miserable marriage to Amber.

Brad's voice broke the silence. "You're awfully quiet."

"I know," I responded, overwhelmed by sadness. I couldn't give up all I had—not even for the man I loved with all my heart. I'd changed from the introverted struggling woman I'd been to a stronger woman involved in a fascinating business where people counted on me.

"I've found out some information for you," Brad said. "Something you may find very interesting."

My spirits lifted. "About my mother?"

"Yep. I've had a chance to talk to a couple of people who knew your mother in AA. You wanted to know why your mother ran away? Whatever happened between your mother and Arinthia was so shattering to her that she vowed never to return. She said it was a matter of principle."

"A matter of principle? Really?"

"Uh, huh. Your mother told a friend she was too weak to go back home, that she'd get sucked into the games that were being played out."

"Hm-m-m-m, interesting. Thank you," I murmured, more confused about my mother than ever.

Brad went on to tell me some of his friends in Barnham were pulling together a baseball team for spring. His excitement made me more and more depressed.

We talked a few minutes longer. Though my heart was breaking, I tried to sound upbeat. I wished him good luck with everything and hung up the phone, numb to the bone. Our relationship was over. I just knew it.

The phone rang again. Listlessly, I picked it up.

"Marissa? What in hell is going on? You sounded as if we were never going to speak again. Is that what you want?"

"Brad? No, I ... I just realized our relationship doesn't have a future. You're tied to your life in Barnham and I've got to see things through for my family. What choice does either of us have?"

"You don't think our relationship is worth fighting for? Is that it?" Hurt and anger vibrated in his voice.

"Brad, I'm just being realistic ..."

"What I'm hearing is that you don't give a damn about us ... you'd just give up without a fight. Think about it. Do you really want that?"

"Brad, that's so unfair ..."

"I swore I'd never again get involved with a woman who wasn't as committed to me as I was to her. Tell me what you want, Marissa. The truth. All of it. Otherwise, I'm hanging up this phone and I won't call back."

"I want us to be together," I began. "But I won't live in Barnham. I can't. You know that. And I realize how much it means to you to be there with your family. I'm sorry now I even came to New Hope. I can't run away from here. I have to stay and do right by my family, my mother."

"Your mother?"

Tears streamed down my cheeks. "Yes, dammit, for her, along with everyone else. You just told me she left as a matter of principle. I can't disregard that."

Brad was quiet for several seconds. "Maybe you're right, Marissa. We'd better call it quits before either one of us gets even more hurt."

"M-m-m-m," I murmured, pressing my lips together to hold back the sob behind them.

I hung up the phone, knowing there would be no follow-up call this time. I let the pain roll out of me in high-pitched wails, tormented by the fact that the family I'd always wanted had ruined the one thing I wanted even more.

The next morning, Becky came bustling into the kitchen from the grocery store, her hands full. She set the bags down on the kitchen counter.

"I bought a pot roast, Simone's favorite. I'll get it started and it'll be ready for you for dinner this evening." She stood still and studied me. "What is it, darlin'? You all right?"

I shook my head. "It's Brad. We've had a fight. It's over."

Becky patted me on the back. "There, there. You just say you're sorry and things will be all right."

I gave her a watery glance. "You don't understand. It's really over."

I blew my nose into the tissue she offered me and decided I'd probably lost the one person in the world who made me feel like the person I'd always wanted to be.

I went upstairs to my bedroom and lay on the bed, reaching out for the empty space where Brad had sprawled, remembering his warmth beside me as we'd laughed and loved. I flipped over on my side facing the wall and recalled our conversation. His news about my mother had been surprising.

I simply didn't know any more if she'd been weak or strong.

Simone swept into the house, shattering the stillness of the late afternoon.

"Traffic was terrible. Simply terrible," she complained, coming into the kitchen and indicating where the driver could place her suitcases.

"You look wonderful—nice and tan," I commented, and gave her a quick hug.

"My sister's place is right near the beach. We did a lot of walking and talking. I've bought a place down there, not too far from hers, right on the beach."

I hid my astonishment. I'd thought Simone would want to remain in Maine, overseeing my part of the business which, apparently, had provided so much to her through the years.

"You said we had to talk, Simone. Is that what you wanted to tell me?"

"In part," she said. "Give me time to get settled and then we can meet in my office."

Less than thirty minutes later Simone reappeared downstairs. "Ready? I want to get things settled between us. I've made some major decisions."

"You have?" I said, wondering at the seriousness of her tone. I'd made some decisions of my own. Like it or not, she was going to give me some answers to my many questions.

Simone turned the knob on the door to her office and, realizing it was open, glared at me. She entered her office and sat behind the desk, her stern expression menacing.

Uneasy, I settled in the chair facing her and told myself not to be intimidated by her.

She studied me with a cocked eyebrow. "Did you take my advice and find out what you could about Rivers Papers?"

"And some of Arinthia's business matters, too." I gave her a no-nonsense look I hoped would convey to her that I was now running the show.

"Ah, yes," she said softly. "The call from George. He was very angry with me. But he doesn't know the whole story, thank God."

"What story?"

"The business arrangement between Arinthia and me."

I shot her a look of surprise. *What was she talking about?*

"That's all it was, you know, a business arrangement." Her features hardened. "People thought we were lovers, but nothing could be further from the truth. In many ways, we hated one another." There was a set to Simone's jaw that worried me.

Her eyes glistening with tears, she stopped talking and stared blankly at the wall behind me.

I clasped my fingers together tightly, remaining silent, not sure I wanted to hear what she had to tell me.

Her gaze returned to me. "It's important for things to continue as they have been. Arinthia and I shared her monthly fee from Rivers Papers. Five thousand each. Sixty thousand dollars a year will be extra spending money for me, in addition to the income I already receive from my portfolio. It's only fair, Marissa. I earned it."

"You shared the fee? Because you worked together?"

"Oh, yes, we worked together, all right." Her laugh was

sharp, mocking. "Except when I decided it was payback time. She never knew about some of the side deals I had with Jake Weatherbee regarding kickbacks she was extorting from him. I tried to warn her to be fair, but she got a little greedy. And nothing I did affected her income. Not really. It just reduced the stockholders' shares by a few cents and gave me an opportunity to even things up a bit."

My mind whirled. *Jake Weatherbee had side deals with Simone?*

"Why are you telling me this? Aren't you afraid I'll report you to someone?"

She chuckled softly. "Not at all. You see, you desperately wanted a family and all the things you never had growing up. You still do have some crazy idea about family. Oh, yes, I know how important it all is to you. That's why I was willing to go along with Arinthia's plans to turn things over to one of her own flesh and blood, instead of to me. I knew you'd cooperate with us."

At the evil smile that crossed her face, a shiver danced across my shoulders. I recalled Brad's words of caution about not being trapped by family. My stomach churned. I stared at Simone, seeing her in a whole new light. She wasn't someone content to run the show; she wanted more than that. She wanted everything Arinthia had. What else, I wondered, had this slimy person done to get it?

"Okay, enough sentimental nonsense," Simone said briskly. "Here's the deal. When you attend the monthly meetings for Rivers Papers, I'll still get half of the fee involved. And you'll let me keep all the money I have. In return, I'll leave, go to Florida, and not bother you again."

Words stuck in my throat. "You keep talking about your money. What exactly are you talking about?"

Simone held up a finger of warning.

My mouth went dry.

"Remember, Arinthia had promised me everything. Then she changed her mind, intending to leave me with just a portion of what she'd promised. I figured I'd go ahead and take my share while I could."

"You'd steal from the woman you worked for all those years? The woman who treated you like family?"

Her eyes glittered, and I had the odd sensation I was staring at a snake. "Family?" she shrieked. "You have no idea what I've gone through, you little twit!" Her words lashed out at me like a venomous bite.

I cringed, wondering if I was about to be attacked.

She drew a breath, calming herself. "A record of all the sales of shares of stock are listed for you. Don't worry. I only took what I needed to end my life comfortably. You have more than enough. After all this time, I'm not about to be idiotic. Nor, I think, are you, when you know the facts."

"You stole from Arinthia?"

She gave me a brittle smile. "No. I took what is mine from you. What makes you think you could come in here and simply take away from me what I've worked so hard for all these years?"

The blood drained from my face. I gripped the sides of the chair. "But you wanted me here. You said so. You told me I had to do this for the family."

Her lip curled. "I wanted time to do what I had to do to make things right. It's done, and it wouldn't do you any good to fight me on this because I'd challenge the will, swear Arinthia was too sick to know what she was doing when she changed her mind. Then, you'd have nothing. And it would hurt everyone involved. Especially your family. You wouldn't want that now, would you? You and I must come to a settlement that will stand up in any court."

My mouth had turned so dry my tongue could hardly move. "What are we talking about in terms of money, Simone?"

Her look of satisfaction gave my stomach a jolt of acid.

"Eight hundred thousand dollars. Not much compared to what you have," she said smoothly, daring me with her hard looks to challenge her.

I sat, stunned by her revelation. The face I'd thought so attractive had turned ugly with greed.

She shook a finger at me. "Cooperate with me, or before I leave, I'll make sure the entire population of New Hope knows what went on in this house. Neither you nor the rest of the members of your family would be able to hold your heads up in this town ever again."

My body turned cold. "What are you talking about? What agreement did you have with my grandmother?"

Simone rose from behind her desk and paced the room, clearly agitated.

Heart pounding, I waited for her to speak.

She stopped her pacing and faced me, her nostrils flared. "I was twenty years old when I came here to work. Your grandmother was pregnant with your mother. Herbert was an affectionate man... He was also handsome, rich and powerful ... and I ... I was young and impressionable ..."

I sucked in air in frantic little gasps. "Omigod! You and he were actually lovers?" I'd suspected she loved him but had thought it was one of those situations where she, the maid, had worshiped him from afar.

Simone raised her chin and gave me a look of triumph. "He wanted to marry me."

"You stayed here in this house, sleeping with my grandfather right under my grandmother's nose? Didn't she know?" My voice quivered with indignation.

"Well, of course, she found out eventually. But by then

there was nothing she could do about it. That's when Herbert helped us devise our business arrangement. Arinthia was given a huge amount of land that belonged to the mill and I stayed in Briar Cliff under Herbert's protection."

I sank back in my chair, trying to take in all she was saying.

"Arinthia and I started out hating one another," she continued. "Herbert was the one who helped us see that there was money to be made by cooperating with one another. What he didn't know was that Arinthia's protests about me were false. She'd grown to hate the man, was glad I'd taken over her ... duties. She was such a cold woman. He also didn't know that Arinthia and I didn't need any help in coming up with a plan that benefited both of us. We agreed that no man was going to dictate to us how to live our lives. In time, we grew fond of one another. Why not? We'd shared so many things."

Nausea gripped me at the idea of my grandparents and Simone living in a *ménage a trois*. "What did people say? Didn't they know?"

"We were very discreet. I understood what my public role would be."

I clasped my cheeks in my hands, my mind whirling. *Did people do that sort of thing?*

"Did my mother find out about the three of you? Is that what drove her away from here?"

A disgusted look crossed Simone's face, turning it ugly. The bridled anger in her voice hit me like a blow to the head. "Your mother was a fool. We could have handled the baby. We'd done it before ..."

I gripped the edge of the desk to steady myself. "What do you mean you'd done it before ... Omigod! Tim ... No, no, you came here pregnant and my grandmother took you in. I saw the photograph."

Simone laughed. A bitter sound that rattled my teeth.

"Arinthia would never have done such a thing. If it hadn't been for Herbert insisting our son live as he should, I don't know what would have happened to us." She shook her head. "When Arinthia discovered I was pregnant, there was nothing she could do about it. Herbert told her she could leave or accept the fact that we loved one another."

"And she tolerated having you here?"

"Oh, yes," said Simone. Her lips thinned. "Arinthia has always been very shrewd about money. And Herbert became ill a few years later. That's when we decided to be friends and live life luxuriously."

"Wait a minute! Tim was always thought of as Arinthia's son. You let that happen?"

Simone sat down and leaned back in her chair, arms crossed in front. "We all decided that would be best."

"But ... but ..." I sputtered, "you gave up your son for money?"

She gave me a hostile glare. "What choice did I have? Tim had a far better life as Herbert Hartwell's acknowledged son than if I'd tried to make it on my own. And, after all, I was there with him, every day."

I shook my head, trying to make sense of it all. "But you all lived a lie."

A look of defiance crossed Simone's face. "Times were different then. In the early '60s, men still pretty much dictated everything. Especially old-fashioned men like Herbert. And public sentiment was still against divorce. Herbert's reputation as a leader of the community and the entire state would have been ruined if people knew he was living with me under Arinthia's roof."

My stomach knotted as she continued. "To keep everyone duped and to maintain Herbert's position in the businesses that supported us, Tim was passed off as Arinthia's son. That's the deal she made with Herbert. And, remember, we had our own side deal going on."

Sadness and confusion did the tango in my head. "So that's what my mother couldn't face, all those years ago. How did she find out?"

"Thea came to us and told us she was pregnant but wanted to have the baby. During the argument that followed, it all came out about Tim and me and her father. Thea got very upset. After all, she'd adored her father and now she saw him for the kind of man he really was. She ran from the room crying. Later, she and Arinthia got into another big fight. They'd always fought, but, this time, it was especially bitter. Thea told Arinthia she was going to leave, that she refused to raise a child in this family, that her whole life had been a total lie, and that it was easier to believe we were lesbians than the greedy, amoral women we actually were."

Simone let out a long sigh that echoed in the stillness of the room.

"Arinthia was furious, thinking of all the things she'd suffered so her daughter could have a nice life. Thea ran away that night. We waited and watched for her. Arinthia was certain Thea would be back in a number of days or weeks. But it never happened. And Thea was very clever, changing her name, moving to a small town where nobody would think to look for her."

"Did you want to find her?"

Simone shrugged. "I didn't really care. I had my son. Back then, we didn't have ways to trace people like they do today. I was afraid if we did find her, she would tell Tim. He didn't know about me and his father, and I was sure she'd make sure he knew, out of spite. He was very sensitive, even as a child. We thought he might react like Thea, and it would have broken our hearts if he'd run away, too. He was always the favorite. We had no idea he'd go and join the Army."

Shivering, I wrapped my arms around my body. No wonder my mother had left. She'd adored her father who'd turned out to be a pig who'd betrayed everyone. And her mother was even worse. No wonder my mother had never felt worthy of unconditional love. She'd never known any. Instead, she'd turned to alcohol.

I got to my feet unsteadily and turned to go.

"Marissa?"

"Don't say another word," I snapped, afraid my anger would crupt in ways I could never accept after vowing to live without violence. "Just leave me alone."

"One quick question," said Simone. "Are we in agreement?"

I ignored her question and stumbled from the room, sick to my stomach.

CHAPTER TWENTY-FOUR

Images of my mother haunted my dreams throughout the night. awoke to find my cheeks wet. I lay in bed, wrapped in misery. The family I'd wanted was a figment of my imagination. It didn't exist ... had never existed. What was real was pretty damn ugly—people twisting wrong into a semblance of right, all for money or pride.

My thoughts kept returning to my mother. She'd changed from a self-confident teenager into a shattered woman, too stubborn to ever return to Maine. Or was it a matter of principle, like Brad had suggested? If she hadn't become addicted to drugs and alcohol, would she have come back to Maine to face the two women she must have despised?

I finally understood how unhappy my mother's life had been, complicated by her addictions and by living with a man like Clyde. Perhaps she'd sent me here to even things up, to get back at her mother and Simone.

A tide of resolution flooded me, washing the shame away, filling me with defiance. I wouldn't run away from the ugly truths I'd just learned. I'd deal with them. I owed it to myself and to the extended family I now had.

I got out of bed and strode to the bathroom. The hot water in the shower poured over my body, renewing me.

After dressing, I called Samantha. She agreed to meet me in an hour.

Simone was already in the kitchen when I walked in. She greeted me pleasantly, though I could read uncertainty in her smile.

"Good morning," I said as if the nasty scene the day before had never happened. "You mentioned you're returning to Florida. When did you plan to go?"

Her cheeks turned bright red. Her expression hardened. "As soon as you and I have a signed agreement. I need only to pack my personal belongings."

"You'd better get started. I'll have an agreement in your hands by this evening." No way in hell was I about to live in the same house with her. She'd get what was coming to her. Nothing more...and perhaps a lot less.

I poured myself a cup of coffee and surreptitiously studied her. In her seventies, she was trim and attractive, a beauty really. What had happened to her that she'd allowed herself to be part of such a sick arrangement? And Arinthia? How could she stand to have Simone and her husband flaunting their love in front of her? What kind of man was Herbert? He'd manipulated them into keeping an arrangement he wanted for selfish reasons. The idea of the three of them conniving together disgusted me.

The sound of a car horn sent me to the window. I waved at Samantha and ran to get my coat.

"See you this evening," I called to Simone. "Becky will be here shortly. She can help you pack."

I left and raced to the car, grateful for Samantha's help.

As she listened to my recital of Simone's story, Samantha's face drained of color.

"It's amazing the three of them were able to pull it off," she commented. "The story in the family was that Simone's baby had died. During that time, Arinthia was bed-ridden with her own pregnancy and didn't want to see anyone." She glanced at me. "The birth of your mother almost killed Arinthia, so people understood why she wanted no visitors for her second pregnancy."

"I'm so damn disappointed. I thought I'd found a wonderful family at last. My family."

Samantha patted my shoulder. "Hey, most families have some sort of stuff they have to deal with. Take mine, for instance." Her soft chuckle couldn't hide her hurt.

"You mean you and your father?"

"I can't get through to him no matter what I do."

Zach Adams, the lawyer Samantha introduced me to in Boston, was a friend of hers. He listened carefully to my story and jotted notes on what I wanted, then accepted the papers I handed him.

"Normally, something like this would take a couple of weeks," he said, "but I owe Sam, here, a huge favor. I'll draft up an agreement between you and Ms. Levesque and will email it up to you this afternoon. It's pretty straight forward. No surprises there. I'll get the rest to you tomorrow."

"Thank you. I want to get everything settled before the board meeting on Thursday. And I want Simone to leave—for good."

"Thank you, Zach." Samantha gave him a quick hug. I smiled and saw the light Samantha's hug brought to his eyes.

He grinned. "You're good, Sam, catching me off guard like this. But, as I said, I owed you big time."

We left his office and drove to Riverton to take care of one last detail before the board meeting.

Simone and Becky were finishing packing Simone's belongings when I returned to Briar Cliff late that afternoon.

"The boxes can be mailed to her, don'tcha know," said Becky, taping a large carton closed.

I was surprised by the small number of boxes ready to be shipped. I'd thought Simone would take away a number of sentimental items from the house.

I checked my computer. Zach Adams had been true to his word. A document was attached to his email. Reading through it, I filled with satisfaction. The money Simone had taken from the business stocks account was to be considered fair payment for having her out of my life, leaving her with no ability to attempt to take more money than she already had. Her power of attorney was removed from every business interest and I was given sole signature authority over it all. Her rights to anything further from the estate were waived, along with her right to remain in the house.

I went to find Simone.

She was standing in Arinthia's bedroom, looking out the window. She turned and studied me a moment.

"You remind me so much of Thea," she said softly. "But you're stronger."

I handed her the papers.

"Everything seems to be in order," Simone said briskly, after reading them. "Now, let me sign the papers and I'll be on my way. I can't wait to leave this place."

A short while later, Becky and I stood side by side on the lawn as Simone got into the limousine that would take her to the airport. With one quick wave of her hand, she disappeared behind the smoky glass of the car windows.

As the limo made its way down the driveway, I let out a long sigh.

"Simone was a difficult person—hard to please, hard to like," said Becky.

I felt sickened by all I'd learned about her. She'd shattered a family and lived luxuriously because of it. But Arinthia and Herbert were no better—selfish, amoral people who'd lied and cheated for money and position.

"Becky? Do you know where Henry is? I need to talk to him." Maybe Henry could make things a little better in my mind, give me something good to cling to regarding the family I'd wanted so desperately and now despised.

She patted me on the back. "He was working on a project in the side yard. A branch on one of the rhododendrons was broken by the wind."

I grabbed my coat and went to look for him, stopping for a moment beneath my mother's "talking tree". I looked up at its wide branches and, remembering my own "talking tree," leaned against its rough bark. Darkness was closing in, outlining the bare limbs in wispy strokes, making them appear willing to hug me back as the wind bent them lower.

Henry appeared from around the corner of the house and waved.

"Just the person I wanted to see." I smiled at the sturdy, weather-beaten face that had endured so many Maine winters.

"Henry, I need to know more about my mother."

He studied me, his features softening. "Let's go inside. Becky can make us some coffee."

In the warmth of the kitchen, I sipped the hot liquid and waited for Henry to finish stirring his coffee with cream. He looked up at me, a sad expression tugging at his features. "Guess you know the whole story."

I choked up, nodding silently.

"I knew early on that things were not normal, but Mr. Herbert, he was good to me, especially after my wife took ill. And the kids, Thea and Tim, well, they needed me."

"The kids came to you after my grandfather was sick, didn't they?" I asked, instinctively knowing how much this simple man must have meant to them. He was decent and honest.

"Thea needed someone to care about her, and Tim needed a man to show him some things. Growing up in that household, neither had what they wanted. I knew when Thea left she wouldn't come back. 'Course, I always hoped she'd let me know where she was. Guess she didn't trust nobody."

I swallowed hard. Heart pumping furiously, I asked the question that still haunted me.

"Did she leave because of me? Did I ruin her life?"

Henry shook his head firmly. "Nope, you were just a part of a whole, big mess. Blame is a hurtful thing for everyone." His gaze penetrated mine. "Letting go of it ain't so bad."

I bit the insides of my cheeks. I knew he was talking about forgiveness and accepting what my mother had tried to do for me.

"She was a good person, wasn't she?"

"Thea had her faults; you know them well. But she was strong enough to get away from the sickness inside this house."

I thought a moment, feeling the weight of resentment ease off my shoulders. Alcohol and drugs had made my mother weak and sometimes mean, but I now believed she'd left Maine to protect a child from a place that was unbearable to her. I let out a quivering breath, feeling as if the weight I'd carried around for years had evaporated.

"Thank you, Henry."

He lifted a finger in warning. "Just remember, it was the people inside the house, not the house itself that turned bad."

I could feel the corners of my lips lift. Henry was right. I could rid the house of the past by living a good life in it, maybe even having a family here one day, if only for summer visits. My thoughts turned to Brad. Somehow, I had to make things work between us.

###

Samantha and I met in Riverton for the monthly Rivers Papers board meeting on Thursday morning as planned. Sitting in the office across from the conference room, contemplating our showdown with Ted, I was as nervous as Samantha.

We'd met earlier with Jake Weatherbee. By pointing out how much money he would continue to make acting as a broker for harvesting the wood from the acreage Arinthia had left me, we were able to convince him to support us. A reliable honest income, we'd told him, was worth a lot more than the possibility of money from a project in Coldstream that might never get off the ground.

Aware that approval for the processing plant proposal was on the agenda, we'd prepared a comparison of expenses involved in locating the new processing plant on mill land versus the land Ted Beers and Samantha's father owned. A daring move on our part.

I swiveled in my chair. "Are you set with all the information?" I asked Samantha.

"As ready as I'll ever be." Her voice betrayed her nervousness.

I gave her an encouraging smile. Defying her father after years of seeking his approval had to be terrifying to her. Yet, we both knew this would set her free—free to help others with her new, start-up consulting business.

"Ladies? You ready to join us?" Jake Weatherbee gave us a knowing look.

Samantha turned to me. "You're sure about this, Marissa?"

I rose to my feet and straightened my shoulders. It was time for the Hartwell women to act.

We entered the conference room and took seats at the long table, aware of the men's focus on us.

Ted Beers' brow wrinkled. "What is *she* doing here?" He indicated Samantha with a nod of his head.

I smiled pleasantly, though my mouth had gone dry. I folded my trembling hands in front of me. "At the end of this meeting, my position on the board will be turned over to Samantha Hartwell. She, not I, will be representing the Hartwell family from that point on. As the largest shareholder, I'll be working closely with her."

Ted's face turned beet red. "Does George know about this? And, Hunter?" He turned to the other members of the board. "She can't do this! I'll see that it doesn't happen!"

The other board members gaped at me with stunned expressions.

I swallowed hard and forced myself to speak firmly. "I've been informed by my lawyer that there is nothing in the written agreement between my family and Rivers Papers to prohibit me from doing this. It's in the best interest of Rivers Papers that the family is represented by a knowledgeable, honest, business person. There's no one better to do that than Samantha Hartwell."

Ted slapped his hand on the table. The sound echoed in the room and rang in my ears. I reared back.

Ted rose to his feet, staring at me with clenched fists.

Though my knees shook, I kept a steady gaze on him.

"Hold on, there, Ted," said Jake, rising and tugging on his sleeve. "The lady has done nothing wrong. That's how you were going to get Hunter on the board."

Ted glared at Jake. "Are you telling me you knew about this?"

Jake shrugged. "I just found out, but I've known Samantha since she was a girl. She knows the business cold. I say give her a chance."

The men talked among themselves, filling the room with

low, anxious voices. I gave Samantha's hand an encouraging squeeze. She sat beside me, a stony expression on her face.

Jake Weatherbee winked at me from across the room, and I began to relax.

A man who'd previously been introduced to me as Wendell Blake spoke. "This isn't a board matter. It's a private issue between Rivers Papers and Ms. Hartwell. If she's already had it checked out by legal, there's nothing we can do about it. Let's move on with the meeting. I've got to be in Boston this evening."

Ted's agitation was obvious as he went through the motions of following the agenda.

Watching him, my stomach twisted and turned.

When he announced the topic of the processing plant, I dug my fingernails into my palms, bracing for the worst.

Ted looked around the room with a confident smile. "We've all previously agreed that the processing plant is a good thing for Rivers Papers, that it will save us a lot of money in the long run."

Murmurs of assent ran around the table.

"Good," continued Ted. "Engineering has drawn up a budget for the project, including the construction of the plant in Coldstream. It's pretty straightforward. You've had a chance to look at the numbers. Any questions?"

Willing my tongue to move, I raised my hand. "During my inspections of the mill, I noticed a number of unused buildings at the northern edge of the property. In talking to Engineering, it was revealed that this would be a less expensive location for the processing plant. I've had Samantha, here, take a look at the numbers and we've come up with a comparative budget."

Ted slammed his leather portfolio down on the table and turned to me. "I'm sure you have the best of intentions," he said in a condescending tone, "but you girls lack experience. You have no knowledge of the workings of this board of directors. I led the committee to develop the plans for this project. We've made our decision and expect the board to follow it. Now, gentlemen," he said, turning away from me, "shall we take a vote?"

Jake held up his index finger, "Hold on, Ted. I, for one, would like to hear what these *women* have to say."

"I would, too, Ted," said Wendell Blake. "You have a fiscal responsibility to do the right thing for Rivers Papers."

The others around the table murmured their agreement.

Ted's eyes rounded. He gazed at each man with incredulity. "I can't believe this! It was all settled. Now, you're going to let a couple of ... of ... *women* disrupt the workings of this board? I bet George Hartwell doesn't know about this."

Ted looked as if he wanted to kill me.

My heart pounded. I was grateful for Samantha's turn to speak. I was too shaken to talk.

Samantha began in a clear voice. "Here are the numbers we've drawn up. I've taken the liberty of having copies made for you. Now, let's begin."

I sat, listening to her present our case. We'd done a careful job of dealing with facts and figures. It was apparent in the way the others listened to Samantha that they respected her for the information we'd gathered.

"Any questions?" Jake asked after Samantha completed her presentation.

"Several," said Wendell Blake. "And I suggest that in light of the self-serving duplicity of what Ted Beers and George Hartwell were about to do, that we take steps to have Mr. Beers removed from the board." He glared at Ted. "Were this a publicly held business you'd be arrested."

"I'd like to see you try!" Ted cried.

"Would you like to attempt some explanation?" Wendell asked him.

Face flushed, Ted looked around the table, in search of an ally. When it became apparent he had none, he got up, stuffed his portfolio in his briefcase and stormed out of the room, shooting me one last dagger-like look.

I swallowed hard. Then a wave of triumph washed over me. I'd faced a man I was afraid of and had persevered. Sitting straighter, I looked over at Samantha and smiled.

Her face aglow, Samantha reached out and patted my hand.

Much later, after the completion of the meeting, I left the mill with a clear conscience about relinquishing my seat on the board. By doing so, I'd guaranteed that Simone would not receive another cent from me and Samantha would, I knew, do a capable job of representing our interests. She and I had agreed to work together overseeing the business, ensuring its success, protecting its workers. The money she'd earn by sitting on the board would help her get her consulting business off to a good start. I thought of my great-grandfather William Hartwell. He'd begun the paper mill with his brother and then fought over it. Now, generations later, the two families were working together to protect what the Hartwell brothers had originally founded.

With this part of my future settled, I headed back to Briar Cliff ready to face the biggest challenge of my life.

CHAPTER TWENTY-FIVE

D oris listened quietly as I told her what I wanted to do. "It might work," she said. "I'll do what I can at this end."

The next day, I drove into Barnham, a different person. Most of my life, I'd struggled to fight my way out of bad situations. In Maine, I'd learned to be strong for a different reason—to stay and see that something good came out of the bad. I'd learned the feeling of success standing up to a bully who threatened not with fists, but with words. No matter the consequences, I was ready to fight for what I believed in.

At the thought of what lay ahead, my hands grew sweaty on the steering wheel. It hardly seemed possible that less than a year ago I was returning to Barnham because my mother had died. I felt her presence in the car as I headed toward Doris's house and the old neighborhood. It gave me a sense of rightness to think my mother might somehow know what had happened in New Hope and realize why I'd chosen to come back to New York.

I pulled into Doris's driveway and came to a stop. The biggest test of my life was about to take place.

I took a deep breath to steady myself. From the backseat, Lady gave me a nudge with her cold nose.

With hands gone cold, I opened the car door. Stepping out, I laughed nervously as Lady brushed by me in order to greet the two people who now stood on the front porch.

My eyes darted from Doris to Brad. I read excitement on Doris's face, uncertainty on Brad's.

"Welcome, Marissa," Doris called, approaching me with

her arms wide open. Brad followed, his gaze fixed on me.

I embraced Doris and stood awkwardly in front of Brad, searching for words.

"Oh, my!" Doris glanced from Brad to me. "C'mon, Lady, I've got a treat for you."

Lady perked up her ears and followed Doris as she hurried up onto the porch and into the house.

Left alone with Brad, I tried once more to think of the right words to say. I gazed longingly up the hill where The Talking Tree had once stood. I needed to make Brad understand that I knew now that money could not make up for love, real love, and that the family that meant the most to me now was the one I wanted to make with him. I was finally free to live my own life and to love him with all my heart.

Please, please make him see it that way, I silently beseeched the skies.

Brad searched my eyes.

I knew how much I was asking of him to make a life with me in Maine. He'd been badly hurt in the past. How could I convince him I wouldn't hurt him again?

As if he knew the thoughts that were running through my mind, Brad clasped my hand and we headed in the direction of the weathered stump of the tree.

Among the tall green firs that separated Doris's yard from my old house, we stood facing one another. I prayed I would say the right thing, words that would let Brad know how much I loved him.

"I don't want to give up what we once had," I began, gazing into his eyes. "When you told me we should call it quits, I was hurt and disappointed, but I'm used to being let down, so I walked away. Brad, what we had was special. You're decent and kind and loving and I trusted you." My voice quavered with emotion. "Do you know what that means to me?"

I took his hands in mine. "I want to make it work. I've never loved someone like you."

Without speaking, Brad put his hands on my shoulders and kissed me on my forehead. Then he stepped back and gazed into the distance as if gathering his thoughts.

Stomach clenched, I waited for him to speak.

"I've done a lot of thinking. It would be easy to give up, easy to remain here in the town where I grew up. But maybe a challenge like learning about paper mills is what I need."

He gave me a crooked smile. "Small town lawyering can get pretty monotonous. I don't know where it will take us, but, Marissa, I want to fight for us, too."

He put his arms around me and drew me to him. I leaned against him, hearing his rapid heartbeat, and smiled as his warm lips settled on mine, smooth and sure.

I knew then I'd done the right thing. I squeezed my eyes shut, blocking tears of relief. Brad was worth fighting for. It might take time for me to prove I was committed to him, that we could have a good life—working together, loving one another. But I'd convince him, no matter what.

Brad's arms held me close. Joy filled me at all the possibilities that lay ahead of us. I glanced at the pitiful stump of the Talking Tree, which had shared so much pain with me in the past. Today, it was witness to my happiness.

Returning Brad's embrace, I hugged him hard. I'd found the home of my heart at last.

I hope you enjoyed *The Talking Tree*. If you have, please let other readers know by writing a review on Amazon, Goodreads, BookBub, or your favorite site. It's so important to any author. Thanks so much!

An excerpt from *Sweet Talk* — Book 2 — follows:

CHAPTER ONE

The sign for Sarita, California, appeared ahead of me. I let out a sigh of relief and loosened my tight grip on the steering wheel. It'd been a grueling drive from Maine.

A car behind me beeped its horn, and I slowed to allow it to pass. I glimpsed a blond-haired man with handsome features. Our gazes met, and then he was tucking his silver Mercedes convertible into the line of cars ahead of me. A soft, giddy laugh escaped. California was the land of beautiful people. That man, whoever he was, had just proved it.

While searching for *Treasures,* the art gallery I now unexpectedly owned with my old college roommate, I drove past the cluster of small colorful shops along the water and continued up into the rolling hills overlooking the village. Her call for help had come at a time when I was vulnerable, following my failed marriage of little less than a year.

The carved wooden sign announcing the gallery beckoned. Second thoughts overcame me as I pulled into the parking lot. I rested my head against the steering wheel. Maybe now, with the New Year beginning, my life would take a wild swing for the better. God, I hoped so. This move had to drag me out of the mental and emotional pit I'd wallowed in for the last several months—months in which I'd despaired of any real happiness, while pretending to be fine.

The drive cross-country had seemed unending. I stacked the CDs I'd all but memorized on the journey and put them in the cubby between the front seats. I crinkled together the M&M wrappers that lay scattered across the passenger's seat and grabbed the empty water bottle. My travel-weary legs supported me as I climbed out of my SUV, stood, and stretched.

The door of the art gallery opened. I tossed the garbage in a trash can at the curb and hurried forward. A tall woman with curly chestnut hair strode toward me with a wide smile that lighted her face. A young girl skipped along behind her.

"Allie!" Kristin Lewis held her arms open to me. "You made it!" Her voice lilted with happiness. "Daisy and I have been watching for you all afternoon."

I returned her embrace, and turned to the young girl hanging back. My breath caught at her beauty--blond curls, wide blue eyes, and tiny, perfect features.

Kristin smiled at her daughter. "Daisy, you remember Allison Hartwell, don't you? She's your godmother!"

"My *fairy* godmother?"

I knelt before her and gazed into round blue eyes, fringed with enviable long lashes. My heart swelled. "Sometimes, it's good to believe in magic."

Clad in pink tights, red shirt and a green plaid skirt, she nodded. I hugged her gingerly, careful to avoid crushing the teddy bear she carried. I hadn't seen her for over a year and she'd grown taller. Her little arms reached around me for a brief moment before she turned away.

I stood and faced Kristin, silently assessing my old friend. Normally vivacious and healthy, she looked exhausted. Dark circles smudged the white skin under her eyes. A smile wavered on her face. "I know, I know. I swear I haven't slept in months. I was terrified I'd lose the business, have to start all over again, and be forced to move Daisy out of the school and her special class."

"Didn't the money I sent help?"

"Yes. It allowed me to pay off enough bills to order more inventory, but our troubles go much deeper than that." Tears shimmered in her eyes. "I can't believe she took off on me."

I filled with sympathy. Last fall, amid heartbreaking sobs, Kristin had poured out the story of her lover's betrayal. Lisa Vaughn had taken off with all their savings, claiming it was her money. It'd left Kristin unable to pay her bills and without the means to build holiday inventory for the gallery. I'd known Christmas season was the best time for retail and had offered Kristin a loan. Instead, she'd suggested a business partnership. I'd jumped at the chance. My short marriage to Willard Jackson III had ended months earlier when he'd left me for his old girlfriend whom he'd kept on the side. Temporarily living at home with my parents after the break-up was not my idea of unwedded bliss.

"We sure know how to pick 'em, don't we?"

Kristin laughed, and her face brightened, smoothing out the lines of worry. "This time it'll be better. I trust you, Allison. You've got a good head for business, and our friendship will make it so much easier." Her lips quivered. "I don't know what I would've done if you hadn't agreed to step in. Daisy is happy at her school, and we have a good life here."

Daisy spun around and around, her arms held out like the wings of a rare butterfly. *Such a precious child,* I thought, well aware that at birth Daisy had been deprived of oxygen and had suffered minor brain damage.

"How's she doing?"

Kristin's lips curved. "Remarkably well. She's a slow

learner, but the teachers say once Daisy's learned something, it's locked in for good."

"Does she miss Lisa?"

Kristin's expression turned grim. "She hasn't said one word about her since Lisa left. It makes me wonder why." Her fists clenched at her side. "God! I was so stupid! Why didn't I see what was coming?"

Wondering how to respond, I teased my lip. I knew all about being made to look like a fool.

Daisy whined and tugged on Kristin's hand. "Mommy? I wanna go inside."

"In a second, honey." Kristin gave me a sheepish look. "I'm sorry, Allie. I got so wrapped up in the past, I forgot my manners. Let me help you bring your things inside."

"Do you mind if I take a moment to go into *Treasures?* I want to look around and savor the moment." Enthusiasm bubbled through me, chasing my fatigue away. "I can't believe I'm part-owner of the gallery. It's what I've always wanted—to have a store full of beautiful things. It's going to be so much fun helping people buy them."

Kristin's expression turned wry. "Oh, honey, believe me when I say that feeling will go away!"

"I hope not," I said seriously. The promise of starting a whole new life away from Maine had kept me driving almost non-stop to reach California. I was out to show everyone I could succeed at running a business of my own. I also wanted to prove I could get along without a man. And while I was working at that, I intended to have a good time.

End of Excerpt ...

About the Author

Judith Keim enjoyed her childhood and young-adult years in Elmira, New York, and now makes her home in Boise, Idaho, with her husband and their two dachshunds, Winston and Wally, and other members of her family.

While growing up, she was drawn to the idea of writing stories from a young age. Books were always present, being read, ready to go back to the library, or about to be discovered. All in her family shared information from the books in general conversation, giving them a wealth of knowledge and vivid imaginations.

A hybrid author who both has a publisher and self-publishes, Ms. Keim writes heart-warming novels about women who face unexpected challenges, meet them with strength, and find love and happiness along the way. Her best-selling books are based, in part, on many of the places she's lived or visited and on the interesting people she's met, creating believable characters and realistic settings her many loyal readers love. Ms. Keim loves to hear from her readers and appreciates their enthusiasm for her stories.

"I hope you've enjoyed this book. If you have, please help other readers discover it by leaving a review on Amazon, Goodreads, BookBub or the site of your choice. And please check out my other books:

The Hartwell Women Series
The Beach House Hotel Series
The Fat Fridays Group
The Salty Key Inn Series
Seashell Cottage Books
Chandler Hill Inn Series
Desert Sage Inn Series

ALL THE BOOKS ARE NOW AVAILABLE IN AUDIO on Audible, iTunes, Findaway, and other sites! So fun to have these characters come alive!"

Ms. Keim can be reached at **www.judithkeim.com**

And to like her author page on Facebook and keep up with the news, go to: **https://bit.ly/3acs5Qc**

To receive notices about new books, follow her on Book Bub - **http://bit.ly/2pZBDXq**

And here's a link to where you can sign up for her periodic newsletter! **http://bit.ly/2OQsb7s**

She is also on Twitter @judithkeim, LinkedIn, and Goodreads. Come say hello!

Acknowledgements

Even though writers sit in a room by themselves writing their stories, I don't believe any book is written without the support of others. I wish to thank my critique partners through the years - among them, Betty, Ann, Gail, Peggy and Lynn, the members of the RWA groups I've participated in, and most especially family members and friends who've read early versions of the manuscript, listened patiently to me talk about plot points or simply cared as I shared my frustrations over the process. You know who you are ... Jen, Jeannie, Shelly, and of course Peter and our boys, Andy and Steve. Your encouragement means so much to me. Thanks, guys!